THE TETHERED GOD

BARRIE CONDON

Printed by Ingram Spark

Photo © Neil Harrison | Dreamstime.com
Cover Design Mercat Design © 2020
All Rights Reserved

Contents

Ancient Days 2566 BC

I watched the knife cut into my father's flesh and felt my scrotum tighten as though clutched by a cold, dead hand. Even the sight of the magnificently groomed Peseshet bending over the body did little to take my mind off the horror. A horror that was giving me such morbid, spiteful pleasure.

Peseshet had felt along Father's rib-cage, finding the lower margin before pushing in the obsidian knife, its blade a startling black against the bright vermilion lacquer of her fingernails. Hennaed fingers either side of the cut stretched the skin, opening it out, revealing bright pink inner flesh. A thin line of yellow between skin and muscle caught my eye.

"What is that?" I asked, my finger reaching out but not quite touching.

As soon as my finger had appeared over her shoulder, Peseshet shuffled aside, fearful of touching me. She turned away from the body, both hands now clasped over the knife at the level of her waist, her head bowed respectfully. Her face was broad like mine, but whereas such breadth made mine look brutal, almost bull-like, her jade green eyes softened the effect. She was attractive, but I had dozens of more attractive women back at my palace. What impressed me was how she had risen to become High Priestess of the Temple of Hathor and Chief Physician to all Egypt.

In her eagerness to turn towards me she had taken her eyes off where I was pointing.

"What, Your Royal Highness?"

"That!" I said sharply, always too impatient with the lower orders. She turned back quickly to look. "That, the yellow stuff," I said as evenly as I could.

"It is fat, Prince Khafre."

"Fat? My father was reed thin."

"There is always fat, Your Royal Highness. No matter how old or how thin or how diseased, there is always a layer of fat."

I tried to keep my face impassive, tried not to show my surprise. I had bathed with the man often enough to know that, even when old, you could make out the corded muscles in his abdomen roiling with every lithe movement.

As soon as I'd spoken, all the priests had ceased their mumblings. Peseshet too was waiting for permission to continue. I was halting the ritual: an unwelcome guest, but one nobody dared disappoint. Noise had faded away in this vast vault of a building; all but our central lamplit nucleus hidden in shadows. The light from oil lamps made the carvings on the walls indistinct, but the flickering made them look like they were dancing. It was like being surrounded by a restless half-hidden army.

"You may continue."

Peseshet's eyes came up, a small smile of gratitude playing across full lips purplish-red with dye from seaweed. The skin under her eyes was green with malachite, almost the colour of her eyes, whilst the skin above was black with galena. Kohl from the soot of sunflowers outlined every single eyelash. Her eyes looked enormous in the flickering flame of the lamp. Peseshet's headdress was more a skull cap, silver with a headband of flared golden serpents. It hardly covered her wig whose tight horizontal curls barely reached down to below her ears. The overall effect was intended to impress and I was surprised even Khufu's dead heart did not start to flutter.

She turned back and again used her fingers to outline the incision. She began to saw away more determinedly, my father's tough old muscle resisting the knife. Finally, when the wound was large enough, she inserted her long thin fingers. She turned to look at me, pleading in her face, but she could not find the courage to say what she wanted.

"Continue!" I commanded.

Her sympathy conquered her fear. "It will not be pleasant, Prince Khafre. For you most of all."

I nodded gravely, though inwardly exulting. "I must be sure my father is treated correctly."

She turned back and pushed her whole hand, fingers straightened, into the wound until it closed over her wrist like a mouth. My father's abdomen moved while she sought purchase and it looked as though a large snake was trapped inside. She gave me a quick, agonised look and then started to pull.

The analogy of the snake had not been wide of the mark for the thing she dragged out of my father's belly looked just like that. Glistening like a reptile slithering out of the water, it slowly emerged. One of her helpers, a thin man old enough to be a grandfather but dressed like a peacock in the finest dyed linens, stepped forward quickly. He held the hawk-headed canopic jar ready, its milky alabaster sides giving pin-prick reflections of the surrounding lamplight. He pulled off the hawk lid and held it open.

Peseshet looked at me fearfully. "The smell will be... unpleasant."

Instead of waving this insouciantly away, I should have listened. The trouble was that I was enjoying myself too much. Seeing my father, the god, having his guts pulled out was giving me the most pleasure I'd had in many a long year.

Her knife made a single slashing movement and the intestine was severed. The stench reminded me of an early and unexpected Nile flood when the fields were full of the rotting corpses of cattle and people. Sometimes the desert winds brought these sickly, overripe smells across the Nile and up to our palaces. I imagined my father's corruption taking a lifetime to make its way through his innards and only now emerging. Even that idea couldn't match this terrible reek.

My breakfast rising to greet the day, I sought for something else to focus on. High on a plinth and looking down on my father's mortuary bed was a bust of Sekhmet, the lioness-headed god of death and disease. Sekhmet's proud head was still held high and lofty even at the sight and smell of my father's insides. Made of black granite, Sekhmet stared down her broad nose at me, her widely spaced eyes and deeply incised whiskers adding to an almost palpable sense of disdain.

Hey, I almost felt like saying, it's not me making that smell!

"Are you feeling alright, your Royal Highness?" Peseshet's soft tones brought me back and I reluctantly turned to her. She was holding up my father's intestine like the body of a headless snake. Hard-caked brown material was poking out of the severed neck.

"Does it always smell this bad?" I found myself asking, immediately cursing my unseemly weakness.

"No, Your Royal Highness. I think it is a result of the Great Khufu's final illness. The contents of the intestine should not be like this." She sounded sorry to say this, as indeed she should be. She had just condemned my father's Keeper of the Royal Rectum to death once the news filtered through to Neferhotep. Inevitably, he got to hear of everything.

This was a shame. By all accounts this particular Shepherd of the Anus had been a good one, spending many years tending to my father's malodorous orifice and to good effect. Even when he reached sixty my father had been as vital and sexually predatory as ever. My brother, Djedefre, who would succeed my father, could have done with the Keeper's help. Djedefre, a thin-faced, spindly stick insect, could hardly keep food inside long enough to do any good.

Peseshet began to feed the cut end of the intestine into the neck of the waiting jar. It was going smoothly, the ugly thing coming free easily enough, but then it stuck. She had not fully severed it on the inside. She gave a tug and then grimaced as my father's body twitched.

"Intef!" she said, in a voice used to command, contrasting markedly with the deferential way she spoke to me.

A male physician priest came quickly forward and gently placed one hand on my father's shoulder, the other on his hip. Giving me a quick look of apology, he bore down firmly and nodded to Peseshet who then gave the gut a good yank. Whatever tissue held it in place parted, Peseshet stepping back smartly so she didn't overbalance.

Such an undignified business for my father. I fought to suppress a smirk.

Even Khufu's lean body managed to subside a little as Peseshet pulled out the rest of his intestine like she was hauling on a filthy rope.

By now the priest holding the canopic jar was struggling with the weight. Other priests were rapidly wiping away the ichor where it had dripped from the neck of the jar and down its white sides. Another was using a horsehair brush to anoint the jar with terebinth, though the resinous, woody odour hardly suppressed the stench.

Meanwhile Peseshet was rummaging away again. The liver went in the jar decorated with a human head, the lungs in the baboon-headed one. Finally, only the stomach remained and she struggled to pull it out of the cut she had made. A priest had brought the jackal-headed jar forward and held it ready, as Peseshet lifted the stomach out. It reminded me of a goat skin water-bag but with two tubes, one for in and one for out, both severed near the ends. Even to my untrained eye one tube was blocked with black, clotted blood. I stepped in closer to get a better look and Peseshet froze. I knew there should be no blood in the stomach because throwing up blood was always considered a bad sign. I had lost other relatives that way.

I must have been absorbed for quite a while because when I finally looked up, I saw Peseshet's frown of concern. "Proceed!" I said.

She gently lowered my father's stomach into the jar. Her eyes found mine but then looked away. "Your Royal Highness..." she began but then words failed her.

"Yes, go on!"

A priest had carried over a polished bronze washbasin full of a liquid reeking of terebinth and turpentine. Distractedly, Peseshet used this to wash my father's filth off her hands. She licked her lips. "The next stage is controversial." Around her I heard a collective intake of breath as the priests, young and old, stiffened. Some actually hissed with displeasure.

Controversial and mummification ritual aren't expressions that sit comfortably together so I should have been shocked but this was, after all, my father we were talking about. I was all ears.

Wiping her hand on a cloth she glanced at me again. "I have performed many studies on tombs looted in Saqqara.

Tombs where the mummies themselves have been stripped of their linen wrappings so the thieves could get at the amulets hidden within."

She put the towel down and paused as though collecting her thoughts. "I have to tell Your Royal Highness that, despite the dry desert air, parts of the mummies had not survived the passage of time."

"What parts?"

"Their heads. The bodies, stuffed with natron and sawdust and aromatics had survived and looked as though they had been mummified only days before. However, the faces had collapsed, eaten away from within."

An eternity without a face; it hardly bore thinking about. The gods would shun you.

"What are you trying to tell me?"

She bowed her head. "I have a theory." There was another general intake of breath. Peseshet was the foremost physician of her day yet her priests were almost in revolt. Blasphemy was afoot. How delicious!

"It is the brain. We do not remove it and so it rots, leaving just the bare skull behind. We know the brain has no uses, after all it's hardly like the heart in which the soul resides. The brain is simply stuffing to keep the skull strong. I feel, and I have Neferhotep's support in this, that we should as routine remove the brain just as we remove the viscera."

A difficult decision! On the one hand we had my father spending eternity without a face. On the other we had the more immediate pleasure of watching Peseshet empty the contents of his skull.

I've never been one for deferred gratification. "Proceed!" I said, but perhaps a little too eagerly. Everyone, Peseshet included, looked at me in frank surprise. I pursed my lips and nodded my head judiciously. "I'm sure the High Lord

Neferhotep has considered this fully and his judgement is always carefully balanced."

I sensed all the priests relaxing. They didn't like this one little bit but against Peseshet and Neferhotep and me they were like fish trying to hold back the Nile.

Peseshet pointed a finger at a stooped priest lurking in the shadow of one of the columns. "Neck block!" she ordered. The priest limped over with a thick piece of enamelled wood. He lifted my father's head and placed it underneath his scrawny neck so that the head fell back.

Meanwhile Peseshet had equipped herself with a chisel and hammer, the stone head tied with twine to the wooden handle.

"You might be best to look away, your Royal Highness."

I shook my head gravely.

She placed the chisel almost at the top of the nose where it met the skull. Two swift cracks with the hammer and she had made a groove, carefully saving the v-shaped piece of bone and flesh that had been freed. It too would have to be entombed with my father along with his umbilicus and afterbirth and the corpse of his wet nurse. The nurse had passed away to the Field of Reeds many years before, had been mummified and kept in a temporary tomb just behind Khufu's pyramid, where she waited to join him in the afterlife.

I watched the process entirely fascinated; breaking my father's nose was something I'd dreamed of all my life.

Peseshet went to a table holding her fiendish instruments and brought forth several golden metal rods of different shapes. Standing over the corpse she gave one quick bow of obeisance and then gently pushed a straight rod into the gap she'd made. When she felt some resistance, she pulled it back a little and then jabbed it hard. Whatever had been resisting gave way and the rod disappeared so far that her fingers were brought up against the nose. I estimated that a middle finger's length of the rod had penetrated into my father's brain.

She removed it, slimy material now glinting along its length. She laid it aside then picked up and inserted another. This one had little glass blades embedded in the end. Intef stepped forward unbidden and took a firm hold on my father's head. Peseshet pushed the new instrument in, twisting it as she did so. When she pulled this out the blades were covered in gore studded with bone fragments.

Now it was the turn of a rod with a hook on the end. The other instruments had made a large enough hole for it to penetrate easily. When it was fully in, Peseshet turned it through a full circle and then pulled it out. What was unmistakably brain matter now adhered to the hook.

Peseshet wiped the hook down with an exquisitely embroidered piece of linen. She repeated the process a number of times before looking at me again. "Your Royal Highness, this is a lengthy process. It will take me several hours to extract all of your father's brain. Then I must fill the cavity with juniper oil and turpentine to dissolve the remnants I have not been able to reach. That also takes several hours, at which point I can turn your father over to let all fluid drain out. Then we must fill the skull and body cavities with spices and natron. It will be morning before we complete that part of the ceremony."

She made a good point and my interest in seeing the desecration of my hated father's body was already waning. However, there was one final service I had yet to administer.

"Send for me when you have finished. I wish to be alone with my father before he is sent to the drying vault." Natron was fierce in its desiccating action and I knew my father would be almost unrecognisable after forty days in the vault.

Only then would they begin to wrap him. For what I had to do I wanted him to appear as he had in life.

Everyone bowed as I turned and left.

Peseshet herself was waiting for me the next morning. Her eyes betrayed how tired she must feel. Already the sun was higher than Father's pyramid and the limestone casing gleamed in the light. The pyramid, Father's chariot to the afterlife, looked ethereal and I almost faltered. Father would be with the other gods soon. Dare I do this?

Peseshet's hands were clasped and her head lowered. "Yesterday..." She hesitated. "Yesterday I was concentrating so much on what I was doing I did not express my sorrow at your great loss. You have lost a father as well as a god."

I let my silence speak for me and finally she nodded in acceptance and turned and led me into the mortuary temple. The large echoing space was empty and the shadows seemed thicker.

"I will wait until Your Royal Highness is finished," she said and retreated, closing the heavy door behind her with some effort.

Father, as ever, was at the centre. His abdomen, which immediately after his evisceration had made him look like a peasant after a particularly hard famine, had plumped out now that it was filled with natron. Peseshet had re-attached the V she had chiselled out of the top of his nose and the whole area was so carefully covered in make-up that I could hardly see the joins.

The smell of spices had by now easily overwhelmed father's stench of corruption. Natron, a bitter-tasting white deposit found in dried lake beds, sucks water even out of the air. The dryness made me sneeze.

I was pleased to see that Father still had his eyes, cloudy though they had become after death. With his body full of natron, the eyes would quickly shrink and so, in a final act of preparation, Peseshet would pluck them out, replacing them with disks of finely glazed ceramic called faience. These would ensure he kept his betel nut eye colour for eternity.

Nice of her to leave his own eyes in for now. I wanted father to watch what happened next.

I hadn't laid hands on him for many years (would that I could say the reverse was true!) and now his body's coldness and looseness stirred no memories within me. Grasping his far shoulder, I pulled him towards me. The natron made him heavy and it was a struggle to pull him over. The hands had not yet been bound together by linen windings, so one hand came over and slapped my thigh. I was more surprised than hurt.

"I'll give you that one," I said.

Now face down, Father's scrawny buttocks were revealed. This was not going to be pleasant. Putting a hand on each exposed cheek, I gently parted them. Father's backside had closed over the wax plug, making it almost invisible. Peseshet had done a professional job so getting the plug out would be tricky. I went across to her table of wonders and rummaged around until I found the golden rod with the hook on the end. It took a bit of manoeuvring to insert it and get it properly positioned but then slowly, carefully, I pulled it out and watched Father's anus open like a raggedy flower as the plug emerged.

As long as the body was intact then the soul, the Ka, remained in heaven. It was vital that all the orifices of the dead were plugged, otherwise insects would find their way in and lunch on the insides, condemning the Ka to an eternity of agony.

I hauled father back over and rearranged him so it didn't look as though he had been touched. I picked up the plug and threw it far away into the shadows.

I looked down at him for one last time. "One final gift to you, Father. It's the least I can do."

Modern Day

*And that was just on*e of my doggy dreams of ancient days. I mull it over, trying to make sense of two confusing worlds as the riverbanks slide by. Why was I behaving like such a bastard? What had my father done that had so offended me?

Meanwhile, the desert is looming, like a monster, all along the Nile. The river, precious, fragile, still brings burgeoning life to a slender strip of land running through this barren vastness. In my heyday, so many thousands of years ago, the river drowned or starved multitudes at its whim. Today it lies tamed and enslaved and the people have become its gods. Waters that once were ever-flowing are now mirror-calm until our bow wave lifts up the reflections of the desert then lays them gently down.

How was the mighty Nile tamed? One mystery amongst many in this new world that I struggle so hard to comprehend. My biggest hurdle has been the strange new Egyptian tongue. How to learn a language when you can't ask questions, can't get someone to repeat what they said? I've had to listen long and hard to decipher their ululating, back-of-the-throat gargling sounds. When I was previously alive - in my human form - the speech of my kind was serene and modulated and underpinned by a bedrock of fathomless authority. Who in their right mind would argue with what we said? Now the people speak like they're getting ready to clear their throats in an argument that never ends.

The struggle was not an easy one. But a dog's hearing is acute and, little by little, I eventually got to grips with their strange tongue and that's why I know my handlers are once again joking about cutting off my testicles. Ragab, thin, nervous, eager to please, is laughing. "At least it would take that superior look off his face. German Shepherds can be so haughty."

Mazan, once athletic but slowly going to fat, laughs and takes a long draw on his cigarette. He's a big, hairy man but there's sometimes an effeminacy about him.

Amr, always my friend and protector, comes to my defence. "Cheops is a good boy. Never howls after bitches, never sniffs where he shouldn't. Always does his business on command."

Talk about accolades! I would blush, if only I could.

"So, no point getting him done," Amr finishes, judgement made, case closed. Like many middle-aged Egyptians he is running to fat and I wish his wife would take more care of him. Without him this old joke might become a reality. And if there's even a chance of that then I'll be gone faster than a beef shawarma in a Cairo ghetto.

"It's in the manual," says Mazan, clapping my head with his heavy hand instead of giving me the gentle stroke his demeanour might suggest. Mazan is not what he seems. What game is he playing?

Amr, a trifle irritated that this issue hasn't been put to bed, crosses his arms and looks stern.

I'm still struggling with their police ranking system but I'm pretty sure he's the most senior, though only just. "It's not an instruction, simply a recommendation. Also, he'd be away for ten days recovering. Do you really want another dog for that long? Do you seriously reckon we could do better?"

Yeah, I think, do you really want one of those howl-at-the-moon, crap-anywhere, blank-eyed idiots?

It's clear they don't and the conversation moves on, as do we. The size of the boat still stupefies me. It's not the length but the height, with not just the one deck but seven or eight. All enclosed, all sheltered and cooled from the midday sun. It's like a palace sailing down the Nile.

And it's full of old people. I take it they are some sort of ruling class, though definitely not royalty, not from the way they dress. In my day you could only be that untidy if you were in mourning. Even then, if you were rich, you paid people to do the mourning for you. Maintaining dignity was everything so you got someone else to wail and smear dirt on their faces and rend their clothing to expose their bosoms. I'm not sure why they did that last bit. It used to make sense but that was so long ago. In my uncanny between-worlds state, making sense of the past is becoming as difficult as making sense of this strange future.

I'd better apologise right now for the quality of my memories. My past life comes back to me only in fractured, though strangely detailed, doggy dreams. I have a vague overall sense of my past but the dreams that colour this in, that provide substance and texture, arrive only at the whim of Seth, the god who revels in chaos and mischief. Nevertheless, over the years of this new life, a story has been slowly unfolding. I want to know more about it. But, given that I eventually wind up as a dog, I'm guessing it can't have the happiest of endings.

Anyway, back to the people on the boat. They aren't royalty but that's how the staff treat them. What's really strange is that they're all so white. Are they ill? We would have put people who looked like that to death. My guess is they're foreigners from lands far, far away. In my time such places were the stuff of myth. Lands where water fell from the sky and people were carried around at great speed on huge creatures. If that's really where these people are from then why are they swanning around my country like they own it? Did they invade and conquer? If they did then why in Osiris's name did Ragab, Mazan and Amr not die defending their homeland?

My handlers, not trained to be ingratiatingly polite like the servants, keep away from the white people. We share one cramped cabin on the lowest deck, almost at water level. We can, however, get out onto this little after-deck where there are machines to pull the mooring ropes taut, and that's where we are right now. The reek of oil is an assault on my doggy nostrils but there are other, more alluring smells, like the fragrance of an aroused lover, that call to me from the river banks.

"I've never seen a dog so interested in everything," says Ragab meditatively. If even a knuckle-head like him can notice that then I'd better tone it down a bit. During my training I had seen quite a few dogs that didn't behave in the way their masters expected. What happened to them took place out of sight but was terminated by a single, eloquent gunshot.

I flick my tail, pretend to catch sight of it, then chase it around in circles.

They all laugh. Mazan shifts his bulk on the mat and readjusts his holster so the gun isn't poking into the roll of fat at his waist. "When do we get to Minya again?"

Amr pulls at his little moustache. "Sunset. Then the fun begins."

I prick up my ears. This cruise may be fun for the old folks but not for us. That's another impediment to picking up a new language: irony. However, I'm getting there and so

I know that fun in this context equals lots of unhappy men with guns.

Amr frowns. "Sisi sent the tanks into Minya four years ago. If we had any sense we wouldn't even be stopping there."

"So why are we?" asks Rajab.

"Money," says Amr, rubbing his thumb over two fingers. "Tourist money. I mean look!" and he points at the nearest bank where decrepit hovels rest on little rises above the river. What happened to this country? There used to be poor people, of course, and their houses were mud brick like these, but they'd be painted white with nice red doors for divine protection against the demons that came in dreams. As well as being unpainted these modern mud brick walls are falling apart, yet in this climate they should last for scores of years. Shoddy workmanship, lack of pride; the countryside simply reeks of poverty and failure.

And I'd thought Cairo was bad!

"And that's why all those senior guys came on board last night," Amr continues. He sniffs and his moustache wiggles.

"They looked so nervous," Ragab says. "Senior police, you don't often see that. None of their usual swagger."

"Their jobs are on the line," says Mazan with a wide grin, evidently relishing his seniors' discomfort. My handlers have little admiration for their superiors.

"So why are we doing it?" asks Ragab. "I mean, a walkabout around the town square. If anything kicks off these poor old sods won't even be able to run for cover."

Amr is always keen to teach the younger man. He must be a good father to his two daughters. "They only recently opened up this stretch of the river between Luxor and Cairo. It was closed to tourists for years because the bad guys were taking pot shots at the cruisers with RPGs and what-have-you. Hundreds of boats were laid up." He's right there, I've seen scores of these grand edifices rotting away all along the river. "But now it's re-opened they can't just restart where they left off. It's a matter of being gradual. First the boats just sail by, then they start to call in so the tourists can travel out in armed convoys to the tombs. The next step, and it's our luck to be here when they take it, is for the tourists to go ashore for a walk..."

Mazan interrupts, "... and that's the problem. The Big Bottoms have to assure the tourists' safety. If even one of these old folks gets a splinter in their pinky..." and he runs a finger over his own throat and makes a gurgling, liquid sound.

My feelings are conflicted. On the one hand I'm pleased because such clear and lengthy expositions are a rarity with these guys and I don't have to rack my brains to figure out what their usually clipped, grunted conversations actually mean. On the other hand, it sounds like a walk looms in my future. A walk along crowded streets surrounded by big men with heavy boots who have no concept of just how painful it is to have your paw stepped on.

"It's going to be operatic," says Amr. "For once I don't envy the Big Bottoms. The region depends on the tourists returning and they're under pressure to make it happen, but if just one tourist is killed by insurgents then it'll cost the whole country hundreds of millions of dollars in lost income. That kind of pressure is some price to pay just so you can sit in an office out of the hot sun."

"For the money they earn, I'd do it," says Mazan.

"I want to be a first lieutenant one day, inshallah," says Ragab. "Then I'd tell you lazy bastards what to do."

Amr smiles at him fondly.

I stick my head out between the metal rails. The sun is about to go down and lazy streamers of red (with my doggy eyes that can only be a guess) lie across the sky and are reflected in the flat calm waters ahead of the boat. On the near shore children are down by the water and waving, a boat still such a novelty. The red sky limns the palms and banana trees. Here and there I can see the strange towers, like the obelisks of old but with a wider, phallic head, thrusting up out of the trees. Any minute now the tinny wailing of the call to prayer will start. Already some of the boat's crew are drifting out and putting down their mats.

My handlers look on. Not for them the forehead to the cold deck, not when they're in uniform, at least. Inshallah, I've learned, means God willing. I've heard all my handlers say this frequently so I'm presuming they too believe in this new religion. I've sniffed my way through enough of their temples to know just how alien they are. Not once have I seen an image of a person or even of a god. In my day temple decorations were all about faces and bodies.

Perhaps their god does not even have a face. I shudder at the thought.

Two of the crewmen are dressed in all-over dirty white garments that reek of oil. Another is a waiter with the black leggings called trousers and a white shirt. They all ignore us as they straighten out their mats.

I hear the tinny click then the strange, amplified cry, like a mother who has lost all her children, reaches out to us across the water. In unison the crewmen kneel, then lower their foreheads to the deck in an act of obeisance.

Mazan and Ragab seem uncomfortable at not joining in but Amr is more serene. He is a man who is at ease with himself and happy with his lot. Mazan must be of a similar age but, whereas Amr relaxes into his life, Mazan chafes. Meanwhile Ragab, eager puppy that he is, is back and forth between them, not sure what role model he should follow.

I catch a movement amongst the nearest men. The waiter has just given my handlers a sideways glance. The merest flicker, too fast to see unless you were a dog. Doggy vision paints the world in a malnourished palette, colours lost as though looking at it through amber. It took me a while to work out exactly why it was different because it's all about absence. Gone are the beautiful red sunsets, shading now into an insipid yellow. Meanwhile, the lush greenery along the Nile is almost white. This new world is washed out, like dyed cloth cleaned by being pounded too often against rocks in the river. Most heartbreakingly of all, both the sky and the Nile are chalky and nondescript.

This is why a desert world is not a good place for a dog: there is so little contrast. I remember once, back when I had human form, being furious when hunting for wild sheep in the desert west of Memphis, spluttering in rage as my dogs walked by two sheep sheltering in the lee of a dune. The dogs' noses twitched like they were full of worms and they darted worried looks all around, but it was as if the sheep were invisible.

Now I know why. Had those sheep moved, had they made the tiniest twitch, then the dogs would have been upon them. For dogs, hunting is about movement and that, at least, is something to which their sight is exquisitely attuned.

So, our waiter friend's barest flick of the eye brings all my doggy senses to bear. I look more closely. He is clean-shaven and his hair is trimmed close to the scalp. He is lean but his face has the smooth, slightly rounded quality of a man who has been well fed all his life.

The prayers continue, the men raising and lowering their heads to the deck as the beautiful reds of the sunset deepen, at least in my imagination. I feel my whole body lean back and realise the boat is slowing. I poke my head back through the railings and see the lights of a town on the east bank of the river. On the other side, steep cliffs rise to an almost plateau-like top. Little black upright rectangles in the sandstone show tombs scattered all across them.

Something unpleasant tugs at my mind but fades away before I can grasp it.

Then again, sights like this, common to both my worlds, always unnerve me. Just for a second I am lost, stranded between two lives, but then the crewmen getting up from prayer drag me back with their chatter. They disappear into the boat.

"You know why they call it Minya?" asks Amr. He lights another cigarette as the other two ignore him. Perhaps they have heard the tale before. Amr doesn't seem to notice or care. "The locals call it the Bride of Upper Egypt as it's dead centre between Upper and Lower Egypt, but it used to have the Old Kingdom name of Men'at Khufu. Do you know what that means?"

I must have given a big doggy blink of surprise because Ragab points at me and laughs. "He heard that! At least he's listening to you, Amr."

Amr claps my head. "Yes, boy! It's named after you because this is where you were born." What the hell is he talking about? The name they have given me is Cheops and being confused with that miserable, vicious old bastard, Khufu, makes me want to bite the fool's hand off.

"Men'at Khufu: the nursing city of the great Pharaoh Khufu," says Amr grandly. The Gods know I'm hardly in a position to be pedantic here, but nobody ever called him Pharaoh. That's some bullshit new word coined since my time.

"So how come he has his pyramid at Giza?" Ragab wants to know. "That's hundreds of kilometres away. Didn't they usually bury the pharaohs where they were born?"

Amr shakes his head. "You ought to listen to the tour guides once in a while, Ragab. You might actually learn something. You're getting confused with the god Osiris who was born and buried at Abydos. It was a place of pilgrimage and burial for the rich but few ever went there as it's too far south."

Ragab clicks his fingers. "That's the god whose dick was cut off, isn't it? Tell us about that, Amr. That's much more interesting."

I can't help a whimper escaping and Amr looks at me oddly. It doesn't stop him, however, and he's soon stamping over my sacred beliefs with his big fat feet. "Osiris was a great king who gave the world farming and laws. All was wonderful but Osiris had a brother called Seth who was jealous. He cut up Osiris into thirteen bits and hid his body parts all around Egypt. Even so, Osiris' wife Isis found them and stitched them back together again. All except the penis, that is, which was eaten by fishes. Isis needed that so she could mate with Osiris. She modelled a cock out of clay, as you do, and fell pregnant. She gave birth to the hawk-headed god Horus."

Ragab, giggling, raises a finger. "Remind we, what are the relationships between gods, kings and pharaohs again? I get confused."

My hackles rise but I calm down by reminding myself why such ignorance is understandable. Sometimes, though rarely, the tourists on this boat speak Arabic and they have guides who provide them with more solid information than I can ever glean from Amr's occasional and inaccurate ruminations. Listening to them I'd finally understood that my time, my first time, was over four and a half thousand years ago. I suppose I should be grateful my halfwit handlers know anything about so long ago.

Amr holds out his hand and wiggles it. "They're all pretty much the same. Anyway, Isis showed mercy to Seth for what he'd done, but Horus wasn't up for it, so he killed his mother."

"Again, as you do," says Mazan, laughing.

Amr nods. "As Isis had been good to him, Seth took her side and plucked out Horus's eyes and threw him down a mountain. Hathor, goddess of love and motherhood, took pity on Horus and cured his blindness by milking a gazelle so the milk fell into his eyes.'

Ragab is laughing and shaking his head. "None of that makes any sense. Surely the ancient Egyptians didn't believe in all that crap."

I lie down and bend my head round so I can bite my own thigh. Don't these silly pricks know what a metaphor is?

"That's not even the wild part. Seth tried to fuck Horus, who managed to catch the semen in his own hands. He showed the spunk to Isis, who cut off his hands and made him clay ones instead. Then, Isis took her son Horus's semen...though how she got it we maybe shouldn't go into... and put it on Seth's lettuce. Seth ate it and became pregnant, even though he was a guy."

By now Ragab and Mazan are crying with laughter and the copper taste of blood fills my mouth. Osiris is good and Seth is evil. Evil strikes at the one thing Egyptians prized above all else: fertility. It corrupts the good as well as the bad, as shown by the terrible thing Isis does to her own son. Hathor, by curing him, is demonstrating that the good must show mercy because only by doing that can good win. By Horus and Seth lying together, it shows that good and evil have been reconciled. However, good corrupted by bad, in the form of Isis, destroys that. The whole thing is about the need for mercy. And as for how Isis got her son's semen...

I stop biting my thigh because I suddenly realise I don't have a clue what the bit about the semen and the lettuce means. I do remember it made perfect sense at the time.

What am I doing here? Why am I not on Ra's chariot, fighting the evil world-devouring snake, Apophis? Why am I in the body of this shaggy mutt, my senses twisted and reshaped, muted and exaggerated at the same time?

Is this punishment? Did I do something wrong? Again, a shadow flickers across my mind but before I can focus on it, it is gone.

I need to think. I need to remember. My dreams are detailed, more like memories, but even so I have trouble understanding them. In my new life as a dog, in the first couple of years before I remembered just who I had once been, the first language I learned to understand was that of my handlers, with their strange notions and ways of speaking. As a result, I think the way they speak. And it is with these impoverished modern tools, with their narrow views and contemporary expressions, that I must interpret my dreams.

Though I may not understand it in the way that I did, I still miss that previous life. Wearily but expectantly, I close my eyes and wait for another doggy dream of ancient days.

Ancient Days 2564 BC

Lesser men lament to the gods when faced with a lack of women. Princes beat their breasts for surfeit of the same. Aside from the jealousies and manipulations, the fights and the feuds, this prince found himself drowning in fecundity.

Thus my palace stank with the piss of infants who ran hither and thither through the rat-run of twisty corridors, souring milk from their wet nurses smeared across their lips and cheeks. Their shrieks and laughter would often startle me from my dreams.

I had my own quarters as far from the centre of this mayhem as possible but, extensive though the palace was, it was still not large enough. Egyptian palaces, and even humbler homes, crammed in as many rooms as possible. This meant each room was small except for those where we feasted and copulated. Even our bedrooms were tiny as we all slept alone lest our dreams, those precious messages from the gods, were contaminated by the dreams of others. We also shunned regularity with the little rooms arranged in a shambolic, arbitrary manner so that getting from one room to another could be a tortuous odyssey. Every foray therefore became an expedition. Countless times I would find myself lost and disoriented in my own palace. Of late I had taken to having a eunuch wait outside my quarters along with my bodyguard, Dedifer. The eunuch, unusually wizened and thin for a ball-less one, knew the palace inside out and was our guide.

Lord of this palace though I was, I had been summoned. Led by the eunuch, and with broad, gruff Dedifer following, we made our way through reed-strewn corridors. Roofed over and windowless, the palace was full of burning tallow which blackened the wall paintings and made the whole place smell of burnt fat. As we trudged along, servants scurrying around on errands would halt and hurriedly slip back into shadowed doorways to let us pass.

I had long since lost count of the turns we had taken by the time we approached the quarters of my wives, bare mud brick walls becoming covered by multi-coloured linens. Khamerernebty favoured red and, as we neared her domain, this colour came to predominate.

I passed the room dedicated to her personal god and glanced in. The goddess Hathor's grotesquely wide-browed statue peered out at me. Wooden penises of inordinate sizes were strewn haphazardly around her feet. Hathor, the lady of the vulva, was much on Kham's mind as I knew only too well.

One more turn of the winding corridor and ahead I saw Kham's maids clustered around the opening to her day chamber, ready to do her bidding. They moved quickly aside when I appeared. Taking a deep breath, I entered.

Kham was naked and wigless and reclining on a golden couch. A necklace with an amulet showing Hathor's head hung on a gold chain. It had fallen to the side, looping over a breast. Peseshet was kneeling between my wife's legs, her backside raised. It was a comely shape, I'd give her that. In this world sex was about fertility rather than recreation and nothing spoke of that more than a large, curved bottom. She was wearing a simple tunic but this had risen up to reveal a thick white linen kilt with an abundance of pleats.

As I came up behind Peseshet, I saw her plucking an onion from my wife's vagina. "In the name of..." I protested.

Peseshet looked round in surprise and made to rise but I held my palm out flat. Whatever was going on, I wasn't sure it would be wise to interrupt.

"My lord is ignorant of women's medicine," said Kham, her voice as cold as the wind on the highest desert uplands in the dead of night.

"It is a common procedure, Your Royal Highness," said Peseshet quickly and defensively, putting the onion aside on a silver tray. She turned back to Kham and held her hands together in supplication. "May I approach, Princess?"

She had just had her fingers in Kham's vagina. How much closer could she get?

Kham nodded regally and lifted a beckoning finger and I could not help marvelling at her cold reserve. My half-sister, our match had been arranged when I was still a child. Her lips were full and inviting but her body was thin, her breasts so small as to be almost useless for suckling children. Her chilliness was an uncomfortable reminder of our father, especially as anger always lurked just below the surface.

Peseshet shuffled forwards on her knees and leaned down over Kham's mouth. For one breathless moment I thought they were going to kiss. Instead Peseshet lowered her head until her nose was directly over Kham's mouth, exposing the most delicate neck.

"Exhale, please, Princess."

Kham blew her breath out between pursed lips. Peseshet's nostrils contracted as she inhaled.

Modern medicine intrigued but baffled me. What in Osiris's name were these two women doing?

Having fully exhaled, Kham breathed back in. "Again?"

"There is no need, Princess. The smell of onions is clear."

Kham smiled at me in triumph. Peseshet turned her head to cast me a worried glance.

I didn't like the feel of this at all. "What's this all about? Why did you ask me here?"

"Tell him!" commanded Kham.

Peseshet, still on her knees, turned fully to me and raised her head, her hands remaining clasped in a servile manner. "I have been investigating your wife's fertility, at her request, your Royal Highness. The most important point to establish is whether her passages are blocked. To this end, yesterday I placed an onion in Princess Khamerernebty's vagina. Today her breath smells of onions so her passages are clear and she is fertile."

Clever stuff. I'd never have thought of that. My admiration for Peseshet's knowledge and professionalism increased. "So why doesn't she get pregnant?"

"Maybe we should get the good physician to look at you," said the Goddess of Cold Air.

"Nonsense! Meresankh spits out children like date stones. She's got...what..." I couldn't remember whether there was four or five of them. Kham and Meresankh, my niece, weren't my only wives and it was easy to lose track. There were children all over the palace. What more evidence of my fertility would anyone need?

"She claims they're yours." Kham's eyes widened as she said this, knowing she had gone too far but had been too spiteful to stop herself.

"Silence," I thundered and even Kham looked frightened. Egypt and the Nile and the bounties of the harvest were founded on fertility. A princess, perhaps one day a queen, who could not produce children was worthless. I knew it was this fear that made her strike out at others.

"What can you do for her, Chief Physician?"

"As you well know, Your Royal Highness, Hathor is the goddess of sexuality and motherhood, but she is also the lady of drunkenness. Perhaps if you and your wife were to drink wine and then to couple, Hathor may hear your prayers. Offerings to Bes and Tawaret may also be efficacious."

My problem has always been a certain literalness of nature. I could not help but see the gods as they appeared, not as the notions they represented. The statues of Bes showed a dwarf with a monstrous phallus, those of Tawaret a hippopotamus that walked on two legs, though weighed down with enormous, saggy human female breasts. Of all the gods they were the least prepossessing. Still, Peseshet seemed to know her stuff.

"Very well, there will be sacrifices. We will next... couple as you suggest." In Egypt there were twelve words for sex, coupling being the most insipid and so the least familiar to my lips. Coupling took place in a special room strewn with cushions and with servants in attendance.

"That won't work." Kham was pulling a blanket over herself and was clearly making ready for sleep. Having an onion pulled out of her vagina had made this one of the busiest days of her life.

"Why is that, Princess?" asked Peseshet, too earnest to sense the bear-trap she was walking into.

"Because..." and Kham held up a forefinger preparatory to letting it droop, but I was much too quick for her. My own out-thrust finger and the fire in my eyes had her quickly burrowing under her blanket.

"I need to get out into the open air," I muttered, the stink of perfume and tallow bearing down on me.

"May I speak with you, Your Royal Highness?" Peseshet asked quietly. "It is about Princess Hekenuhedjet. I am concerned for her health."

"Of course. Come out onto the terrace! It will be cooler by now." I turned and strode off down the corridor, but had to step aside quickly as my daughter, Shepsetkau, ran by screaming pursued by my son, Duaenre. Or was it Hemetre being chased by Nuiserre? For a second my head spun and it took me a while to realise Peseshet was saying something.

"What?" I turned to face her.

She looked frightened but remained resolved. "I think you will find it is this way, Your Royal Highness," and she pointed back the way we had come.

Of course, she was right. I glared at the eunuch who, seeing me stride away so purposely had no doubt been too frightened to ask where I thought I was going. Peseshet may have been a physician, the highest ranking in Egypt, but the wives and children of the various royal families took up most of her time. She knew our palaces better than we did.

I nodded and followed her. Soon we were stepping out into the evening air. The sun, low in the sky, was a baleful red. A blissful breeze off the river was like a cool wet towel to my forehead.

The terrace was made of the finest red granite hewn from quarries around Aswan. Scattered around were many bowers screened by trellises covered in climbing plants with flowers of all hues. Deeper shade was provided by palms and fig trees. All around, little pools were stocked with large slow-moving fish that the children could torment to their hearts' content.

The only thing I could not tolerate, though it was common in the other Royal Palaces, were caged birds. I did not care how sweetly they sang. To hear my wives complain about this uncharacteristic delicacy on my part, one would think I had demanded they walk around naked in front of commoners.

I walked across to the balustrade that looked down onto the Nile. Across the river lay lush farmlands with dusty farmworkers making their stooped, tired way home. Palm trees jostled right up to the edge where the bank fell away into the water. To right and left the royal palaces lined this side. Single-floor and sprawling, they grew like living things from one harvest to the next.

I had always been struck by the contrast between the temples we made for the gods, and the houses we built for ourselves. The former soared, cool and spacious like heaven itself, while the latter were cramped and smelly. The temples and pyramids were made of granite, limestone and sandstone and would last forever whilst our mud brick homes and palaces fell down around our ears like apples from trees.

Perhaps this was to reflect the permanence of the gods and the transitory nature of human existence. Lost in admiration at my own perceptiveness, I had forgotten about Peseshet until she cleared her throat. I turned towards her and it struck me that the plainness and formality of her tunic and kilt suited her cool professional manner.

"So, what's this about Heke?" I asked. Hekenuhedjet was from Kush, the daughter of the chief of the largest tribe. As with many of my wives, the marriage was to ease diplomacy. In theory it helped foster understanding and avoid war. That, at least, was what father had believed.

Pretty, with skin darker than pitch, Heke had already given me one child, though right at that moment I could not recall its name.

"The birth of your son Sekhemkare was a trial for her, Your Royal Highness," Peseshet said gently. "She was barely sixteen and less developed than a girl of her age should have been. She tore badly..."

I held up my hands so that I would be spared the details.

"I know this is not my place but she is a sweet..." I think Peseshet was going to use the word 'child' but wisely went instead for "... person. I fear for her life if she falls pregnant for a second time so soon. In a few years perhaps..."

Though I take great pains to hide it, I think my heart is more tender than others in my rapacious, backstabbing family. Heke was indeed a sweet child and I would not wish to do anything to hurt her but my wishes were as nothing in a family dedicated to manufacturing gods. Gods mattered, the Egyptian people mattered, but one little person did not matter at all.

I turned back to the river. The sun was so low and so red I could stare directly into it without pain. "I would... I can't..." I stopped myself. If my father had heard this hesitation, he would have beaten me like a drum. My little finger, as well as my pride, had been permanently bent where it had been broken fending off his blows.

I steadied myself and turned to face her. The sun dyed her robes a gentle red. Just for a second her broadly spaced eyes, full breasts and generous hips made me wonder about her husband. Whoever he was, he was a lucky man. What must it be like to couple with such an intelligent woman?

I rarely felt the need to explain my actions but something about Peseshet made me speak frankly. "Chief Physician, you must understand that children for a royal couple are even more important than for a farmer who needs sons to tend his farm and look after him in his old age. It is about alliances, it is about peace, it is about avoiding wars that kill thousands. We, my brothers and my sisters, are married to people from lands beyond the Western Desert and north of the Sinai. From Sumeria and Mesopotamia, Khor and Babylon and Canaan. We are all under constant scrutiny, not just for the number of children we produce but also how often we couple with our spouses. Servants..." and I indicated around, though I had not been aware of them. I noted that, whilst we had been talking, they had magically appeared with beer and fruit juices, bread and dates, all on silver platters. They had placed these on two gold embossed tables I had not noticed them carry in. Two of the servants stood within earshot, heads bent, hands clasped, waiting for any instructions.

I hesitated, a little stupefied by the strength of my own point. I made a gesture of dismissal and they left. "Servants keep count of these things and that information is bought by Neferhotep's minions. And, of course, our allies hear about it from our spouses."

"I understand, Your Royal Highness, but perhaps I may suggest a solution. There are methods, known to physicians like myself, that can prevent conception. In that way you could couple with the... appropriate frequency without the Princess being with child and risking her life. I think your wife would be happy with the arrangement."

"What are these methods?"

"The one I would suggest would require your wife inserting a material into her vagina just before you couple. Afterward, she simply throws it away. I can supply as much of this material as is required."

"What is it?"

"Crocodile dung exposed to the sun for thirty days."

How did physicians know these things? Peseshet continued to amaze me with her arcane knowledge.

"How does it... I mean why..." Khufu must be turning in his sarcophagus and not just because insects would be chewing at his insides.

Peseshet didn't seem to notice my hesitation, or the demeaning way I was seeking information. Instead her eyes had lit up with enthusiasm. "I have performed some research, studied the action on a man's essence when brought into contact with the dung. It is absorbed completely, sucked up by the dried material. I prescribe it for many of my patients. For some, five or six children is enough, especially if they are wealthy. For poorer women it is a different matter; they are made to kill themselves with myriad births." Her face looked red, though whether from the setting sun or from anger I could not be sure.

I sensed an underlying heresy, hardly something she should mention to me, of all people. Again, this spoke of her enthusiasm. What she was suggesting was not how medicines were supposed to work. Medicine was all about essence. This much I understood. Animal dung, from hippos and monkeys, lions and cows, pelicans and ostriches, lizards and cats were commonly used in medicines, the idea being that they captured the essence of the animal. Hippo dung was for power and given when an illness had been especially weakening, antelope dung for wasting diseases of the legs to give them strength and speed. Sobek, the crocodile-headed god, was the god of semen, but also a god of protection. In the minds of other, more conventional, priest-physicians some fusion of these two properties would be how it worked to prevent pregnancy.

Yet what Peseshet was suggesting was a much more prosaic mechanism. Heresy has always been a heady drink for me. I found Peseshet's notion intriguing, something that made sense without any reference to the gods or their essences. I wondered what other strange ideas lurked behind those clever eyes.

"Let us proceed as you suggest, Chief Physician." As we were alone, this was an opportunity to seek information on an even touchier subject. I leaned forward and lowered my voice. "Chief Physician, I am concerned about my brother, Djedefre, the King. His cough is worse and he gains no weight. He hardly eats at all, whatever delicacies are put before him. What ails him?"

Her forehead creased as though I had said something hurtful. This close I could smell her breath sweetener, a ball of cinnamon and myrrh, if I was not mistaken. The smell was strong so it had been recently removed. I hadn't seen her pop it in or out of her mouth, but was pleased she had taken the trouble.

"Your brother is no longer your brother. He is a god. I cannot speak of his health."

Brothers and sisters hide little from each other, even in royal households. That had all changed on the day my father died and my scrawny, breathless brother became a god, or at least a god-in-waiting. He had withdrawn from us as inexorably as the waters of the Nile retreated in the winter, protected from his friends and his family and all mankind by the fearsome High Lord Neferhotep.

"No matter how different his life now, he still has the same cough that plagues many of our countrymen. The same cough that my elder brother Kawab also had. He died, as you know."

This little trick worked and I found myself disappointed at how easy it had been. Peseshet's enthusiasm overcame her professional reserve and she was more than happy to talk about Kawab, though everything she said would be applicable to Djedefre. "Prince Kawab had a condition which indeed is common amongst us. I have looked into this with interest. As with many of my profession I am an adept at mummification and I find the contents of the viscera deeply revealing. I treat these with full respect, I assure you, your Royal Highness. I merely inspect them before placing them in the canopic jars."

I nodded. "Of course."

"I find I cannot pass up such an opportunity to look within the bodies of the dead as this can afford great insight into what caused their deaths." She leaned forward, so earnest and serious. "Prince Kawab fell ill from coughing and weight loss. After he died, I prepared him as usual but noticed that the insides of his lungs were black, not pink. I scraped out a little of this black substance and studied it later. I washed it then dried it and do you know what I found?"

She was leaning far forward now, her hands clasping so tightly the knuckles were white.

I shook my head.

"Sand!" she said triumphantly. "It was sand coating the inside of his lungs."

"Sand killed my brother?" I hadn't been expecting this.

"I think - and remember, this is just my theory - that sand kills thousands. Sandstorms come and we breath the sand in. We can't help it. Most of us can somehow rid ourselves of it," she held up her hands palms towards me. "I do not know how, Your Royal Highness, so please don't ask me. Others, like Prince Kawab, cannot rid themselves of the sand and, over time, their lungs are damaged. This condition is found very often in quarry workers who cut the sandstone and granite for our temples and tombs. You know how dust-filled the air is in our quarries."

"Indeed, I do," I said though, of course, I had never been to such a place.

"And I think that is also what does such damage to our teeth."

I frowned.

She hurried to explain. "Our teeth are poor. They wear down too quickly."

"Compared to...?"

Perhaps I spoke too sharply, or perhaps she remembered at last who she was talking to. Our civilisation was clearly the mightiest in the world; implying Egyptians were in any way inferior to others was another heresy.

She fell to her knees, head bowed. "Forgive me, Your Royal Highness!"

I stooped forward and grasped her upper arm and pulled her upright. "I appreciate your honesty, Chief Physician. I have an appetite for the truth but so few people dare speak to me frankly. Please continue. You have nothing to fear from me."

She lifted her head and risked a glance, her eyes blinking in surprise. I smiled as reassuringly as I could.

"Continue!"

A deep breath. "I have interrogated and physically examined slaves from the far south whose skins are blacker even than ours. They say the desert does not go on forever. Beyond Nubia and Kush the land becomes greener. Their teeth are big, strong and alabaster white. Ours are yellow and stubby and pain us. I believe it is the desert sand and the grit that gets in our food, especially our bread, that wears down our teeth."

"And what would be a more suitably priestly explanation for this?"

"They do not even acknowledge it is a problem. Our teeth have always troubled us this way."

I noticed the servants had returned to light oil lamps and I realised how dark it had become. I should have dismissed Peseshet but found myself asking her many more questions about her profession. This turned into a long and easy conversation, both of us seeming to forget the differences in our stations in life. We talked thus for many hours until, finally tiring, I sent her away.

After she left me, I lingered for a while on the terrace. The air was still and clear and I watched the endless belt of stars wheel across the sky. It was peaceful enough but when I went to bed all I could think of was of my brother slowly choking to death on Egypt's endless, swirling sands.

Modern Day

Ever been lost in a world of smell so rich, so profound, so satisfying that you forget every other damn thing?

No? Then try being reborn as a dog.

These old people eat more than you would expect. The boat needs to be constantly re-supplied with a breath-taking range of comestibles, and I can smell every single one of them. Both when they go in and when they come out. Right now, what is going in are the smells of cumin and coriander, lemon and lime. But these are just the polite patina below which lurk the arousing just-starting-to-decay aromas of meat and fish.

I am at the boat end of the metal gangplank they throw down whenever the boat docks. Sweating crewmen stagger past carrying the provisions: muslin-wrapped sides of beef, whole carcases of lamb, boxes full of fish immersed in this mysterious substance they call ice. Smells radiate away behind all this like the wake of a boat. The impulse to shove my nose into all of it is more imploring than any mistress I have ever known.

Stationing me here is a form of cruelty to which my handlers seem oblivious. Rather than salivating to death like me, they stand bored, hands on hips, trading insults with the crew.

Can you drown in your own saliva? If you're a dog, I'm pretty sure you can. I stand bug-eyed as mountains of meat waft over me. I was well-used to the heavy butcher's block smells as I passed by in my sedan chair through the dusty reed-covered alleys of Memphis. My stomach would churn at the flies crawling over the exposed flesh, giving it a rippling black skin. The dense smell of corruption was always a presence.

Meat does not smell nearly as bad now. I'm also aware of other discernments. Fat and flesh are quite different and each excites my doggy palate, the sweetness of the fat moistening my tongue, the coppery waft of the meat making my jaw muscles bulge, eager to rend and tear.

It's all too much. A whimper escapes me.

"What's his problem?" asks Mazan. "Did you remember to feed him this morning, Ragab?"

My communications with my handlers are basic but unequivocal. A bark means I smell explosives so draw your guns and start shouting. A whimper means I'm just being a silly dog.

"Of course I fed him." Ragab could be a handsome young man but the overall effect is undermined by a spindly and singularly ill-advised moustache. "There's probably just a bitch around here somewhere."

There isn't. If there was, blood would already be hammering into my canine cock. I know little about canine anatomy but I'm pretty sure there's a tube that goes from my nose directly to my penis. One whiff of that entrancing furry, sweaty, bloody, vaginal, faecal stench and my heart contracts, my stomach churns and the bright yellow (though, in the context, I'm guessing it's actually pink) tip of my penis comes poking out of my furry foreskin.

This has got to be cosmic punishment. That dream, when I removed my father's bottom plug, suggests I may not have been a very nice man. What I did was definitely bad but surely not worthy of such damnation?

The really weird thing is that if I actually catch sight of the goddess producing this exquisitely seductive stink, then all I see is a scraggy mutt not fit to be squished under the boots of my bodyguards.

Does this make my penis retract into its rancid, unwashed shell? Not even close. Instead all the blood drains from my heart into my bursting organ.

So, it turns out I'm all smell and cock. In fact, you can use that for my second memorial. Cheops: all smell and cock.

"You guys need any help?" asks a sweating porter as he staggers by under a sheep carcase.

"Fuck you too," says Amr amiably.

As ports go on this river, Minya is quite pleasant. The jetty seems to lead directly onto the town square, or at least a wide tree-lined promenade. Beyond that the narrow, car-ridden streets crowd in.

Cars, that's another thing I can't comprehend. They growl, they screech and they move at blistering speeds even in these twisty little streets. Are they designed specifically to kill dogs?

I'm hoping I won't have to go on this walkabout, that I can stay here and sniff away. However, the big men with boots are already assembling. Some are dressed in blue uniforms like my handlers, others in what looks like white but could be green. Put it this way, if they were hiding in the trees, I wouldn't be able to see them unless they moved.

There are a couple of groups of men dressed in black, one lot hunkering down in a black van. One man stays out in front but behind a heavy shield. His assault rifle is resting on top of the shield and pointing out into the street. People walking by must pass the muzzle of the gun at the level of their temples. Some are brave and walk by, others flinch, some duck a little. Nobody's digestion is improved. As part of my training I've seen a number of these guns come to life, spitting like cobras as they released their devils, plumes of fire and fury bursting out of their mouths.

In the past I've heard my handlers talk in awe of these men in black. They are Special Weapons and Tactical, though I'm not sure what that means. As far as I can see, they appear whenever things look like they might kick off, as my handlers would say.

The loading seems to be trailing off. If it stops altogether then they may drag me with them on the walk. I don't want to go because of the boots and the cars, but there's another reason and that's the state of the dogs that slink around towns and villages. Don't get me wrong, I'm not identifying with these three-legged, one-eyed, limping monstrosities with matted hair and clouds of flies round their backsides. What I don't like is the reminder of just how limited is my freedom of action because downtrodden and detested though they are, at least they don't spend their lives on a lead.

In my previous life we had animals as pets and my palace was full of pampered cats and even a few of the better-behaved dogs. Nowadays dogs aren't pets and Egyptians seem to regard us as unclean. We're functional, like my old hunting dogs. If dogs aren't working then they are strays. Indeed, the state of the stray dogs is why I don't make a bolt for it, leaving my leaden-footed handlers far behind. Doing that in Cairo, where I'm normally stationed, would mean more or less instant suicide. Cairo doesn't do stray dogs. One happy, tongue-lolling mutt breaking free from the oppressive hands of its owner will be instantly predated by the treacherous Cairo traffic. Cairo's roads are colonically blocked by stationary metal for hours or even days at a time, except in the instants when they are not, when the cars travel so fast they are just a blur even to my exquisitely motion-sensitive doggy vision. They come at you, horns blaring, forming rivers of instant death for escapee dogs.

The further from the big city you get, the lighter the traffic and the more stray dogs there are, but they are so spavined and worm-eaten that nobody in their right mind would envy them. The Egyptians let them live - perhaps they keep the rats down - but they are unforgiving if the mutts misbehave. The dogs must slink in the shadows, scavenging from one reeking midden to another.

So, unless I can figure out a brilliant plan, I'm stuck with my handlers because at least I get fed.

The last porter is leaving the boat and I notice the squirrelly waiter from earlier is with him. He's awash with scent so strong it makes my eyes water. His white shirt and black trousers are clean and stink of what they use to wash them. It has a sharp, tangy odour but I can still smell his sweat under the soap.

His eyes are on my handlers as he passes me and they don't look friendly. Of course, my handlers don't notice. They're too busy checking out a woman who has come through the gate and is heading their way. It's an all-male crew on the boat and so any woman below fifty is a rarity.

As he passes, the waiter looks at me and winks. What the fuck is that all about? He makes his way through the gate and disappears amongst the crowds in the square.

The approaching woman is in black trousers and a lighter jacket. A black head scarf covers hair which is no doubt dark, lustrous and plentiful. The thought of it almost makes me swoon. As she steps onto the gangplank my handlers' eyes swivel to track her backside, which is well-rounded.

"I miss my wife," says Ragab sadly.

Amr nods his agreement. "Thirty days away," says Amr. "It's too long."

"We will soon be home, inshallah," intones Ragab.

And if you believe that bullshit, that sexual satisfaction lies only days away for my handlers, then you'll believe anything. Here's a deep, dark secret: Egyptians don't have sex. They never really did.

Yes, I have to admit there are quite a few people around, certainly far more than in my day, so I'm forced to admit there must be some vaginal penetration going on but, if so, it's as rare as an even-tempered hippopotamus.

And I should know. Even when I had a man's nose, I was aware that semen and vaginal secretions had a smell. The latter could even on occasion be entrancing, but those smells were like a faraway candle on a misty night compared to the coruscating rainbow brilliance revealed by my doggy nose. Unless they scrub themselves down afterward, I can even estimate how recently they did it and how excited the woman had been.

Cairo could be a city of eunuchs for all the sex they seem to have, except at the big hotels where some younger versions of these strange white-skinned foreigners live. To my new nose they reek like sex. Do the foreigners do nothing else? I would stand stunned at the checkpoint where I sometimes sniff for bombs in the cars coming into the hotel, desperately trying to concentrate on my job.

Even worse is when the women, often with hair so pale it's like gold, stop as they are walking out into the city and crouch down and gently rub the top of my head, crooning in languages I cannot even begin to comprehend. Their pale eyes come close to mine and the scent of their recent arousal overcomes me and I have to lie down to conceal my erection, resisting all efforts by my handlers to pull me to my feet.

My guess is that these strange foreign people don't have big families, or they send their children away to wet nurses and tutors and thus clear the way for unrestrained and continual sex. Meanwhile, the poor Egyptians from time immemorial have lived with generations under one roof, where the opportunities for privacy have always been rare.

The well-built woman halts in the main reception hall and the boat's overseer comes over to her. The overseer marks himself out as different from the rest of the crew by wearing what I've come to identify as a suit. They begin to talk and in doing so reveal everything that feels wrong to me about this modern Egypt.

It is as if the woman is surrounded by an invisible shield which the man tentatively approaches but then bounces off. He is tall and lean with kind eyes and it is clear he likes her. His smile is genuine but all the energy he might like to put into touching her spends itself on rolling shoulders, dipping head and the clasping and ringing of his hands.

Behind me I hear Mazan whisper, "He is fucking her. You can always tell."

Oh, Mazan, I think, you complete idiot!

What happened to this country? It had been very tactile and it still is today but only when men meet men. They clap each other's shoulders, drape hairy arms round necks, hold hands, kiss on meeting. But when a man meets a woman it is as though he has stumbled across a deadly viper poised to strike.

"Imagine her letting down that lustrous hair all over your chest. It would be like a river flowing over your nipples." This is the final leg of two return trips but, even so, I expected better of Amr.

"That is not the flow you most want to feel," says Ragab, wise beyond his years, if only within the confines of his own skull.

"And smell," says Mazan.

I'm glad the woman does not have ears like mine. These men look tough, they have cultivated the cold, faraway looks of police and soldiers throughout the ages, but they talk like little boys.

The woman keeps glancing away as the man bounces around her. I don't smell arousal but I'm pretty sure she likes him. They stand, barely an arm's length apart, but separated by the length of the Nile.

Disgusted by this silly, stilted, self-defeating charade, I look away.

The old white people have been congregating in the entrance hall, milling around like sheep. Now they are starting across the gangway and they all pass by me. Apart from the bald ones, everyone has their own hair yet they seem untroubled by nits and fleas for they rarely scratch their heads. And, unlike my police friends, they pay attention to perfume. Too much, perhaps, because the complexity overwhelms me. I smell flower oils like jasmine, rose and lavender, but also coconut and vanilla, sandalwood and pine. There is cinnamon and lemon and rosemary. Most redolent of all are the traces of frankincense and myrrh. That's all very pleasant but the fragrances are bound together by underpinning notes of sulphur and seaweed and many other smells that I have never experienced before. Like the explosives I have been trained to detect, they don't smell like they come from this world at all. They have a bitterness amplified by my dog nose so it feels as though my head has been stuffed with burning coals.

I can't help whimpering.

Unlike most Egyptians, these old folks don't seem to regard dogs as unclean and some scratch my head as they pass, much to Amr's disapproval. He feels it detracts from our dignity, our martial invincibility.

As if. The man has no idea what dignity means. Then again, now that I'm a dog, it's hard for me to take the high ground on this one.

As the last elderly tourist crosses to shore, the gangplank is withdrawn. We follow the old folk, leaving local cops to guard the ship. We pass through the main gate guarded by the SWAT team dressed in black from feet to helmeted head. A black mask obscures their features. They climb out of their truck and join us.

The square I find myself in is tree-lined and contains one or two little stalls selling fruit. The line of tourists snakes across it, flanked on either side by more SWAT guys. At the head of the line, and also bringing up the rear, are the usual security contingent, ordinary cops dressed in green uniforms and all with assault rifles. Embedded within the line are the plain-clothes guys, give-away pistol butts sticking out of pockets or tucked in waistbands at the back of their trousers. Ever alert to tiny changes of expression, I can see how anxious they all are and that's what scares me the most.

With all the movement, and with my low viewpoint, it's difficult to accurately judge numbers but I'm guessing the thirty or so tourists are far outnumbered by their security detail.

We cross the square and dive into a road overshadowed on either side by five and six-storey buildings. At ground level there are little shops, just like the bazaars of old but selling stuff I mostly cannot recognise. I can make out those that sell clothes, the flat disks of bread, vegetables and shoes. On one stall, oranges hang in nets framed by fruit like long yellow fingers that weren't around in my day. Whatever they sell, the goods are piled up in an abundance I still find so alien.

On the faces of buildings and hanging between poles are the images of the Pharaoh. I know this because the men talk about him all the time. His name is Abdel Fattah el-Sisi but he's like no god-king I've ever seen. For one thing, he smiles. God-kings don't smile; instead they regard the workings of the little people with god-like serenity. Smiling makes you look like a market trader, a point Khufu would often hammer home by way of his fists or, if you were unlucky, his cock.

Meanwhile, the real market traders seem too stunned by this procession through their midst to rush forward and sell their wares. Equally shocked are the passers-by who stand stock still, mouths open. Some clutch little children to their chests. The kids laugh and point. One or two of the parents also begin to smile and one or two to wave. The old white folks smile and wave back enthusiastically.

The plain-clothes men's eyes search everywhere for threat but the townspeople, though surprised, seem glad to see us. Perhaps for once Amr, with his dung beetle's eye view of the world, is right. The townspeople are poor and the white people are rich and this may be a sign their money is returning.

Suddenly a man steps forward from the crowd of onlookers, hand outstretched. The plain-clothes guys leap forward, hands on their pistol butts, but an old tourist guy beats them to it. He's very tall with hair almost as pale as his skin. He grabs the outstretched hand and shakes it enthusiastically. The police freeze, conflicting emotions skirmishing across their features. By the time the handshake has finished, the Egyptian guy is surrounded by police, all leaning in close.

I feel a peremptory, deeply undignified and vastly annoying tug at my throat. I must have stopped to gawk and Ragab has yanked on my chain. Reluctantly, I turn and follow.

At least the old folk are wearing soft, open shoes that are rather less ornate than the elaborate gold-embossed sandals I'd worn when I had feet. The police are a menace though, their heads swivelling from side to side, not looking where they're putting their heavy boots.

Little kids have been following us and the braver ones have dashed into the tourists, grabbing the nearest withered hand. The tourists look delighted, the policemen less so. A few of the local cops peel off to shoo away other kids before they do the same.

I check back automatically to make sure one of the ubiquitous cars hasn't crept up on me prior to running over my head and suddenly I realise there aren't any of the damned things. Glancing round I see that at every crossroads a SWAT guy is standing right in the middle staring them all down, gun cradled in his arms. The cars wait patiently, their owners neither shouting nor gesticulating nor making their cars squeal in outrage. Silent, respectfully waiting Egyptian traffic is an unnerving sight but I know where they're coming from. I've seen how angry those guns can get.

Meanwhile, our walk is turning out to be a circuit and we soon find ourselves back on the square that sits by the river. Ahead I can see the lights of the boats. With safety so close yet still so far, I can literally smell the policemen's tension. As a human, fear smelt like piss because that's what happened to me when my father went into one of his rages. As a dog, fear reeks of something different. I don't really have the words, but it's like a piercing, shrill high note but made of smells. It's unpleasant but also viscerally exciting. If I smelt it off a herd of animals, like sheep, I would find myself killing and killing in brutal doggy exultation. Smelling it off a herd of heavily armed policemen: not so much!

Even so, the smell of their fear keys me up, so much so that I can see the trouble coming. Ahead of me an old white woman is stepping up a kerb, but I can tell she isn't going to make it. Her toe catches, she staggers and falls, but three plain-clothes officers, thrumming with stress, instantly leap forward and catch her, breaking her fall so she lands like a feather. They help her up but then back off quickly, too inhibited to dust her down.

When we return to the boat, they've put the gangway back across. We stay on the jetty until all the old folk are safely on board. The sense of relief amongst the policemen is palpable across all my senses, and they start clapping each other on the shoulders and laughing.

Amr unclips my lead and points at some bushes over in a corner and I go and take a quick dump. Crapping in the sand is no novelty but once upon a time the sand would have been in an exquisitely ornate and perfumed bowl which a slave would empty as soon as I'd finished, the smell not daring to disturb my nostrils.

Not now, though. The noisome digested smell of whatever the hell it is they feed me follows me all the way back to the boat. Amr clips me up again.

Some crew are returning and I sniff them frankly, something I've learned from bitter, painful experience not to do with the white people. The crew's dirty secrets are shamelessly revealed as they slope aboard trailing behind the miasma of their sin. I'm sick to death of my handlers complaining I'm not a proper sniffer dog because I've never been trained to smell drugs, but I'm not stupid. Kief is everywhere in this country and some of the men coming back aboard reek of it. Others reek of women, some of other men, some just of tobacco and alcohol. Interesting, but nothing worth a warning bark.

Then, coming through the gate, I see my squirrelly waiter friend. He's looking unconcerned but I instinctively trust him as much as I would a Nile crocodile and pull forward on my lead as he approaches the gangplank.

"Someone's keen tonight," says Mazan. "What have you been up to, Masud?"

"Nothing," says the man.

"Then Cheops must like you. Look at the way he is sniffing at your crotch. You must be his type."

"Can't you keep your mutt under control?" I'm still sniffing hard but there's nothing except sweat. The lack of evidence of sin is itself unsettling, but my barking vocabulary isn't sufficiently nuanced to convey this to my handlers.

"Oh, this is him under control, Masud. Just one word and he'll open your throat as easily as you open the zip of your trousers." Mazan says this with relish, though it's a fantasy. Jobs are parcelled out just like they were in ancient Egypt, passed from father down to son. I have no recollections of my canine parents but my furry dad must have been a bomb sniffer dog too. Other dogs may sniff for drugs or blood-thirstily attack people with their teeth but that's not what I do, either through training or inclination.

Nevertheless, I look directly into Masud's eyes and bare my teeth ever so slightly. For a second his eyes widen in alarm and I can tell he is forcing himself to stand his ground. He has backbone. I've seen him through the boat's windows serving the old folk but there is nothing of the servant about him now.

Ragab tugs me back. Masud throws me a look of contempt and then strides aboard, the gangway flexing up and down with his heavy, angry steps.

"What's got into the dog?" asks Ragab, lighting a cigarette.

"Perhaps we've got Monthu instead," says Amr and they all laugh.

As Ptah endures... I think, the old expression of disgust coming readily to mind. Being a dog is bad enough but I'm considered an inferior one to boot. Monthu: the fucking Wonder Dog. Monthu whose exploits are written up breathlessly in the papers my handlers read. Monthu: the scourge of the Muslim Brotherhood. Monthu: protector of the innocent, disemboweller of the guilty, saviour of mankind, god provider of fertility to the testicle-less and so on and so on.

Monthu to whom I am always being compared. And, sure enough, he does look like me: big and hairy with lots of teeth and a lolling tongue. What my disparaging handlers don't see is that while my brain is the size of a pyramid, his would be dwarfed by a grain of sand.

We're both German Shepherds, after a fashion. We're well-muscled with black fur on our backs and sides that turns lighter on our bellies and shoulders and legs. We're nothing like the dogs of my day, who were skinnier and shorter haired with long thin legs so they could run like demons after prey. They were either hunting dogs or scavengers and they hung around in packs. You wouldn't dream of petting one if you wanted your hand back.

Monthu plays to the crowds, something in which I have no little expertise myself but wouldn't dream of doing as a mutt. Cutting through the bullshit as best I can, his reputation seems to have come from being on a job near a big government building. He sniffed a bomb. Summoning his mighty intelligence, he gave the signal bark.

Er... and that's it. Yet for days there were more pictures of him in the flimsy paper Amr reads (what happened to papyrus which lasts for ever?) than there ever were of Pharaoh Sisi. Maybe it did save a hundred lives but all he did was his job.

A couple of the crew that deal with the gangway have appeared. "Knocking off time," says Amr with evident relief.

"Come on, Monthu," says Ragab, giving my lead a tug. We walk across the gangway and back onto the boat. There is a grating sound as the gangway is pulled back for the night and soon the boat is drifting away to a safer anchorage downriver.

Ancient Days 2563 BC

The Goddess Renenutet, flattered, placated, sacrificed to, had granted us a wondrous harvest. The Nile had risen in the spring, a great beast stirring gently, its inundating waters arriving slowly, respectfully, like a slave waking his master. No villages were washed away as the waters surged in, hidden by the night. No rafts of swollen, drowned cattle swirled around its eddies. Most sublime of all, when the waters receded, they left behind the thickest skin of fine dark silt that none but the very oldest had ever seen. For a full month each farmer took to his plough, its underhanging end digging like a phallus deep into the fertile, loamy earth, churning the new soil into the old. It was said crops began to rise even before each furrow had been finished.

And now, months later, had come the harvest and the feast to celebrate. From across the river I had seen excited children collecting papyrus and reeds, tiny figures dragging long thin stems many times their length. Before I had left for the Royal Feast, columns of black smoke from cooking fires all across the river valley rose up bamboo-straight into the still sky until toppled by the high desert winds.

Now the sun was setting and our own feast had begun. The third year of the new King's reign and the harvest had been more bountiful than for decades. Djedefre, already eased into godhood, had decreed that our royal harvest feast must be suitably emblematic.

Thus, before me lay a madman's dream of the Nile valley stretching for the length of twenty men along one side of the palace square. Cucumbers fashioned as crocodiles lurked in its dark waters. Quail with figs for heads and cinnamon sticks for legs were hippos gambolling in the shallows. Honey cakes studded with roasted nuts formed the royal palaces whilst broad beans, grapes and lettuce were the fields. Sprigs of coriander hung with tiny red berries were the pomegranate trees. Further beyond, mounds of chickpeas and lentils made the rising desert.

And through all this flowed a river of the finest Theban wine. All evening slaves had been collecting this in the buckets of their long-poled and carefully counterbalanced shadoofs. They took the wine from the lower reaches where it spread out into the Delta and hurried it back to the reservoir at the inland end. They had done their work well for the river of wine flowed more smoothly and continuously than the Nile ever had.

Across the whole marble square drifted the rich, fatty smell of cooking meat. Geese and ducks and smaller wildfowl that I could not even recognise, turned on spits over crackling fires. Other spits held dismembered hippo and ox and sheep, black and brown and dripping with precious fats, collected in troughs by slaves and used to baste the meat continually. Not a single drop was lost.

Despite its magnificence, the river valley was merely a decoration to which few paid attention. Instead we lounged on divans in our finery, gossiping away as servants offered us tasty morsels from platters stacked high with meat and fruits and cakes. Some tottered under huge trays bearing cups of beer and wine decorated with brightly painted designs showing scenes from older times.

I signalled to a servant holding a tray with a roast ox-head. He leaned down so I was looking into the roast onions filling its eye sockets. I pinched its cheeks as I would pinch a lover's and the tender, slick flesh came away. I dropped the fat sweetened meat into my mouth.

"I can't eat that sort of thing. Not when its eyes are looking at me." Kham, reed-thin even after giving birth to my new son Menkaura barely three weeks before, was the only one in the whole of Egypt not enjoying a feast. On her plate lay just a few morsels of bread dotted with cumin and sesame seeds. A side-bowl of plain chick-peas, each gently and painstakingly carved to accentuate their hawk-faces, had not even been touched.

"Then don't," I said.

This was supposed to be a family affair but, even so, there was a surfeit of generals and high priests and officials with job titles too long to enunciate without falling asleep. With such a vast administration, even whore houses had official licences, their doors marked with the seal of the Royal Administrator of Pleasure Houses, Bawdy Parlours and Genital Massage Establishments. Even crumbling huts in the most flyblown of towns offering holes through which a man in anonymity could place his organ to gain simple release had such a seal. Woe betide any whore who worked without it.

For an instant, a breeze made the beautifully dyed hangings flap like the wings of a giant vulture. The hangings were at the far end, the Nile to the left and the row of fire pits to the right. The near end of the square was being cleared by men in toughened crocodile leather tunics, signalling the entry of our god. Already late, I was sure Djedefre would even now be dithering about what to wear.

Neferhotep emerged from the Royal Palace with his chief of security, Kamwase. Poacher turned gamekeeper,

Kamwase had been a thief who many years ago had been caught stealing perfume from a merchant. This merchant had brought his wares, more precious by weight even than gold, from lands so far away they had no names. Maat, the goddess of truth and justice, was the touchstone of all High Lord Treasurers and balance was all. To this end Neferhotep had had Kamwase's nose sliced off, leaving a ghastly gaping hole from which globs of mucus would sometimes drip. If Kamwase ever looked like he might sneeze, packed rooms quickly cleared.

In one of those ironies so common in life, rather than hating Neferhotep for his mutilation, the heavily set, almost bear-like Kamwase had shown nothing but abject obedience ever since. Beat a wild dog often enough and it will recognise you as its master. If Neferhotep was the right arm of the King, then Kamwase was the nail-studded bludgeon grasped in the fist.

Divans and low tables were laid all the way around the Nile valley centrepiece. The further you were from the Royal Palace, the lower you were in esteem. As the King's next eldest brother, I was on the first set of divans to the right of the gold throne. This was raised up so that my brother could look down on the whole tableaux like Ra himself.

The High Lord and Kamwase were casting their searching eyes over everything, checking for the faintest sign of trouble. Both men were tall, taller even than the Ethiopians sold in the slave markets who were destined for the mines and quarries. Neferhotep favoured bright blue makeup made from ground lapis around his eyes and with heavy lines of kohl across his forehead as though he was perpetually frowning with the darkest anger. His face was hard and weathered, not at all what you would expect from someone performing physically effortless work in the shade. Whatever life he had led before my father lifted him to greatness, it had taken its toll, seasoning him like wood and making him hard and dark.

Both men, having completed their surveillance, stood at the back of my divan, waiting for the god to arrive. Neferhotep's dark eyes turned to look down on me while Kamwase's danced this way and that, daring someone to endanger the High Lord.

I am uncomfortable being looked down on so I stood, though I was still a good hand's length shorter than Neferhotep. When I was a boy, and even sometimes as a young man, he had beaten me when my father, the god, was too busy.

"Prince Khafre," said Neferhotep, "May you complete a hundred and ten years upon earth, your limbs being vigorous."

"High Lord Neferhotep," I said, matching his dead rote-like tones as closely as I could. "May the fecundity of your wives bring you children without number."

The pleasantries dispensed with I indicated to his right, away from the divans and the listening ears of my wives. "May I speak with you on a personal matter?"

Neferhotep glanced back at the entrance from which the King would enter. A guard waiting by the drapes saw Neferhotep looking and shook his head. Djedefre, fluttering around indecisively, would inevitably be ridiculously late.

Neferhotep looked back at me. "I can spare you some time, Your Royal Highness."

These men had known me so long, had seen me crying my eyes out and soiling myself when they'd chastised me as a child, that they could not bring themselves to regard me as a threat. Kamwase, who usually stuck as closely to Neferhotep as a fly to a pile of horse dung, didn't bother to accompany us as we moved further away than the length of his sword.

Our movement interfered with a servant carrying a shadoof heavy with wine buckets for the wine river. He had to swing around us in a careful, elongated pirouette so its long poles did not touch us. It was clumsy and ungainly but he didn't spill a drop.

Just as well, as his life had depended upon it. Neferhotep was nothing if not unforgiving.

Our own relationship had always been a complex one but, with the death of my father, it had changed. Neferhotep had seen only the worst of me and his blows had, amongst other injuries, left a discolouration under my left cheek that I would take to my tomb. Until Djedefre's sons were old enough to pick their noses unaided, I was now a heartbeat away from being a god myself. However, we had different mothers: his mother Meritities was still alive and it was likely she would be named Regent until Djedefre's eldest son matured. Thanks to that bastard Khufu my own mother, Henutsen, had suffered a much less deserving fate. Unable to bear him any more children he had banished her to the Delta where she had died from fever. Out of pure spite he had not allowed her to be mummified. I would never see her again, even in the Field of Reeds.

Can you wonder why I hated the vicious old bastard so deeply?

Meritities would not last forever and there was an outside chance that I could be named as the successor, especially if the sickly sons of sickly Djedefre did not survive childhood. For the first time in all my years, Neferhotep had to be careful in how he dealt with me.

Had he been a normal, easy-going man, I might have felt sorry for him. I hadn't been the sweetest and most obedient of children. It was in my nature to mock everyone, mimicking their speech and manners and the way they moved, Neferhotep not least of all, though never within his sight or hearing. However, one day the wild streak in my nature had got the better of my sense of self-preservation and I had aped someone even more dangerous: my father.

When I had been seven years old, Khufu had built yet another temple to Horus. As any good god-king knew, you just couldn't have enough of these for they were the personification on earth of that fearsome hawk-headed deity. Newly painted, the carvings of scenes of the gods glared out in blazing reds and blues and golds. Fifty sweating slaves had carried father's golden chair up the twenty steps to the temple. The chair and its supporting poles had been far too long so the slaves at the back had to stand on tiptoe, muscles corded and veins standing out on their temples, in order to keep the chair level lest father should be tilted back in an ungodlike matter. The overseers with their whips of twisted and seasoned hippo leather stood ready.

Father looked splendid. A lapis mask of Horus hid his soulless calculating eyes and narrow unsmiling face. A cape of bright red threaded with gold covered his body except for the arms that held the golden crook and flail of Osiris. The crook showed he was the shepherd of the nation, the flail the scourge he would use to make sure the people behaved properly. Osiris had been our first king and, on his death, had become King of the Dead.

Somehow, despite bursting hearts and with muscles and tendons snapping like lute strings, the slaves manhandled the chair up to the temple entrance. The chair was then rotated so the King faced the people. It was lowered most gently and Khufu waited while the slaves, their bodies hunched and broken by the effort, were led away on shaking legs.

The temple rose high above us, the roof resting on hypostyle columns so thick that five men holding hands could not encircle them. Representing the stem of the lotus, the columns widened out with their granite flowers supporting the roof. All this the people had the rare opportunity of seeing through the heavy doors that had been flung open. Soon these would be closed and the people would be herded out of the high-walled enclosure round the temple, never to return. Temples were for the God-King and his priests, not for the common people.

The whole royal family was up there with Khufu. My siblings and I were all so young we still had our top-knots, braided to one side so they hung down over one shoulder. Neferhotep, Kamwase and the High Priest of the new temple were standing with us. A hundred soldiers, their crocodile leather breastplates looking like jade, formed a column down either side of the steps and across at the bottom, a barrier between the people and their god.

The High Priest came forward and addressed the crowds. Of course, I paid not the slightest attention to what he was saying. Father remained seated, as he would throughout, his face hidden under a mask of solid gold. I had sneaked a look at the chair earlier at our palace, before father had taken his seat and was carried up the long avenue to the temple. The red and gold cloak that father wore was really for another purpose. It disguised the supports which held up the heavy mask. I had watched, peeking around a corner, as Father had wormed his way up and into it in a very un-godlike fashion.

The temple was south facing so there was no hiding from Ra's heat and light. The family all wore the finest linens which had gleamed a breath-taking white when fresh but had quickly darkened with our sweat.

The High Priest droned on and I vaguely realised he was talking about the godly duties of Horus, while Father was alternately making shepherding motions with the crook, and whipping motions with the flail.

Father had damaged his shoulder while hunting ibis as a young man. He had taken the impact of a charging animal full on one shoulder. Since then the range of movement in that arm had been limited. Now, while Father could thrash away with the flail in lusty style, most of the movement of the crook had to be with his wrist and it looked, it has to be said, a little effeminate.

Hot, bored and most important of all, extremely stupid, I mimicked the gesture. Father's cold calculating eyes, his slight sibilance and this restricted movement were standout features for any self-respecting mimic like myself. Oh, how I had entertained my siblings on many a night, their guilty laughter such a satisfying prize.

Unfortunately, none of them were laughing now. Looking round in surprise I saw their dark pupils outlined by white as their eyes had widened in alarm.

Neferhotep grabbed me, or so my siblings later informed me for he came at me from behind. I found myself lifted off my feet and carried away, my family parting before me like earth before a plough. Though the pain in my upper arms was unsettling, just for a second it was nice to feel like I was flying.

Within a couple of seconds, I had rounded the corner of the temple, a flight of marble stairs leading down to my left to a large man-made pool. I found myself descending the stairs but I never got to the bottom. Half way down, I found myself lifted even higher as a hand shifted from my arm to my leg.

Then I really was flying, somersaulting end over end across the marble balustrade and over the side of the pool. I crashed down into its green waters. My fall, from a height of perhaps five men, made hitting the water feel like crashing into a wall. All the air was driven from my lungs and filthy stagnant water surged in to replace it. I felt myself sinking like a stone, too winded and paralysed by shock and fear to resist. Fear because some animals were sacred. Crocodiles, hippos and cobras were worshipped. In some temples, serpents slithered amongst the columns, whilst in others pools were set aside for the water dwellers. Was this such a temple? How I wished I'd paid more attention.

Far away through the murky waters I saw movement. Something thick-legged was churning its way towards me. Hippos kill more people than crocodiles; their lower teeth, thick as a woman's wrist at the base but curving up to fierce points, can tear a man in half with one bite.

I gulped in fear, more water entering my lungs, sinking me deeper.

The thick black legs came crashing towards me. Even through the water muffling my ears I could heard the creature's roar. I felt something close on my top-knot and drag me towards its gaping maw.

Then, instead of heavy teeth spearing through me, I found myself back in the air and flying once again. This time my landing really was against stone, the impact squirting a jet of water out of my mouth and sending it splashing over the marble.

Whole seasons seemed to come and go as I coughed and choked, air and water gurgling in my throat and lungs. Finally, I was aware of something large looming over me. Black against the blazing sun, hands on hips, thick arms bent in anger and indignation, I realised the hippo had been my Nubian maidservant Mashnga. Wet nurse for the first three years of my life, she had remained with me ever since, giving me more love than all of my family put together.

"What is wrong with... how dare you..." she was spluttering. Then, for the first time in my life, and to my infinite surprise, she slapped me hard across the face.

So, to say that Neferhotep and I had history is rather an understatement. As soon as he had launched me into the air, he had turned on his heel and stalked away, vastly indifferent whether I would land on marble flagstone, or marble balustrade, or on water.

That had not been the end of his punishments for my blasphemy. It is surprising that I lived at all. I had many brothers from father's first rank and second rank wives, never mind from his harem and from amongst his multitude of slaves. There were plenty more where I came from.

The only thing I still marvel at is how obtuse I had been. I had been taught by everyone, in a thousand direct and indirect ways, that my father was a god and must be treated as such. I knew only too well that he wasn't so I must have come to consider this pretence just a game. My flight showed me just how dangerous and deadly that game really was.

Now, all these years later, Neferhotep faced me, and the circumstances had changed. My chances of becoming a god were not quite as remote as they had been. I had been the fourth eldest brother but Minkhaf had died in battle in Kush, and Kawab, according to Peseshet, had been killed by sand.

Instead of contempt in Neferhotep's eyes I now saw appraisal. His hands were metaphorically steeped in blood, not a little of it innocent, for Neferhotep's justice could be bought if you stuffed his mouth with enough gold. If I ever did become king and decided to appoint someone else for High Lord Treasurer, there was more than enough justification to put him to death.

"How can I help Your Royal Highness?" he asked almost pleasantly.

"My father's death. I have questions about it."

His eyebrows rising a hair's breadth was the only sign of surprise. Neferhotep's face was almost always impassive, though one sensed the implacability of the will that lurked beneath it. "Questions?"

"I visited the preparation table immediately after my father's death..."

This time the eyebrows rose by several hairs' breadth.

"... out of respect."

Neferhotep bowed. "Of course."

"I noticed clotted blood in my father's stomach. Was he poisoned?"

The corner of his thin-lipped mouth curled by the tiniest amount. I was seeing the full range of the High Lord's expressions today.

"Forgive me Your Royal Highness, but your father died almost three harvests ago. Why are you asking me this now?"

It was a good question for which I had no satisfactory answer. Obviously, there had been distractions since. Moaning wives, squealing brats, thrilling hunts, carousing with my friends: it all hardly seemed sufficient as an explanation. The truth is I did not really care how my father had died and this was little more than idle curiosity. Perhaps I simply wanted to unsettle the High Lord out of sheer devilry.

"I have my reasons," I said with a regal sweep of my hand.

Neferhotep hesitated, an unusual sight, as he made his calculations. Djedefre was visibly ailing, his eldest son was barely three years old and the High Lord had a lifetime of misery inflicted on me to atone for.

"Your father was a vigorous man and, apart from a few physical injuries, he had never suffered from an illness. Yet he died suddenly and very quickly. I must confess it was surprising."

It seemed he intended to leave it at that.

"Are you saying he was murdered? A god was murdered?" I prompted.

"Not at all. Stomachs become diseased like any other part of the body and they can bleed. High Priestess Peseshet says so and so do other physicians I have consulted. Your father was so full of life it was easy for all of us to forget that he was an old man."

That is just what Peseshet had told me but, for once, I had found her explanation not entirely convincing. "Is it at least possible he was poisoned?"

"It's true that perhaps not everyone loved your father," said Neferhotep, his expression altering not a whit. If this was him trying to be funny, it was the only time I had ever heard him attempt such a thing. "But really, nobody had a chance to administer poison. Every morsel he ate was first eaten by three tasters who were then watched as closely as mice are watched by hawks."

There had always been tasters for our kings. They worked in the kitchens. Nobody was better at supervising the preparation of food, and ensuring no poison was added, than someone who would have to eat it themselves.

Just then the horns sounded, the drapes at the back were parted and Djedefre entered.

As long as I could remember, my brother had always been a weakling, always the one who was sick, always the first to be caught as we had chased each other around the harem when we were children. He was thin, with an uncertain smile, never sure enough of himself to relax. He made an unlikely god. I am by nature a jealous man, as my other siblings would readily attest, but Djedefre's manifest weakness was so disarming I never really felt that way with him.

He was struggling under a heavy cape woven with enough gold thread to encircle the whole country. On his head the double crown weighed heavily, accentuating his slight stoop. The central white crown of Upper Egypt, bottle shaped, was within the tapering red crown of the lower, downstream Nile lands. The whole thing was of felt and was light but was adorned with the solid golden heads of a vulture and a cobra. Under this Djedefre wore his usual heavy black wig to hide the scrofulous growths on his neck. He was clearly battling to keep his neck upright.

"He looks magnificent!" I turned in surprise to find not Neferhotep but Peseshet beside me. When had this happened? Sometimes I drink too much, even for family feasts. Perhaps this is why my next comment was so uninhibited.

"Do you really think so?"

She turned to look at me, her green eyes widening in surprise. "Of course. He is a god."

In a world such as this I had never developed tools to argue against blind faith. It would be like a fish arguing against water. God-kings, like Djedefre and my father, had ruled Egypt for hundreds of years. In this land the things they had created, the temples and pyramids, loomed large and terrifying over farmland and mud brick hovels. A land governed by implacable power, held by the god-king but wielded by the High Lord Treasurer. A land at the mercy of the river, a fickle, deadly mistress with whom only the god-king could intercede via the gods.

"Of course," I said, keen not to disturb those beautiful, trusting eyes. In my heart I was secretly dismayed. I had been impressed by her focus on mundane explanations for how her medicines had worked, rather than on something dependent on the gods. Yet, even clever Peseshet could not step aside enough to question the gods themselves.

Not for the first time I wondered what was wrong with me. As ever I felt alone, the only one doubting that poor scrawny Djedefre straining under a heavy cape and crown was a god.

I cast around for a safer topic. "The harem...?"

Peseshet immediately reeled off the fertility status of my wives. Her advice had been wise and Khamerernebty had produced Menkaure. Meresankh was with child again whilst Hekenuhedjet wasn't - and to the relief of all concerned. I continued to have sex with her, purely for the sake of maintaining cordial foreign relations, but the crocodile dung had done its work. Two lesser wives were also pregnant and two others were being treated to enhance their fertility. I already knew all this but there was more. One of my lesser wives had just the previous night accidentally tipped a lamp onto one of my daughters - called Hemetre - and had badly burned her arm.

"Hemetre?"

"Three years old, small purple birthmark here." She pointed to the right side of her chin.

This didn't help me place her. "Has the child recovered?"

"Yes, my remedies proved efficacious. There may be a discolouration but no permanent scarring."

I nodded in approval and, of course, what she said had excited my curiosity. "And what were these remedies?"

Peseshet's intelligence always lurked below the polite surface, a crocodile eager to emerge. "There is a five-day regime. On the first day we apply the blackest mud we can, obtained from the final hollows where water has been trapped when the Nile receded. On the second day we apply fresh goat excrement, on the third a mixture of carob, acacia and fir oil. On the next day we cover the burn with papyrus and wax. Finally, we use copper flakes, red ochre and carob."

"It seems so... complicated. How do all these things work?"

She nodded her head and her enthusiasm took flight. "That is such a good question, your Royal Highness. Even though many of these remedies have been used for centuries, how do we know that any of them really work? I can understand the use of black mud for that contains the silt on which all Egypt thrives. It helps our plants grow so, of course, it should help damaged skin regrow. And, though I don't understand why it works, I know that applying acacia, fir oil and other substances like willow leaves and frankincense reduces suppuration in a wound. But as for the carob and papyrus and wax..." She shrugged.

"The goat excrement?"

She lifted her hands. Her eyes alight like this, I found her quite alluring, but I pushed the thought away. She was married and I had more than enough women to contend with. "We use excrement because it contains the spirit of the animals which are totems of the gods. For example, hippo excrement..."

"Yes, yes, I can understand that. I can also understand that dried crocodile excrement can soak up the juices of a man. But why, for example, do we use infant excrement to treat eye disease, why goat and sheep excrement for burns?"

She looked around then leaned close to me, her voice barely more than a whisper. "How do we know they really work at all and... can this be possible... how can we be sure they do not do more harm than good?"

A brave idea, even braver to confide this to someone like me. I was flattered that she trusted me and I wondered what I'd done to earn such trust.

"I would know more," I found myself saying. Even to be around such enthusiasm was refreshing. The concerns in the royal palaces were all so narrow, so confined, so inward-looking.

"I would be honoured if you walked with me when I visit the harem."

I waved this notion away. "Not the harem, anywhere but the harem."

She looked surprised but then, very briefly, a wry smile flickered across her lips. "There is another possibility, though your presence amongst such patients may be overwhelming. I treat the poor of Memphis, in a small house near the fish market. The conditions my patients present with are satisfyingly wide-ranging."

"How do they pay?"

"They don't. Alms are provided by the physician temples of Sekhmet, Selquet, Duau, Hathor and Tawaret. The high priests donate the medicines for the condition those gods represent. For example, Sekhmet for remedies against the plague, Selquet for bites and stings from reptiles."

"That sort of charity... I had no idea."

"Oh yes. All the food and gifts worshippers leave are used, even if it is simply to barter for medicines."

We both fell silent, she waiting for my next question. Filled with heady thoughts, not least of escaping my gilded cage if only for a few hours, I found myself saying, "Of course, if I were to visit, it would have to be kept secret."

Modern Day

Another thing I miss as a dog is the stars. If they were moving, I'd see every single one of them but, hanging almost motionless in the clear night sky as they do, they slip below some threshold and have vanished. Sun and moon, yes, but that myriad splash of stars, either the spraying milk of the Goddess Nut or the spurting semen of Ammon-Ra (take your pick!), are gone.

The redness of dusk, itself the blood of Atum, has also faded from my disappointing eyes so there is little to see on the small open deck where I spend my nights. Instead, I lose myself in the sea of smells washing over me. I savour the richness from the dung fertilising the fields, the ungodly heaviness of whatever they burn to run the pumps that draw water up from the Nile, the tang and bitterness of the fires from the reeds they burn that would otherwise choke the now placid Nile like a strangler.

Alone, too scared to communicate, half blind but spooked by the smallest movement, I am like an orphan abandoned in the desert. Osiris, Ra, Isis, Nut, Seshat, Thoth, was I that bad? Why do you punish me like this? In my dreams I've hardly been a kind man, and I certainly never respected my father, but these sins were nothing compared to those of so many others. Why am I not in the Field of Reeds living in happiness and fulfilment for eternity?

Thoughts like this obsess me for I have little else to occupy my busy mind on those endless nights when sleep does not come. The only comfort I can muster concerns Khufu. If I'm in the body of a dog then where must the gods have put him? I've thought of this long and hard and my best guess is that he languishes in the body of a blind, three-legged rat lost and stumbling through endless reeds with only the smell of the nearby crocodiles to keep him company.

I hear a door open behind me. Ali, one of the cooks, likes dogs and brings me leftovers to eat. My ears perk up and instantly saliva slooshes into my mouth. I turn but it's not Ali; it's that squirrelly little runt Masud. What's he doing up at this time?

My handlers don't trust me enough to leave me untethered. They fear the smell of some faraway bitch will have me leaping over the side. Little do they realise that what would really send me into the waters of oblivion are the sleepless nights where I probe every aspect of my conscience and rarely like what I find.

Masud approaches but stays beyond my reach. He puts his hands on his hips and looks down at me, yet one more aspect of being a dog that I loathe.

"Don't look at me like that, you filthy mutt," he whispers.

He's not a striking-looking man, he's just like any one of the countless numbers bustling through the streets of Cairo, but somehow that makes his malevolence even more terrifying.

He kneels down, still keeping his distance, and points a finger at me. Could I bite it off if I dashed as far forward as my tether would allow?

"I'm going to shoot you right between your big doggy eyes," and he makes a movement with his thumb above his pointing forefinger.

Just for a second, I panic. If he tried to kill me by any other means he would have to get close and I'd have the bastard, my big sharp teeth ravaging his soft flesh. But, if he's got a gun, he could stand back and do the damage from afar. I quickly smell the air but the only artificial fumes are from the metal and oil in the deck winches. He hasn't got a gun. I relax and give a little growl.

"And fuck you too," he says. "And fuck your friends, especially that fat one." Masud smiles grimly.

Taunting chained-up dogs, even big, fierce-looking ones like me, isn't unusual. There are bullies everywhere. A dog that can't reach them gives such weaklings a rare treat. They can be nasty to something stronger than themselves with impunity. It must harden their little dicks.

Somehow, I realise this is not what is happening here. There's no excitement in Masud's voice; instead all I glimpse is a vast and implacable hatred and the surprise makes my lips pull back to bare my teeth. What have I ever done to warrant this? And Amr, he's an asshole sure enough, someone who thinks he knows more than anyone else, but why would Masud hate him so much?

"I'm going to blow this boat right out of the fucking water but before I do that, I'm going to shoot you through your doggy face. I ordered a silenced gun just for that pleasure. As soon as I get it aboard, I'm coming for you, you mobile shit machine."

Well, that was unkind!

Maybe my brain isn't the size of a pyramid after all because I've only just worked out that Masud isn't a pissed-off waiter taking his rage and frustration out on a helpless mutt. No, Masud is the Enemy, red in tooth and claw.

During my training, at some big military camp the gods know where, my trainers had talked about little else. My handlers had listened, bug-eyed, at all the terrible things the

Enemy would try to do to them. The Enemy were basically all the demons rolled into one. They were the ones who planted bombs in cradles, who raped the maidens, who slit the throats of captured policemen, who wanted to bring the good Pharaoh Sisi down and send Egypt's mighty new civilisation crashing into dust.

I have to say, given all the build-up, that Masud doesn't live up to the reputation, but I have to respect his hatred even though I don't have a clue what it's all about.

A real dog at this point, sensing the Enemy, would bark like fuck. My handlers would come running, Masud would shrug and say he was only trying to pat the dog and it had gone wild. My handlers would shout at me and Mazan would whack me and then they'd all go back to bed. And then we'd all die. Whatever hope of expiation I might have, assuming this is what this whole sorry doggy mess is all about, would die with me and next time round I'd wind up keeping ratty three-legged Khufu company down among the crocodiles.

Now is definitely the time to use a brain that may or may not be as big as a pyramid, so I don't bark. Instead I make my tongue loll out and snuffle like I'm pleased to see him.

"Pathetic!" says Masud. He goes to the side of the boat overlooking the river and peers down into the water. What is he expecting?

Minutes pass then his head jerks up just a little and I guess he's seen what he's looking for. He glances around then heads up the stairway to the next level, but I can then hear him climbing further until he must be on the top deck. This is out of bounds to the crew during the night, probably so their stomping around on the metal deck won't disturb the old folks in the cabins below.

Something is really messed up here and it looks like I'm the only one who can do anything about it. I find myself hesitating and, for a second, I can't think why. Slowly it dawns on me that after only a few years in the body of a mutt, I have turned into one. My handlers tell me what to do and I do it. Just like Neferhotep and my father did in my past life, in fact.

Now, for one of the few times in perhaps two lifetimes, I have to act unsupervised and on my own initiative. I feel fear but also an unfamiliar excitement. Whatever I've got to do, I have to untie myself first.

The end of my lead has a teardrop-shaped loop of metal but a little bit of it is hinged. Mazan would whack this against the metal rail and the loose bit would open on its hinge and then close after the loop was through. To unclip me, Mazan would use his fingers to open the hinged bit and slide the loop back off the rail.

I'd watched this operation hundreds of times. Opening the clip is simple in theory but, of course, I don't have any fingers.

That's problem one. Problem two is that if I do manage to unclip myself then my handlers will work out I was way smarter than all of them combined. If they realise that then I don't give much for my chances.

Back in my day, if a dog had shown itself to be so smart we'd have assumed it was a demon and crushed its head with a rock. Would my fate be any different now?

Then again, if I don't do anything, I'll definitely wind up dead.

Cursing Masud for putting me in this position, I place a paw on the metal lead so it's pulled taught against the railing, clearing the little hinged bit. I lean in and pushed my tongue against the hinge. Annoyingly, a dog's tongue isn't like a man's, it's squishier and less muscly. Dogs don't stick their tongues out like humans because they just can't. If the tip of the tongue protrudes for more than a finger's breadth then it immediately droops like a drunk's cock.

Poking away with the tip only gives me a nasty metallic taste and barely depresses the hinged metal at all. No good. I lean my head back and try to think this through.

I can't control my tongue well but it's quite big and heavy. I lean back in but tilt my head and let my tongue loll out the side. I turn my head slowly, bringing the side of my tongue against the hinge. It yields under the weight.

That's all well and good but now my tongue fills the loop, blocking the hole it has just made. Now what am I going to do?

I hesitate for a second then slowly pull back my head so my tongue starts to slide out. Tongues taper and as it comes out, it gets thinner over the hinged bit, opening up the space.

Too much, I'd pulled it out too far. With not enough thickness and weight to hold down the metal, the hinge closes and expels my tongue out of the side of the loop.

So, I try again, and again, and again. By now I'm so angry that even if I get free, and even if Masud has been bullshitting about killing everyone, I'm still going to sink my big teeth into him.

Then, on the fifth attempt, the space looks big enough but now I have to push the loop up so it can slide over the railing and come clear.

My troubles really begin now because all I have to push are these big clumsy paws.

So, taking the weight on my other three legs, I lift up the fourth and try to gently nudge the loop upwards.

If I'd drunk a barrel of beer, I couldn't have been any more clumsy. My paw slams against the loop, pushing it up. The loop comes off the railing but the hinge snaps shut on my tongue. The hinged bit is sharp and digs deep into its underside.

I stagger back in agony. Gallons of saliva gush into my mouth, the droplets pattering to the deck. Panicked, I find myself pawing at the lead, jangling it, but it only drives the point deeper. I yelp, stumble, and just as I fall forward, my other paw comes down on the end of the lead lying on the deck, trapping it. The hinged bit rips out of my tongue before my head even hits the deck.

I'm free but in agony. I clamp my mouth shut to stop myself howling. A new metallic taste washes over my tongue and I can feel it start to swell.

I haul myself back to my feet and immediately the metal chain rattles over the deck. If I try to follow Masud he'll hear me coming a Nile's width away.

What could I have done in my past life to warrant this? I lower my head and agonisingly use my abused tongue to bring the lead up into my mouth so I can carry it.

I can do fury, but it's of a cold, calculating kind and that doesn't seem to have changed much over four thousand plus years. Best to be prepared before I rush in, teeth snapping. I pad to the river side of the boat and look over the railings to see what had been of such interest to Masud.

The movement makes it easy for me to spot. It's a faint bubbling of white on the surface of the pitch-black Nile. It's by the boat's side about twenty arm lengths forward. Movement above makes me look up and I see Masud lowering a rope down towards the river.

Is Masud simply fishing? Has my agony been for nothing?

Then there is more movement at the surface and a black-clad arm rises out of the water to grasp the rope. I watch, the cold of the chain soothing my ravaged tongue, as the arm ties the rope to something just below the surface. Masud hauls and the thing emerges. It's a net holding several objects wrapped in some material, one of them long and thin and assault rifle shaped.

I turn and pad slowly up the steps, taking great pains to keep the chain lifted clear. My heart is hammering and I've never felt so alone. I climb up three decks to the top, which is open to the air and where the crazy old people spend the day lounging in the sun. Nothing marks their foreignness more because that is precisely the last thing any Egyptian would do, unless they were completely insane.

As I get to the upper deck I slow down and peek over the top of the steps. The net must be heavy because Masud is struggling, leaning over the rail then heaving back and scrabbling hand-over-hand on the rope before the load slips back down. Preoccupied, he does not see me slink onto the deck. I use the cover of the chairs and loungers to get closer until I am just behind him.

One final heave brings the net to the edge of the railing and Masud lets go of the rope and lunges forward to grasp it. With a grunt he pulls the net up and over his head and turns, teetering under the weight.

Perfect! I drop the lead and sink my teeth into his exposed groin.

I'll say one thing for German Shepherds: they sure can bite. I feel my teeth go straight through the thin fabric of his long tunic and deep into his flesh. As soon as I have a good grip, I jerk my head back hard, feeling the big muscles in my neck bunch up. Masud gives a dreadful wail. It could be my imagination, but I think I feel one of his balls pop.

Pulled forward by his nether regions, the heavy net above his head is suddenly unsupported and crashes down on him, sending him to the deck and dragging me with him. I worry away at him urgently, shaking my head from side to side, feeling tissue tear. I know my tongue must be hurting but in all the excitement I can't feel a damned thing.

Somehow, despite his agony, Masud brings his knee up sharply into my side. He's struggling to push the net off so he can get his hands on me. All the time his blood-curdling screams are assaulting my exquisitely sensitive ears. The net clumps to the deck and he pulls himself upright, his fingers reaching for my eyes.

I let go and step back, partly to escape his reach, partly in fear at the terrible rage on his face. He looks down at the dark stain of blood on his trousers, then his hands are scrabbling at the net and I know he's going for a gun.

I lunge forward and bite hard into his hand then try to shuffle back, but his boot catches me in the ribs and sends me smashing against the railing. One hand is still good and is already inside the net. I bark hard and bare my fangs then lunge again but his boot catches me in the head, fending me off. He keeps kicking away at me as he pulls the long gun free of the net. It's covered in that thin material these people use, more transparent than the finest linen. He won't be able to fire it until he gets that off but that's not what he has in mind. The butt end comes swinging round and hits me on the side of the head and I smash back into the railing.

And that's when I suddenly see the stars once again and they're all wheeling around in crazy spirals. I lose my balance and clump down on the deck. I hear the rustling and tearing as Masud pulls the material off the gun.

Dizzily I struggle upright just in time to see the toe of a heavy boot connect hard with Masud's temple. The light immediately flees from his eyes and his head crunches down onto the deck.

"Use the fucking torch!" I hear Amr shout.

Ragab and Mazan are stumbling along the deck, half-dressed but carrying their own assault rifles. Mazan fumbles with a torch and the beam lances down into the water.

Amr scoops up Masud's gun with one hand and throws it aside as Ragab's gun tracks the circle of light that jerks around over the water. "I can't see anything," he yells.

"There's no boat. Maybe it's a diver with an aqualung. Look for bubbles!"

Still dizzy, I struggle to my feet and poke my head through the railings.

"There!" shouts Mazan.

I've noticed that firing these guns isn't straightforward; there always has to be some preparatory pulling and poking, perhaps some supplicatory act to propitiate the demons within. I haven't figured out exactly what you're supposed to do and apparently, in the heat of the moment, neither has Ragab. His gun just gives a feeble click.

"For fuck's sake!" roars Amr. He pulls his pistol from its holster and takes aim at something in the water.

"Sorry, sorry," wails Ragab. He fumbles at his gun, there's a couple of clicks then the crash of full auto gunfire, a flickering bulb of evil yellow flame licking out from the muzzle.

The river erupts in gouts of water. Meanwhile, Amr has started to fire, slowly and deliberately.

My training has accustomed me to gunfire but I still don't like it. It's excruciatingly loud. To my dismay, I piss all over the deck.

Amr's and Ragab's guns make clicking sounds and the terrible noise stops. Mazan's light is moving back and forth again. He seems to have lost whatever he'd seen.

"Do you think we got him?" asks Ragab excitedly.

Amr scans the water. "I can't see anything. He might have dived deeper. Keep looking!"

He turns away and comes over to me, reaching down and putting a hand on my head.

"So, Cheops, old son. What the fuck have you been up to?"

Ancient Days 2562 BC

Like a foreigner carried to Egypt from some fabled land far away across the Great Green Sea, I strode overwhelmed through the streets of my own city, making little sense of what I saw.

Yet the dusty streets of Memphis and the palace I had come from were separated by no more than a gentle stroll. Sometimes, through breaks in the buildings, I could still glimpse the great sprawling palaces on their bluff across the river.

It was not that I was unaccustomed to travelling, but when I did it was with my family and an entourage the size of an army. We travelled to pay homage at the temples and tombs at Thebes, to Sneferu's tomb at Saqqara. Sometimes we feasted in the houses of rich merchants in the better parts of Memphis, carried there in sedan chairs down streets emptied before us by troops.

Now, in this single walk through Memphis, I had seen more people than I had ever dreamed lived in the whole of Egypt. They jostled and shouted and insulted, bought and sold, haggled and argued and denounced. Dogs barked from every household and cats chased scurrying rats from midden to midden.

Even the middens were a revelation. I was stunned to realise that wherever the royal family went, an advance party of servants and slaves must have doused the middens and shit-caked streams in buckets of rosewater. Memphis, it transpired, did not smell sweet at all. Who would have guessed?

Adding to my unease at this strange yet familiar world, I felt naked without my wig. At Peseshet's instruction all my finery had been removed and I was dressed in a long white robe held up by a white strap over one shoulder. A white skull cap covered my bald head. My best flint blade had made my scalp raw from close shaving. My face and body felt as though they had been slapped, for the purity of priests required all hair to be removed. It was a good disguise but I was paying a high price for my curiosity.

Two of my more discreet bodyguards, also dressed like priests, walked before me shouldering away anyone who strayed across our path. Most people respected priests and automatically moved aside as we approached. However, some of the rougher men, unshaven and smelling of beer and piss and stubbornness, made to stand their ground only to find themselves facing two of the biggest and most formidably muscled priests they had ever seen. They too finally stepped aside, leaving it to the last moment to preserve as much surliness as possible.

My life up to then had been too tame, too controlled. The chaos wrought by the god Seth had been but a concept. Now that I saw the city in its raw disordered form, I felt my panic rising. Only the god-king could combat the depredations of Seth, a task for which I realised Djedefre was starkly unworthy.

Tiny alleys, covered with reeds to shelter them from the sun, led away to either side of this main thoroughfare. There, amongst the beggars holding out empty bowls, crouched sharper-eyed men. One was looking at me frankly and I felt my anger rise at such an outrage. I'd had a lifetime of the lower ranks casting their eyes down in my presence. This man's gaze felt like an assault.

I took a deep breath and kept walking, shooing away the flies swarming from flensed animals lying shipwrecked across butchers' tables. At one, a small crocodile was being heartily dismembered by a thickly muscled man. Tied to a stake at the end of the table hung the heads of many more, their jaws wide and arranged like a posy of open flowers. As I watched, the butcher slid a spoon into an eye socket and levered out the big green orb, its black vertical slit staring balefully out into the world. In one well-practised flick he sent the eye into his mouth and began chewing with evident satisfaction.

Every household spun flax to make linen, though usually to make rough everyday clothes, but here on the main thoroughfare skilfully embroidered kilts and tunics and shawls hung ready for sale. Tables held vegetables and fruit being rudely prodded and poked by housewives and servants from the larger houses. Something about the fruit caught my attention and, just for a second, I hesitated. Many of the apples were misshapen, hardly the perfect spheres I was used to. The pomegranates were mottled, some almost black.

The merchant had seen me looking. He spread his hands out over his fare. "Have you ever seen better, priest?"

I hurried on as my guards, too intent on forward threats, had not seen me hesitate. Even as I caught up, Dedifer, my most trusted bodyguard, stopped to ask directions of a well-built woman with a child on her hip. The child's top-knot swung back and forth as its eyes moved from the mother to the looming priest. The woman's accent was so broad I could barely understand what she was saying.

Dedifer nodded to her and beckoned me into a reed-shaded alleyway. "Stay behind me, your Royal Highness. Leris will be directly behind you."

I noticed the beads of sweat on their temples and their worried, darting eyes. I had assumed they could handle any problems but I suddenly realised how little our light, sheer linens hid. "Are you armed?" I wondered, belatedly.

"Knifes strapped to our thighs, your Royal Highness. Short swords hanging in sheathes between our legs."

"Yet you seem concerned?"

Dedifer's eyes, studiously averted until now, found mine for a fraction of a second. "If the slightest harm should befall you..."

I raised a hand and gave a little nod. This trip was a whim for me but it meant life or death for these men.

We continued down the alley for only a few steps before we came to a queue of people leading to an open door. They coughed and sneezed, some groaned in pain. Some were supported by relatives, others had sat down on the shaded ground. Nobody stopped us or even spared a glance as we pushed past and entered the building.

The smell of sour beer testified that this was usually a tavern. Yellowing reed mats covered the floor. Peseshet sat cross-legged in the centre, her long plain kilt stretched tight between her knees. She was leaning forward, staring intently at a woman who was kneeling in front of her. As we entered, Peseshet looked up and made to get to her feet but I waved a hand to stop her.

I walked across and sat down beside her while my bodyguards stepped back into the shadows. The dried reeds were rough on my thighs.

"High Priest, may Osiris guard your slumbers," said Peseshet, inclining her head. "It is kind of you to join us and give us your guidance."

I nodded. "Thank you for inviting me, Chief Physician. May Sekhmet guide your healing hand. What is it that afflicts this lady?"

The lady in question was in her twenties and, though her features were fine, she was broad shouldered with heavy breasts that tugged the neck of her tunic forward. The linen of her robe was coarser even than those worn by the lowest slave in my household. Her wig was old, worn and stained a garish blue. Thick yellow fluid leaked from the sides of her right eye and, though she periodically wiped this away with the back of her hand, the smears had dried over time to look like the tracks of yellow tears.

"Her eye," I said before Peseshet could respond.

"Indeed, High Priest. May I continue?"

I nodded and Peseshet turned back to the woman. "And how did you offend Duau?"

"I cannot think, Chief Physician." The woman's voice was earthy, its huskiness faintly alluring.

"The moon, the god Duau's eye, sees everything. He sees what you see. Something you have cast your eye on has caused him to take away his protection."

"I cannot... there is nothing." The woman was a poor liar.

"You must be truthful lest you seek the barren succour of Mechenti-Ri, god of the blind."

The woman took a deep breath but kept quiet.

Peseshet leaned forward even further until they were almost eye to eye. The woman turned away but Peseshet grabbed her chin and pulled her head back round. "You have a lover. You are an adulteress."

Clearly there was a lot more to this medicine business than I had thought!

"Never!" said the woman.

Peseshet sat back, a smile of triumph on her face. "But you have seen someone, haven't you?"

The woman moaned and leaned forward until her forehead was on the ground. "I just... he was so... but we have never... Forgive me, please!"

Peseshet nodded her head. "The treatment is clear. Alms to Duau for your eyes, to Hathor and Isis for your marriage. Meanwhile..." and she snapped her fingers, "... Tadukhipa!"

From the time I had entered, my eyes had been only for Peseshet and her patient and I had not noticed the mound of earthenware pots of every size, colour and description to my right. A woman stood up from behind them and bowed. "Chief Physician?"

"A fine paste. Lizard, crocodile and, I think, pelican."

Tadukhipa, small, skinny and brown as baked clay, had already been reaching with one hand for the jumble of pots before Peseshet had finished speaking. Meanwhile, the other hand had fished out an earthenware bowl. Ingredients from the pots went into the bowl and then a dash of water from a goat skin. A stone, almost spherical in shape, was pressed down to grind everything into a paste. When she had finished, she set the bowl down in front of Peseshet and I caught the whiff of spicy-smelling shit.

"Hold still!" commanded Peseshet, grasping the woman's jaw once again. She hooked an index finger into the mixed excrement and gently rubbed it into the sides of the woman's weeping eye.

When she'd finished, Peseshet smeared the medicine from her index finger onto the side of the bowl. "We're finished," she said.

With abject thanks, the woman backed away on her knees before standing and disappearing rapidly out of the doorway.

"Impressive," I said. "How did you know?"

Peseshet smiled wryly. "I could almost smell the need for sex coming off her. I had been questioning her before she arrived. Her husband is old, very old."

"And the mixtures of dung? I was taken with your explanation of the crocodile dung and how it prevented pregnancy by soaking up the juices of the man. But how does dung work for the weeping eye?"

Peseshet smiled shyly and she lowered her voice. "You remind me of my heresy. I should not have been so indiscreet."

"Heresy intrigues me, especially when argued with such intelligence."

"You flatter me, High Priest. But, to answer your question, I do not have an alternative explanation as to why dung cures such eye disease. Or why tortoise brain mixed with honey helps cure cataracts of the eye. The sacred scrolls in our temples mention only that the essences of these animals contain the essences of the gods. I use these ancient treatments for want of anything better."

I shook my head in puzzlement. "But crocodiles, pelicans and what-have-you, what have their essences got to do with eyes?"

"The scrolls do not say. Perhaps once the answers were so obvious that nobody thought to record them."

"Which temple do you serve at again?"

"I take turns, a year about. Sekhmet for plagues, Selqet for the bites of venomous reptiles, Duau for the eyes and, of course, Hathor for childbirth."

"I thought physicians specialised in only one disease and so served at only one temple."

She raised her eyes. "I know I am being immodest but the truth is I am not a normal physician. It is hard enough for these poor people to see any of them, never mind one who is also a priest for the god associated with their illness. I am the best they can hope for and so I must be all things for them."

I nodded. "That you do this for the poor, and without payment is..."

She waited, eyebrows raised.

"... insane."

She laughed, her head coming back to show the smoothness of the skin over her throat.

I laughed too. "Well, madwoman, let me see more!"

And more I did see. A young boy, eyes unfocused and bleary under a skull with a ridge of raised, bruised flesh showing where it had been broken. I watched as Peseshet smeared powdered ostrich eggshell over the boy's head. Even I could see how that would work.

As the morning wore on even my bodyguards felt compelled to join in. With Peseshet and Tadukhipa we all chanted:

Flow out foetid nose!

Flow out son of foetid nose

Flow out, you who break bones,

Destroy the skull and make ill the seven holes of the head.

to treat a chap who was a sniffling, snuffling, sneezing mountain of erupting mucus. Later, my burly guards held down a brawny man who had broken his arm. The yell he gave when Peseshet bore down on the break, resetting it, was one I will never forget. He whimpered like a child as she applied a splint of bamboo tied with reed.

At midday we broke off for beer and olives and bread, perhaps the simplest, plainest meal I had eaten since I was a child. Never had I witnessed such deprivation and suffering. Never had I been so interested in what I was seeing.

A servant came in and whispered in her ear.

"Send all the others away!" she said and the man went to the door.

"Finished," he shouted. "Come back in one week."

I could hear the groans of despair but Peseshet seemed unmoved. "It might be best if you left now, High Priest."

I was starting to stand and about to offer my thanks but that might made me hesitate. "Are there no more patients?"

She looked away. "There is one but what will happen is not for your eyes."

"Why not. Another heresy?"

She shrugged. "Taboo might be a better word."

I smiled. "That was a mistake. If you had said it was something boring and ordinary, I would have been gone in an instant."

Her eyes met mine and, for a second, I felt a shortness of breath. "This is serious, High Priest. It is taboo because I am going to open the body of a man during life."

"Why in Seth's name would you want to do that?"

"It is a very special case. The patient's body is submerging part of itself. I am going to try to reclaim the original."

This wasn't making much sense but I felt my excitement rising. I had wanted to see something different and Peseshet was not disappointing me. I began to think aloud. "Taking from the body is taboo because we need the body to be intact in order for us to survive in the afterlife, to walk among the

Field of Reeds. Extracting something from within the body during life would end that possibility but..."

Her heavily inked eyebrows rose. "But?"

"... but if the body itself has changed and you were to allow the original body to emerge, then that might not be taboo at all."

I heard a commotion from outside in the alleyway. She turned away to look, but saying, "Exactly, though I'm sure many of my fellow physician priests would take an entirely different view."

Two people entered, one whose body was so grotesquely distorted I leaned back in appalled surprise. It was not that I had never before seen the effects of elephantiasis, the curse of the foreign elephant god for whom we in Egypt had no name. Someone so cursed would never have been allowed within the royal palaces, but I had seen them many a time languishing on the riverbanks as we sailed by in our royal barges. Women with legs as thick as tree trunks, each step requiring one leg to be flung wide to get around the other, men with scrotal sacs the size and texture of breadfruit.

That indeed was the problem of the man who now entered. He was accompanied by his wife. The couple were tiny, malnourished, the tops of their heads barely coming up to my shoulders. He was cradling the head-sized mass hanging from his crotch, the penis fully submerged within his ballooning scrotal sac. All this was revealed as he lifted his cheap, unpleated kilt.

He was not old, certainly less than thirty, and that meant the mass must have started to become evident in adolescence or even before. Yet his wife had married him and they had had time for one child before any more became impossible, as Peseshet told me afterward.

I watched as the wife's night-dark eyes swung from her husband to Peseshet and back again. For him she showed love and concern, for Peseshet she showed frank amazement.

Peseshet turned to me. "This is Harwa and his wife Ineni. I have explained to them how dangerous the treatment is but they are sure they wish to continue."

The couple did not speak but bowed their heads.

A fresh mat was laid across the old ones and Peseshet's assistants, who had come back into the tavern after getting rid of the queue outside, were using sticks to batter holes in the reed roof so that bright sunlight lanced down into the room. At Peseshet's instruction, Harwa lay down on the mat, Ineni beside him, flicking the flies away with a bunch of dried grass.

"Tadukhipa. Milk of the poppy and bring me the Fang!"

Peseshet pulled off Harwa's kilt without preamble. I could barely bring myself to look at the terrible engorged fruit nestling in the man's loins. Like breadfruit, the skin was coarsely grained with a multitude of little lumps.

The apothecary brought a milky solution in an earthenware pot and also a contraption the like of which I have never seen before. It looked like some kind of thorn but at one end a small bladder was attached, perhaps of a cat. Peseshet placed the sharp end of the thorn in the milky liquid and squeezed the bladder until it was flat. Air bubbled out of the milk then she let go and I heard a faint sucking sound. Peseshet then laid the point carefully against a large vein in the crook of Harwa's arm before pushing it gently in.

"Stay still!" Peseshet's tone was unequivocal. Once again, she squeezed the bladder. This was all too reminiscent of magic, too much like witchcraft. I heard my bodyguards shuffling uneasily behind me.

Turning his head to look at Peseshet, Harwa gave her a weak smile.

"What did you just do?" I asked warily just as Harwa's eyes closed and his body slumped as though life had fled. A last lengthy exhalation of air eased out of his lungs.

"Is he dead?"

Peseshet put a hand against his neck. "I hope not. I can't tell you how many goats I killed until I found an animal with just the right bladder size to take up the correct amount of poppy milk."

What would Neferhotep say if he heard I had been consorting with a witch? Suddenly I found myself in too much of an adventure.

She nodded her head. "He lives. Milk of the poppy to send him to sleep. Drinking it is too unpredictable and it's easy to give too much. With this I can give an exact amount, but for the drop or two that escapes." She pointed to the pale pink globule of blood and milk standing proud of the little wound. "The thorn is hollow all the way through. See!" She held it up so that I could make out the tiny hole in the end.

I didn't know what was more upsetting: her matter-of-factness or the witchery. "You use this all the time?" I squeaked.

"Of course not, High Priest. I resort to it only in cases where the patient would die. Very bad breaks of arms and legs, or in pregnancy where the only way either mother or baby will survive is if I cut the foetus out. And here. Harwa would not survive otherwise."

She turned to the apothecary. "Honey and acacia, cinnamon and frankincense for after."

Now it was the turn of her other assistants. "Start the fire!" she commanded and with this she picked up an expensive dark wood box covered in elaborate carvings of

Horus and Selket and Duau. Opening it, she revealed bronze and obsidian blades. Nestling amongst them were two large bronze spoons. These managed to be both familiar and sinister.

As she prepared her tools, I tried but failed to detect any rise and fall to Harwa's scrawny chest.

Peseshet pulled out other tools from her box and handed them to a servant. "Heat them!" she commanded. We watched as he waved them through the flames.

Then, without further ado, as though it were a trivial task she did every day, she took an obsidian blade and made her first incision, cutting straight down between the two huge testicles, pulling apart the jelly-filled halves to reveal something I dared not recognise. It was like a small snake that had been beaten with sticks: twisted, reddened, bruised black. Its skin was mottled and gnarled.

Belatedly, I realised Peseshet was smiling at me. She had the delightful little crease across her forehead that spoke of concentration. "You see how the skin of the penis lacks the wrinkled leather appearance of the testicles. I think that's a good sign. I think the curse has not reached there yet."

She started to scoop away with the spoons. Under the thickness of the skin, the mass was gelatinous, like the contents of a sheep's eyeball. Spoonful after spoonful was ladled out and slopped into a pan. Finally, Harwa's real testicles were revealed. They looked like pink baubles, the sort of thing you might find dangling from a beauty's ears.

It was a windless day and the smell from the fire was making my head spin. Peseshet was pointing with a finger at something but I had difficulty bringing my eyes to bear.

"I need good skin to re-cover his penis and testicles and I think he is in luck. Look!"

My spirit fled my body and I crashed to the ground.

Modern Day

Dishes like the heads of sunflowers are fixed to all the buildings in Cairo. However, unlike sunflowers, the heads do not track the sun but stare at some distant point in the sky. Like so much of this new world, I have no idea what they do.

If I had to guess I would say they had religious significance, like the ankh symbol that used to adorn our own homes. Whereas we would bow to these as a matter of course, modern Egyptians don't even seem to be aware of the dishes' existence, just as they are oblivious to the rubbish that litters their streets. Perhaps the dishes are for an old religion that has passed out of favour, like the statues of ancient gods nobody remembers.

Or perhaps, rather than sunflowers they are actually artificial eyes and, Ra knows, the city needs them. Many buildings soar into the sky for twelve or more storeys and all have many openings but these are blank and the rooms within empty. They look like eye sockets of the long dead. Mile after mile of soaring edifices peer down with these blind eyes. Are these their new temples, the public kept out of them just as in my day?

I see all this again as we drive along, me chained in the back of one of their open-backed vehicles trying hard not to piss myself in the raging traffic. What magic propels these things? The conversations of my handlers are too sporadic and, I suspect, too ignorant to provide anything like a decent education for an attentive dog.

I am feeling sorry for myself and my cluelessness when suddenly, out of the blue, the mystery of the eyeless buildings is revealed! Amr and Ragab are in the back with me and we are all hunched up under a little metal arch that keeps the sun off our heads.

"Why all these empty buildings?" asks Ragab. "There's what... maybe twenty million people in this city but it looks like there are almost as many empty apartments. What's that all about?"

Around us cars jostle and moan in their high-pitched way, every moment just an instant from disaster. It's like being strapped on the back of a bull during a stampede. The cars are full of resentful Egyptians. Even by Cairo standards Mazan is a rubbish driver, but this is a police vehicle and nobody is going to shout or make rude gestures as Mazan veers from one lane to the other seeking the most minute of advantages. If there is a gap in the speeding traffic, however small, he will go for it. Cars screech in alarm as they take evasive action.

Amr doesn't seem to notice. Maybe all police drive like this. He loves to lecture and so that's all he'll be thinking about, no matter how closely death is shadowing our every step. He leans back against his metal seat and lifts a hand to wave airily at the buildings. "You still live with your parents, don't you, Ragab. And on your copper's salary..." He lets it hang in the air for a second. "I guess you won't be buying somewhere anytime soon. Do your parents rent?"

"Sure," says Ragab. "That's what everyone I know does."

"All these empty apartments are for sale and were built by rich men as an investment. It was a craze, a boom, and that made them build far more than was needed. They filled the apartments with crap Chinese refrigerators and sinks and washing machines and cookers and whatever. People would move in, they'd turn on the stove for the first time and it would catch fire. Buyers got wise to this and so they insist on doing all their own interior work. Now the apartments are sold empty, without even glass in the windows."

Ragab has the attention span of a minnow. He points. "The pyramids. We're almost there."

Anger wells up in me and I have to close my eyes and try to still my racing heart. I still cannot believe what the modern Egyptians have done to my beautiful pyramid.

I hunker down so my head is below the little metal wall that surrounds the back of this vehicle. I can't bear to see this.

"Poor old Cheops is tired," says Ragab.

"Maybe we should change his name to Monthu."

"Or Monthu Two," says Ragab and they both laugh.

Hey! I wish I could say, not only am I royalty but now I'm a hero as well. Show some respect!

And a hero I am. I'd saved the lives of everyone on the boat, including those of my ingrate handlers. Apparently, I'd also saved the country billions of dollars in lost tourist income. I'm pretty sure that's good, though I'm still not clear what dollars are, or what a billion is.

A herd of Fat Bottoms had said all this when they came on board, constellations of gold stars on their epaulets. Not one of them was carrying a gun, that's how senior they were. They clapped my head and shook Amr's hand. I'd never seen Fat Bottoms smile before. Civilians stood around clicking those little things they spend all their time saying prayers into. Sometimes I'd heard the things answer back and I'm guessing that, like their guns, they've trapped demons in there too.

Masud had been carried off the boat on a canvas sheet supported by two poles. Other policemen, and some of the crew, had punched and kicked at him as he went by, perhaps to help him take his mind off his torn groin.

It took a while for Amr to realise the blood in my mouth wasn't just Masud's. I guess the giveaway was that it kept falling to the deck in bright red globs. I should have been more careful and just swallowed it because as soon as Amr caught on, he started intoning the name of that most pitiless of demons: The Vet.

We'd stopped at an army camp just outside Cairo where nobody could even be bothered to brush away the sand, fingers of the desert seeming to grasp the roads and sidewalks. I'd been taken into a place that smelled of the stuff we used to pickle our dead. As usual, and without a by-your-leave, the Vet had shoved something up my backside.

The Vet left whatever it was up there to marinate. Meanwhile, Amr was holding me tight, one arm over my back and under my stomach, the other round my neck. Nobody had ever held me tighter and it wasn't with affection. I'm not painting a happy picture here but I have to admit that this modern medicine does its business. In my day if a dog got sick or injured, he usually died. Even in my brief new life I'd had my fair share of both of those and the Vet had always come through.

Finally, the Vet plucked the thing out of my bottom and peered at it myopically. "His temperature's OK. Now comes the difficult part."

Amr and the Vet, both wheezing with the effort, eventually managed to prise my jaws apart. "Nasty cut," said the Vet. "I'll give him an anti-inflammatory and an antibiotic. I'll go for a leg vein. Hold him down!"

Amr's a heavy bastard and, for a second, I thought he would crush me to death as he slammed down on top of me.

So preoccupied was I with getting in enough sweet air to cling to life that I hardly felt the pricks in my skin.

"There, that wasn't so bad, was it, boy? I'll give you some pills, Corporal. One pill, once a day. Don't feed him for twenty-four hours otherwise he'll just bite his own swollen tongue and make it worse."

The Vet looked into my eyes. Tufts of thick chest hair poked out over the open neck of his off-white shirt. His big brown eyes, expanded to amulet size by the glasses he wore, regarded me reflectively and I couldn't help meeting his gaze.

The Vet smiled. "I've heard what he did. He's an intelligent-looking fellow, isn't he?"

"He sure is," said Amr proudly. "We still don't know how he got loose." This managed to be both a lie and the truth at the same time. Amr, privately, had berated Ragab for not clipping me to the railing properly. Publicly, with the senior coppers and now with the Vet, he took a more mysterious line. Indeed, one of the senior policemen had said, this is the work of Allah.

Who Allah is, and what in Osiris's name he had to do with anything, is beyond me. OK, I'm kidding. I've picked up who Allah is. I've worked out that this is their peculiar singular god. What an odd concept! Why should there be only one?

Amr has a question. "There's a big deal at the pyramids later today. Press and photographers from all over the world are going to take pictures. Will he be OK for that?"

The Vet nods. "He'll be fine but, like I say, don't let anyone give him anything to eat."

And that's when I realised where we were going. I'd seen the pyramids often enough but only at a distance. Close enough, however, to curse their terrible fate. In my day they had been encased in exquisitely carved and brilliant limestone, but over the ages this had been hacked away.

Occasionally our duties had taken us to tourist hotels near the pyramids but never at them. Now it appeared I was going to see their degradation up close.

And that's what was happening now. Mazan has turned off onto a smaller road and the full glamour of Cairo is being revealed. In the old world, papyrus was almost sacred in itself and was stored carefully for the benefit of the ages. This new form of paper they use is strewn all over the place with careless abandon. It forms into heaps, taller than a small boy. Indeed, some boys spend all their hours rooting through them looking for Horus-knows-what. Paper covers the sandy earth and the pavements and the roads. As vehicles pass it whirls upwards in spirals, flapping like flocks of birds.

Half-finished, roofless buildings with brown metal sticking upwards like thorns loom over us on either side. Dusty little shops sell a variety of goods beyond my imagining.

"Are you nervous, Amr?" asks Ragab suddenly. He's young, still not much more than a boy, and often sounds as naive.

Amr, a man, ignores him even though it might be true. Whatever is about to happen is some sort of ceremony and I've had a previous lifetime of those. I am curious, though. My dog's life to date has been entirely bereft of anything like it.

I look at the passers-by who step in and out of the traffic as they wend their way past the tiny shop fronts, their path blocked by parked cars and cycles and motorbikes. Gone are the loincloths of the workers and shendyt skirts that higher class men would wear. Nowadays it is trousers and jackets, though quite a few wear the sort of floor length linen shirts they call gallebayas that haven't changed much in millennia.

The women, of course, hide their beautiful hair with scarves. Their dresses are long and, for the most part, shapeless.

What a joyless society this is!

I catch sight of the pyramids and flinch. To me they are symbols of all that is wrong with this world.

We make another turn onto a road ramping upwards. We halt at a checkpoint and the soldiers come to peer at me. One salutes, the others laugh.

I'm not sure how to take this. I've always had the visceral sense that revealing my intelligence would only end in death, so I'm uncomfortable at being so conspicuous. On the other hand, adulation, however ironically given, strikes a welcome, cosy chord.

The pole rises and our truck drives through. The closer we get to the pyramids, the worse they look. Only on my pyramid, way up there at the apex, are the remnants of the limestone that clad the entire edifice in pure ethereal white. Cladding that made these the greatest man-made objects the world had ever seen, and that I doubt have been bettered since.

Don't get me wrong, their sheer mass still takes the breath away, but now just the rougher sandstone blocks lie revealed. Cracked and crumbled by the change from the cold of night to the heat of day, their edges have been rubbed away by the desert wind. These blocks were never meant to be seen, their quarrying lacking the perfect precision of the limestone. A mighty edifice that once had been sublime now looks impoverished, ramshackle, approximate.

We pull up and Amr gets out and lowers the tailgate. Ragab, my lead in his hand, jumps down. I follow and he walks me across towards Khufu's pyramid. A large group of men and women cluster at the base but they turn excitedly as we approach and click their votive objects at us. All around are heavily armed police. Up on the higher steps of the pyramid, their uniforms blending in so well against the sandstone, only the slight movement of the Special Forces give them away to my new eyes.

I shudder. Normal police laugh and joke when their gangmasters aren't around. Special Forces never do, their dead eyes constantly scanning everybody and everything as a potential threat.

A senior Fat Bottom steps forward, hands outstretched. "Behold, mighty Cheops," he intones. There is clapping. A man in a perfectly cut jacket and trousers has been bending in close conversation with a smaller man, but when he hears the applause he spins round and steps forward quickly, outpacing the policeman and getting to us first.

"Welcome, Cheops," he says, his voice a rumble in his thick chest. He reaches out and Ragab gives him my lead without question.

The smaller man has meanwhile clapped his hands for attention. "Abdul Ibrahim, our esteemed Minister of Defence, will say a few words."

The man holding my lead inclines his head. I turn to look up at him, the first chance in my new life to observe real power up close.

I am disappointed. In my day power marked you, supported you my means of a vast theatre dripping with masks of gold and lapis and legions of slaves and servants and soldiers. This man looks like any other scurrying through the streets of this teeming city. Receding grey hair and beard. Glasses, though not as magnified as the Vet's, reveal flat brown eyes. He is squat and powerful and I guess that once he was a soldier, but now he seems drawn and harried and eager to please.

Neferhotep would have had this man's guts for fishing line and his testicles for bait.

The Minister is looking down at me with something approximating affection though I suspect this may actually be an emotion with which he is unfamiliar. It is still early in the morning but a bead of sweat is running down one temple.

He turns to the mob. "We are here today to honour a mighty hero with a mighty name. Cheops, as you know, is the Greek version of the name of the magnificent Pharaoh Khufu who created this, the greatest of pyramids," and his arm sweeps back to take in the vast sandstone bulk behind him.

I didn't know that at all and my big heavy jaw drops open in surprise. These bastards have named me after my father! For years I have been answering obediently to the name of the man I despise most of all.

My rage doesn't end there. My pyramid, the one standing right next door, is obviously higher and is in better condition than my father's, if only because those thieving zealots haven't been able to get at its remnant crown of limestone without it falling down and squishing their bodies into the dust.

As to the size issue, I'll be the first to admit that from base to apex Khufu's pyramid is technically bigger, but I was smarter and built mine on higher ground so it looks the biggest. Not only that but it used only a fraction of the stone. If that's not splendour coupled with sagacity and prudence then I don't know what is.

I look across at my desecrated pyramid where my mortal remains are entombed. My mummified body should have allowed my passage to the afterlife. However, instead of bargaining with the gods for the fate of mankind, I'm on the end of a lead with my paws in the dust.

Again, what did I do that was so wrong? As Khafre my sins were a trickling stream compared to Khufu's raging torrent. Whole countries had been decimated at his cruel command.

I look back at his pyramid and I notice something that has me blinking in alarm. The entrance high above is still sealed but, down from this and barely six layers up from its base, there's a dark space. A soldier steps out of this and looks down at all the people below.

It's a tomb raider's rat hole! Fingers of ice clutch at my heart.

"And this dog, this mighty dog," Ibrahim is intoning, "risked his life and suffered grievous injury to protect our people as any good Arab would."

I'm not an Arab and neither are you, I think. We're Africans. Who are Arabs anyway? From East across the Red Sea is my best guess. Their skin may be lighter, though not quite as light as the old people from the north, but plenty of African blood still flows through their veins.

Ibrahim goes on about my bravery and the dangers that the Daesh pose, whoever they are. The Enemy has many other names and I must have heard them all during my training: Iranians, Americans, militants, Shiites, apostates, Muslim Brotherhood, terrorists, Israelis, dissidents. I'd quickly come to realise that these come and go like the desert wind or court fashions. I have no idea what any of these have done to warrant such hatred and fear.

This world is certainly a tricky place.

Even though praise is a novelty in this life, it's all I ever got in the last so I find my thoughts quickly turning back to the rat hole which may as well have been bored straight into my own heart.

Because I haven't been listening, I'm surprised when I feel the tug and find myself being led by Ibrahim towards the pyramid. I can hear others following behind. Little steps have been cut into the lower blocks and we climb up these, then along the blocks to the left, then up more steps. We wend our way back and forth across the lower face of the pyramid but there's no doubt where we're heading. The soldier who has been watching us steps aside and we enter the rat hole.

The first thing I notice is the smell. Countless people have come this way, their sweat condensing out on the cool of the walls. The passage is roughly hewn and twisting and the floor is uneven. I fear where we are going and, sure enough, we emerge into the Grand Gallery which rises steeply up into the heart of the pyramid. A sloping wooden floor with little ridges for steps has obligingly been laid. The gallery is high and tapered but, as we approach the entrance, even Ibrahim has to stoop as the ceiling there gets too low. He climbs, his back bent like a farmer carrying a sack of grain.

The smell is even worse here. Many thousands have been this way to disturb Khufu's sleep. I hated the man but I still feel sick to my stomach. This is the worst desecration of all.

The Grand Gallery leads unerringly up into the King's Chamber and I find myself seeing things I thought I never would again: the huge red sandstone blocks that had taken many months and multitudes of men to quarry and drag up here.

The place is lit by modern lamps but it can't drive away the darkness that is more than simply a lack of light: a darkness made of three parts infamy and one part heresy and it all fills my throat like sand filled Djedefre's lungs.

The tomb has been emptied of grave goods and all that remains is Khufu's sarcophagus, tucked away at the back like an afterthought. The lid is gone and a corner has been hacked off. I can't help myself, I strain towards it, dragging Ibrahim behind me. He resists at first but then wisely judges that it would be undignified to resist a creature so forceful.

I scrabble to the sarcophagus and put my paws on the edge then push myself up on my back legs.

The sarcophagus is empty!

I sense Ibrahim leaning in to look as well. "Gone, boy," he says. "All the pyramids are empty and the bodies disappeared ages ago. Where they went nobody knows. Burned on a fire, or chopped up to get at the amulets hidden in the folds of their wrappings. If only you'd been there to guard them, eh boy?"

All the pyramids are empty! The world spins and I feel sick. A whimper escapes me and a viscous line of drool falls from the side of my mouth and into Khufu's empty sarcophagus. There are flashes of light and I think I am dying, brought back to life only to have this last outrage thrown in my face. Then I realise the crowd is arriving and it is their votive objects that are flashing.

A soldier steps forward, hand raised. "You cannot take pictures in here!"

Ibrahim raises his own hand, waving away the man's objection without a word. The flashing intensifies as more eager, shoddily dressed people arrive. Ibrahim is smiling. "If only Cheops the dog had been here to protect his namesake," he says again, but for the benefit of these others. It is clearly a thought that has tickled him.

If all the pyramids are empty then where is my body? I wonder. Where in the whole of Egypt?

"Perhaps the dog could sniff out where the mummy went," shouts someone to general laughter. Like I could follow a four-thousand-year-old scent trail overlain by millions of dog shit covered shoes worn by sweaty, farting multitudes.

I want to cry but dogs can't do that.

"Get him to put his paws on the sarcophagus again!" someone yells and Ibrahim pats the lid. I'm too weak to refuse so I dumbly comply.

"Cheops on the job. Great headline!" says Ibrahim. "Feel free to use it, guys."

Stars erupt all over the tomb, each extinguished in an instant. I peer down into the mockingly empty and age-blackened interior of the sarcophagus and struggle to find my footing on a new world, the old one having finally crumbled away beneath my feet.

The body is everything. Without it the spirit fades even after death. One cannot walk or talk or eat or drink or have sex in the afterlife if the body back in Egypt has been lost. That's why we took such pains to preserve it after death, with our unguents and our finest linen bandages and our amulets and our labyrinthine tombs complete with traps to squash and drown the raiders.

And perhaps this explains everything. My body destroyed, my Ka has been wandering these many years and has somehow found a host in the body of this dog. Maybe there's no cosmic plan here, just a sick spirit finding succour where it could. Instead of parleying with the gods, an advocate for all of mankind, shielding them from plagues and floods and droughts, all I'm useful for is as a well-trained nose.

I sink back on my haunches and lower myself so my jaw is on the cold stone floor.

"He's praying," someone yells and the stars sparkle again.

Ibrahim, wincing with the effort, crouches down and pats me on the head. "Good dog," he says. "Good dog."

Ancient Days 2560 BC

I had seen less grandiose military campaigns. We could have captured a whole city with the force that left Faiyum that day. A thousand fighting men, their loins barely concealed by cloths, like farmers plodding to their fields, had, at the first faint lightening of the sky, trudged away into the wasteland. Left behind were their crocodile leather breastplates, their hippo-hide shields. Gone were the banners, the plumed headdresses and gleaming bronze helmets. Only a few carried shields and spears, the oldest and most battered the army could find, whilst others carried drums like a horde of itinerant musicians.

All Egyptians fear the desert. The delicate thread of life that is the Nile lies sandwiched between two great desert beasts that one day, restless in their sleep, may roll over and extinguish it, like a mother numbed with drink may smother a baby.

In the early light the death beast on this side of the river was revealing itself. Here and there the pale yellow of the sand was broken by outcrops of black granite trailing sooty veils of eroded fragments. Conical hills rose and were cut by slabs of sandstone like blades slicing into anthills. On the other rises, sand had fallen away to form a gentle slope, broken only by blocks of harder rock curved and creased by the desert wind into thuggish, craggy shapes, like the foreheads of frowning giants, unimpressed by the feeble efforts of mere men such as ourselves.

My sedan chair, one amongst twenty others, rolled as the slaves' feet slid away beneath them on the yielding sand when we descended into each gully. The sun had not yet risen but I could make out the gleam of sweat on their backs in the mother-of-pearl pre-dawn light. Up and down, up and down we moved like scarabs over the undulating desert. Ahead, fearlessly leading the way, was my brother on his huge golden chair supported on the shoulders of forty slaves. Even here, seen only by his family and friends, he wore the twin crown of united Egypt. Over the backrest of his chair I could see its red and white tops nodding with the movement.

Fifty metres around us on all sides were soldiers, these fully kitted out for fighting, making a cordon around us that only the suicidally foolish would try to cross. Not that there was anyone else in the desert to attempt such a thing.

I felt for my bow, sleek and beautiful and made from black antelope horn strung with corded strips of lion gut. My arrows, precious wood brought north by traders from Kush, were tipped with the sharpest obsidian and fletched with the finest goose feathers. Hunting was a royal tradition and our tombs were decorated with heroic tableaux of our exploits slaughtering crocodiles or hippos or even just birds in the fields. Two artists had been brought along on this hunt to capture the details that would adorn Djedefre's own tomb, their leather bags full of papyrus, quill pens and paints. Prepared for a long walk on shifting sands they had almost swooned with delight when they too had been provided with sedan chairs just like the royal party.

To our left the tip of the sun appeared like molten metal, stretching out the shadows of the soldiers to impossible lengths.

Ahead and just to the right I saw Cetes, governor of the Atef-Pehu province, raise his hand to halt the caravan. The slaves lowered us and, though they risked the whip if they made a sound, their groans were unmistakable and I cast a disapproving glance at the gang-master who looked away guiltily. He tapped his short-knotted leather whip against his thigh in irritation. It would be busy tonight.

I had known Cetes for years. He was a tall, dignified man who had a reputation for fairness and integrity. Though he had little time for me, dignity and integrity not being my strongest attributes, I had nonetheless respected him. The only problem was that when he was with the King all his dignity fled, like a cat caught eating a cake. Right now, as he was coaxing the King to follow him, his back was bent and he was wringing his hands as though cleaning them with sand.

I stepped down. My sandals, the red leather so beautifully patterned with gold inlay to show Horus and Ra back to back, were not meant for walking around the desert. They were also not meant for hunting but this was like no hunt I had ever seen.

Sand is cold in the morning and I did not enjoy it trickling between my toes. Annoyed, I strode over to Cetes, who had stopped a little way from the caravan and was pointing at the sand. Something long and thick lay there and it wasn't until I got closer that I was able to separate the shadow from the object casting it.

I stopped in my tracks and shook my head, wondering if this was a dream. Before me was a skeleton or, more precisely, a spine but one that was as long as ten men laid head to toe. Had I cupped my hands, touching finger to finger, I couldn't have encompassed its breadth.

Djedefre looked more sickly than usual at the unexpected sight of the huge bones. The God-King was suddenly no longer in command of all he surveyed.

Cetes, unaware of his error, was talking excitedly. "We find these sometimes after storms when the desert winds blow the sand away."

"What are they?" Djedefre's reedy voice could barely be heard. "Are they giants?" He looked around quickly.

Expecting awe and finding only consternation, Cetes manner changed like a man strolling through a wheat field then finding himself amidst a nest of snakes. "It's not a man Your Highness. No, we think it is a fish."

A fish. I chuckled and Cetes allowed an instant of annoyance to flit across his patrician features. I shook my head. "I've heard of perch found just before the First Cataract, where the waters are deep and still, that grow to the length of a man but no more. Probably even that is a lie. And fish need that thing... what's it called... oh yes, water." I spread my arms and turned full circle. "Where is the water?"

"Perhaps it is a crocodile," said Djedefre and I felt embarrassed to hear the dread in his voice.

"Again, water," I said as gently as I could. He had been the only one to show kindness to me as a child. More kindness than I deserved. "Also, crocodiles can be up to four or five man-lengths, never more to my knowledge."

"Unless this is the skeleton of Sobek, the crocodile god," said Djedefre with a horrified wince, oblivious to the blasphemy.

"It is not a crocodile," said Cetes quickly. "With other such skeletons we have excavated and found no bones for arms and legs."

"A serpent then," said Djedefre queasily. "Perhaps the snake god Apophis himself."

What was to have been a triumphant hunting trip was becoming, in my brother's febrile mind, a saunter through the graveyard of the gods.

"No, Your Highness," said Cetes as humbly as he could. "The rib-cage of these things is huge, bigger even than a hippo's. This is no snake. If we were to dig out its skull, which is almost birdlike, though the length of a man, it would have only the smallest of teeth."

So, a big thick body but no arms and legs and small teeth. Whatever it was it couldn't have run very fast so I wasn't worried even if there were living versions still lurking around. Djedefre didn't look anywhere near as reassured.

"How did it get here?" Neferhotep had joined us. I hadn't noticed his approach or indeed that of the wealthy hangers-on in the party who now considered themselves Djedefre's closest intimates. The High Lord was not a man to ask idle questions. The furrows on Cetes' worried brow deepened.

"I am simply telling you what my First Accountant thinks. He collects the bones the sands reveal. He has many strange thoughts. To him the sand of the desert is like that on the shores of the Great Green Sea. He thinks that the sands of our deserts show that once the Great Green covered all of this land."

"But Egypt is eternal," said Djedefre simply, certainly, faithfully.

"Presumably you have had this man strangled for blasphemy," said Neferhotep mildly.

Cetes, too honest to lie, was at a loss for words.

"You and I must talk of this further," said Neferhotep icily. "After the hunt."

We returned to our sedan chairs, our hunt off to a less than auspicious start. How could the gods not have been angered by so much careless talk?

We took our seats and our little group of gilded scarabs resumed their rolling path over the desert. Looking back towards the Nile I could make out the faint glimmers of light on the battered old spear points of the warriors. They formed a line stretching along the Nile almost as far as the eye could see before curving round like pincers into the desert.

Ahead of us rose cliffs riven with more horizontal frown lines and we were heading towards the only break in this impenetrable facade. It formed a valley leading up gently into the highlands. For a second, I remembered Cetes' notion that once this was all under water. I visualised the waters receding, revealing the skeleton of the leviathan we had seen and I suddenly realised that over the ages water would carve valleys like this, river valleys just like the Nile itself but on a smaller scale. Could Cetes have been correct after all? I found myself relishing the heresy.

The valley had been chosen with exquisite care. Whilst my father might have stalked and chased animals for days, more account had to be taken of Djedefre's unspoken limitations. As the red sandstone valley narrowed, an outcrop of darker granite formed both a choke point and a platform commanding it. At a shout from Cetes, the slaves lowered our chairs and we all stepped off. Salas, my personal servant, had been walking behind and he rushed forward to gather my hunting gear. As we trudged towards the outcrop, the slaves lifted the chairs and retreated back out into the desert.

Fresh reeds had been carried all the way from the Nile and were supported on bamboo poles to make shade on the platform. The ascent was too steep for a sedan chair, no matter how many slaves were lifting it, so Djedefre had to scramble up, though with the help of many hands. His hairy, scrawny legs, revealed as his tunic rose up, could not have been less god-like. Ever since he had ascended to godhood, his every appearance had been carefully managed by Neferhotep, the King's dignity being sustained at all costs. So effective had this been that I had found myself going along with it, albeit half-heartedly. But now, scrabbling up in his ungainly manner, the gilded mask slipped away and he was once again just my clumsy brother. Like Cetes and his desert sea, I felt my illusions dissolving. I stopped and took a deep breath.

"Can I help, Your Royal Highness?" The man speaking was tall and lean and earnest but was stooping humbly so his head was below mine. I recognised him as a high official, the Royal Commissioner of Winemaking if I was not mistaken. He had misjudged his attire. Rather than aiming for spectacle and wearing his finest decorated linens, he had gone for sand-yellow leather leggings and tunic, the better to wrestle dangerous taloned beasts. That was the very last thing any of the rest of us were intending to do that day.

"No thank you..."

"Hapiwer, Your Royal Highness."

"Of course. No, I do not need help, Hapiwer. I am simply reflecting on how glorious the King looks today." I hadn't really thought this through because Hapiwer looked down at his coarse hunting gear, a stricken look playing across his face. Not that I really cared how he felt.

I started to climb but more slowly. It wouldn't do for any of us to overtake the King. "How's the Shedeh, Hapiwer? Will we have plenty tonight?"

"Of course, Your Royal Highness. All five great wines will be available at the celebrations. The Shedeh is from the harvest five floods ago and is the best I have ever tasted."

Shedeh was one of the few things I felt thankful to my father for. A wine so red it looked too similar to blood to sit easy with previous kings. It was said that the vines in the Delta grew only on ancient battlefields. Drinking blood was for heathens, like the benighted inhabitants of Kush, but Father had liked his wine more than the ancient superstitions and had insisted it be drunk at all royal feasts. Sated with beer and palm wine, and even the white wine imported from the fabled northern lands across the Great Green, I had taken to all of the five great red wines, though Shedeh was my favourite. So rich and heavy, I could indeed believe it was made from the blood of slaughtered heroes and that made its savour even sweeter.

I reached the platform, Hapiwer a respectable step behind despite his long legs that could have carried him to the top in barely ten strides. Leather-bound seats formed an arc near the lip of the outcrop and slaves waited with trays of food and drink. I took a seat as far to the left of Djedefre's central position as possible and beckoned Hapiwer to take the seat beside me. Looking back down the valley and far across the desert I could see a long arc of river glinting in the glancing red light of the sun.

Behind each seat stood a bamboo rack holding flint-tipped lances and arrows. A simple wooden bow, less ornate than my own gleaming curve of horn, was already strung and waiting lest the string of my own bow broke. Both bows were a little shorter than a man's height and had single gentle curves. My horn bow had been tailored to my unimpressive strength but when I tested the draw on the wooden bow, I found it had been made for someone more robust. I put it back, a look of distaste on my face as though its aesthetics had offended me.

I surveyed the company. High officials, senior scribes and accountants, my younger brothers Baufra and Horbef, the two painters and several others I did not recognise. I had arrived too late for the introductions but I guessed the older man would be Ramose, a wealthy merchant who owned vast tracks of fertile land in the Delta. He had a daughter who

Neferhotep thought would make a good wife for the King. Perhaps the younger man beside him was his son though his physique was not that of a scion of wealthy merchants, or indeed anyone else in this hunting party. His tunic, though capacious, was stretched tight over an upper arm with muscles like entwined pythons.

"This is so exciting," said Hapiwer, stringing his bow unaided.

"Don't get too carried away. It would not do to be more successful than the King."

Hapiwer's look of surprise made we wonder how a man moving in such high circles could be so naive. Egypt was ruled and regulated to within an inch of its life, locked into an administrative system that had governed for hundreds of years and would no doubt rule for thousands more. High officials, controlling everything from warehouses to whore houses, were more plentiful than vermin. Too many to all come to a single feast or hunting party, they received invitations on a strictly rotational basis. I was guessing this was Hapiwer's first and probably his last.

Neferhotep stood and slowly looked around. Our armed escort, half with bows and half with spears, were arrayed in a half circle behind us. The platform sloped upwards and the soldiers at the rear were well above us.

"Are you ready, Your Highness?"

"Begin!" squeaked Djedefre.

Neferhotep waved his arm in a complete arc. Soon black smoke was billowing into the sky from the top of the sandstone bluff across from us. Somewhere, one thousand men would be starting to move, banging drums or spears against shields. All this was too far away for us to see or hear as yet.

I took a mug of milky beer from a slave and waved Hapiwer to do the same. The beer was beautifully cool and I guessed it had been stored somewhere nearby in the chill of the desert night. "I knew your father, Setka," I said. In Egypt jobs were hereditary, sustaining generation after generation. Fall foul of Neferhotep or any of his deputies, have your job taken away and you would doom generations of your descendants to penury. If, that is, Neferhotep didn't just slaughter the lot of you and be done with it.

Hapiwer bowed his head. "He comes unbidden to my thoughts every day though he died these three floods past."

"As such thoughts should." Not only must the body be preserved through mummification, but the Ka, the soul, must be sustained by thoughts and prayers otherwise it will fade. My father had built no less than twenty funerary temples and employed over a thousand priests in perpetuity to do just that. In the unlikely event I became King, I would raze every damned one of his temples to the ground and bury his memory as carefully as a desert rat buries a nut.

"He was a wise man. In everything I do it is as though he is at my shoulder, a shadow cast from the grave, advising me."

"And is the advice any good?" As I recalled, Setka had been a bibulous man, always good company and so a frequent guest, someone who seemed to take genuine pleasure from my father's bitter jokes.

Hapiwer seemed troubled that I would even ask. We Egyptians have more respect for the dead than ever we had when they were alive. I could imagine that Setka's advice might be nonsense, coming as it would from a drunken ghost, but in life he might well have made an amiable and perhaps even loving father. For an ungenerous second, jealousy, always coiling within me like a viper, made me resent this jumped-up commoner.

"My father's advice is always sound, Your Royal Highness. He was the Royal Commissioner for thirty years before he left for the Field of Reeds. He knew every clod of earth in the Delta."

After thirty years in that marshy hole he must have been King of the Mosquitoes. I was amazed he had had any blood left to swell out his substantial frame.

I was startled to see little bits of the desert begin to move, this movement swift and darting. I realised that jerboa, tiny long-eared, long-legged rodents that had been hiding in plain sight were now scurrying to their holes and crevices in the sandstone bluff before us.

Even as I watched I felt a tickling sensation in my ears as though a far-off flying insect was approaching. Hapiwer heard it too and his long thin eyebrows dipped in the middle with puzzlement. The chattering party fell silent and we watched as the first faint dust clouds began to swirl up out of the desert. At first the little clouds were few, but as time passed they multiplied and merged until they formed a curtain hiding the river and the green of the crops. The curtain formed a vast semi-circle which even as we watched began to shrink as the dust clouds funnelled towards us.

A man dressed in full hunting gear who had been standing back came forward diffidently and whispered in Neferhotep's ear.

The High Lord stood and turned towards the nobles and their guests. "Please prepare yourselves my Lords, Your Royal Highness."

My bow was already strung so I simply transferred some arrows to the leather tube attached to the armrest of the chair. I was selecting an arrow when I heard the thudding of hooves and was just in time to see a single oryx streak by in the defile below, its long grey horns repeatedly jabbing at the air with each stride as it galloped past. Before anyone could even notch an arrow, it had gone.

For a second there was complete silence and then everyone laughed. "Quick off the mark. He'll live to rut another day," said the King and everyone, well nearly everyone, laughed. Neferhotep wasn't capable of laughter and I couldn't be bothered.

Far away the dust cloud was like a net dragging in its catch. The noise was still faint but rising, a cacophony of brass-on-brass and the deeper thudding of stone on stretched leather as the soldiers drove the game towards the funnel of rock and our ambush.

Wild bulls had been terrorising Faiyum, flattening crops, smashing down fences and attacking, goring and trampling to death anyone foolish enough who tried to stop them. The God-King, so concerned for his people, had decreed the hunt to rid the region of this pestilence. At least that's what Neferhotep had made widely known.

Several red foxes, moving so quickly they looked like fire arrows streaking across the floor of the defile, provoked a few ineffectual arrows. One from the King was so feeble it didn't even stick in the sand but just fell over. Meanwhile the foxes had disappeared where the canyon curved to our left.

An ibex came next, heavy in body and with horns which curved round over more than a half circle. It must have been near us when the beating noises began for ibex are not fast runners. This time the archers had time to aim but with equal lack of effect. Pudgy fingers and arms, strengthened only by lifting papyrus from one shelf to another, sent arrows on wild, weak trajectories.

A *ssstt* sound next to my ear startled me as air was parted violently by an obsidian-tipped arrow and a scything bowstring. So powerful was the shot that it hardly curved in the air before striking the ibex just below the shoulder. It stiffened in mid-stride and came to a faltering stop. As the other men fumbled to notch new arrows, the ibex looked round confusedly, took a couple of experimental steps then thumped to the ground. Its chin lay cradled by the sand, horns erect, a hazard for the animals that would come next.

I turned to look at Hapiwer with new respect. He smiled shyly. "Game in the Delta is plentiful. I am well practiced."

Some hyenas now appeared, their ungainly loping strides matching the ugliness of their faces. To me hyenas look half dog and half man with their short legs and long arms and I detest them. Egyptians had over two hundred gods for just about every animal except this revolting creature.

Well worth killing! For the first time I took a shot but the arrow sailed into the sandstone cliff, a hazard only to cowering jerboas.

More foxes, an ostrich, some wild sheep, an addax, all ran the gauntlet. Not interested, I took the time to look at my fellow guests, assessing their technique. I noticed that the strange, muscular chap was more interested in what the King was doing than in the hunt. The King was waving around his bow with its notched arrow, ineffectually choosing a target then changing his mind. However, a limping ram caught his eye and he swung round to aim. In synchrony the muscular man swept his bow round and loosed his arrow within an eye-blink of the King's.

Like my own efforts, the King's arrow at best spoiled a desert rat's day. Meanwhile, the muscular man's arrow had driven clean through the ram's eye and the tip was now sticking out of the back of its skull, dropping the animal like a stone.

Rams, I reflected, had thick skulls.

The hard claps of Neferhotep's hands could be heard even over the rising noise from the canyon. "Excellent shot your Majesty! Instant death, worthy of Neith herself." Neith, our most ancient of deities, guides the hunter's arrow, and we had sacrificed at her temple in Memphis before we had set out.

My brother, whose poor vision had probably lost sight of the arrow as soon as it left his bow, held up his arms to warmly receive his due praise. We all bowed and murmured our prayers, the muscular man not least of all.

I began to wonder what other aspects of my brother's life were so skillfully engineered by Neferhotep. Did the equivalent of the muscular man, perhaps one with a penis like a stallion's, service the King's wives? Did someone with an arsehole like a tomb entrance take monumental shits on his behalf?

Suddenly there was a terrible commotion as the first of the wild bulls arrived, bellowing angrily. We'd been too busy celebrating my brother's marksmanship to prepare so we watched helplessly as the bull galloped by to safety.

The floor of the defile was now full of animals and the guests started to shoot wildly into their midst. Neferhotep was just about to congratulate the King for bringing down a dorcas antelope by proxy when rising thunder drowned him out. A murky wave of brown, like the Nile in flood, washed into the valley, the heavy stamping hooves of the bulls shaking even the granite outcrop on which we stood. The antelopes and the sheep and the goats swerved into the sides of the canyon, clearing the way for the bulls. In a solid mass they surged forward, their thudding hooves raising a turmoil of dust, but not enough to prevent me seeing two of my own shots striking home.

Then the wild bulls, whose demise was the whole point of this extravagant charade, had made it through the defile and the thundering diminished. I peered through the dust. Had we brought down a single one?

There was at least one body down there that was bigger than any of the other animals that had come through. Beside me Neferhotep was claiming Djedefre had brought a bull down with a single shot but, as he extolled such hunting prowess, his voice was drowned out by more thundering. It was coming from the left and I turned to see the wild bulls charging back the way they had come. Even as they did so, from the right two lions bounded into the canyon. I blinked in surprise for lions were rare this far north, being ruthlessly hunted by dogs and men if they killed any livestock.

Suddenly it was a though everyone was wading through the Nile, its heavy waters slowing all movement. The lions travelling too fast to stop before the charging bulls ploughed them down, swerved to their left and came bounding up the bank towards our platform. In the blink of an eye they were amongst us.

While the rest of us froze, Djedefre in blind panic dropped his bow and staggered back. The movement was like a lure to a hungry fish: both lions' heads swung towards him.

Something hit me on the upper arm, impelling me to the side. Hapiwer, his long legs thrusting his body forward, threw himself between the King and the nearest lion just as the animal leapt, knocking Hapiwer backwards. As they crashed to the ground the lion's wide-open jaws closed on his head.

In an instant, the lion transformed into a porcupine. One arrow nicked my ear, another went through the accountant's neck. We'd been standing in the line of fire of the army bowmen behind us. On the other side of the platform, another guest had been between them and the second lion. He tumbled to the left, an arrow sticking through his thigh.

Agony exploded onto Hapiwer's face as the lion collapsed on him, its jaws not closing but its teeth sliding across his forehead and opening his flesh.

How I got to his side I do not know. Why I got there is an even greater mystery. To my surprise I found myself with handfuls of fur and pulling them with all my might. "Help me!" I roared.

Even the most dull-witted of the fifty guards had got the message by now. Being helpful would be the best strategy to avoiding strangulation later, though, if the King had been injured, it would all be a moot point.

The lion was lifted off Hapiwer as if it was a toy and thrown down into the canyon. The other lion was down but still alive. It seemed so puzzled by the shafts appearing from its side that it didn't even turn to look as a guard stepped forward and thrust a spear deep into its chest.

The whole side of Hapiwer's face was covered in blood and his lips were turning blue. Without thinking, I did what Peseshet had done with a breathless patient, turning him on his side. The weight of the beast had driven the air from his lungs. Blood wasn't bubbling from his mouth so at least his ribs had not been broken and his lungs pierced.

Hapiwer suddenly took a deep breath, so much so that I saw the dust rise and get sucked into his mouth. This set off a coughing fit that would be agony with bruised ribs. At least he was alive.

I looked across at my brother, whose chief injury appeared to be confusion. He was standing unaided and his linens were as free from blood as when the slaves had put them on this morning.

"Salas!" I yelled, "Get my travelling box!" I moved quickly over to the wounded accountant, whose blood was pulsing out and was soaking into the sand. But for the sand it would have been all over our shoes, for he was losing a great deal of it and so very quickly. His eyes had already glazed over. I muttered a brief prayer to Osiris and went over to the guest with the arrow in his thigh. I recognised him as the Curator of the Royal Placentas. His face was pale and his teeth were gritted.

"You!" I pointed at a soldier. "Hold the arrow front and back. You!" to another, "cut the shaft at the front! The rest of you hold him down!"

The arrow had gone through the thick muscle of the thigh, missing the bone. As the bronze knife sawed away, the curator screamed and tried to writhe but hairy arms held him firm. Once the barbed arrow head was removed I pulled the arrow back through the wound and threw it aside.

By now my travelling box was beside me. It was strange that I had included all the paraphernalia I used when I went to Peseshet's clinics. Perhaps the gods had guided me for once. "Keep hold of him!" I yelled. Somehow, at the first attempt, I threaded the cat gut through the eye of the needle. It's not easy to make a sharp ivory needle - the holes it punches can be bigger than the wounds themselves - but the wound had to be closed before the man became very white and very dead. The curator screamed like a little girl and I had to use great force to push the blunt needle through his flesh. Six thick stitches gave me enough purchase to pull the wound closed and stop the welling blood. I sat back and, looking up, saw a circle of soldiers staring down at me in evident puzzlement. Peseshet's stitching technique was a radical new approach, far more effective than the prayers intoned on the battlefield to cure the wounded. What I had done had taken even these battle-hardened warriors by surprise.

Once the curator had calmed down and it was clear the stitches would hold, I returned to Hapiwer and his lacerated forehead. Peseshet had let me try stitching wounds many times since I had started coming to her clinics, but only under her close supervision. However, drunk with expertise,

I did not hesitate. To a man of my talents, Hapiwer's little cut was trivial.

Hapiwer seemed less convinced. "Do you know what you're doing, Your Royal Highness?" he asked fearfully.

"Of course," I said. "I've had the best teacher. Hold him!"

It didn't wind up looking pretty but I sewed up the gash in his forehead without a problem and within a few minutes the bleeding had stopped entirely.

In all the excitement I hadn't noticed that the canyon had filled with soldiers, the beaters having finally all converged. In the middle of this the King's sedan chair was waiting and he was being helped down the incline. I was surprised that Neferhotep was not at his side and, when I looked round, I saw him standing to my left and staring at me, his look that of a starving man who had caught sight of a juicy steak. I turned quickly away, not sure what to make of this.

After the King had departed, surrounded on all sides by a line of soldiers five men deep, I clambered down from the platform and walked up the canyon, curious as to why the bulls had come thundering back. I had to step around carcasses, most crushed under the hooves of the bulls. There were many antelopes and goats brought down by arrows, but there was only one dead bull, a single arrow sticking into its chest just below the left shoulder. The muscular bowman had done his work again.

There was a turn in the canyon ahead and when I walked round it, I found myself facing a barrier of fur-covered flesh, the different colours forming a tapestry. A hundred archers were sitting on the lips of the canyon, their work done. Below and on the other side of this field of death, butchers and flensers were already at work. I wondered if a single animal had made it through the gauntlet.

As for the bulls, their way blocked by this wall of death, they'd simply charged back the way they'd come. The beaters didn't have bows and the bulls would have crashed through them easily. Even now the bulls, the target of this magnificent spectacle, would be back down at the Nile munching the sweet young corn.

Modern Day

The night is still heavy with the heat of the day. Cairo slips by as our little truck wends its way through streets that have finally quieted, most of the crazed drivers now in their beds. No doubt they dream of driving still, steering their imaginary vehicles to crush harmless dogs under unforgiving wheels.

I'm not at my best. It's as though my guts have been scooped out. My life as a possible god-king had been one with purpose where I might one day have occupied the fulcrum point, gods on one side, man on the other. There could be no more important role and I had been trained for it all my life, though nobody had ever really thought the training would be needed.

This was one reason it had been so hard waking up as a dog, but I had got it into my head that I was still serving some greater purpose. I had no clear idea what that was but it was the only way I could cope. Now, even this wispy veil had been torn aside, leaving me naked and unmanned. With my human body gone, just so much dust spread by the four winds, I am never going to intercede with the gods.

What I am now, when all is said and done, is just a stupid, tail-wagging dog. Worse, it now seems clear that my new life can only be one of punishment. I don't understand as I haven't done anything very bad yet in my dreams, except for showing a breath-taking lack of respect for the dead. I wonder if Peseshet may be a clue for why else would a mere physician feature so prominently in my dreams?

I watch dully as this strange city rolls by. Some districts are full of lights, some are made dark by looming empty buildings. Sometimes a single lit and inhabited apartment can be seen, the first soul brave enough to move into these hulking, ghost palaces.

The mud brick palaces of my day are now also ghosts long since crumbled into the restless sands. Only temples and tombs of granite and sandstone remain. Rain in Egypt has always been a startling event. Years can pass without a single drop, so these temples and tombs have hardly changed. The hieroglyphs and carvings on their walls look just as they did in my day though the paint has been chipped off over eons by motes of sand flung by the desert winds.

What must modern Egyptians think of us? All that remains of our once mighty civilisation are almost perfectly preserved buildings devoted to gods and to death. All that smacked of life and vigour and joy has faded like a memory. They must think us obsessed by death yet nothing could be further from the truth. We loved life, loved it so much we wanted to keep living for eternity. However, all that remains now is beautiful but morbid. No wonder they don't seem to understand us.

Then again, though the desert has yet to sand it away, I struggle to grasp anything of this new world. I can't even understand my handlers though they are, to put it as politely as possible, simple souls.

However, even I can sense that something is definitely up with them. I'm all alone, tied up in the open back of the truck while the three of them have squeezed into the single row of seats in the cab. Mazan's a giggler but now they're all at it. I can't make out what they're saying over the roar of the engine but their girlish laughter reaches me well enough.

Suddenly an evil thought pierces my melancholy. Am I finally for 'the snip'? Are we heading for the dreaded Vet's? Is that what they're finding so funny? Could they be so cruel after my bravery, after the selfless act that saved their miserable lives?

Again, I am presented with definitive proof that dogs can't cry because I would weep buckets if I could.

Woefully I peer down between my legs at my cock and balls. These hairy appendages are pretty repulsive, yet I have spent countless nights locked in a battle to stop myself licking them. I know it would give me pleasure, but I have to draw the line at licking a dog's cock, even my own.

Call me prideful if you must, but that's something royalty should never do.

I shake my head angrily, sending the self-pitying thoughts flying away like water droplets after my much-loved, though infrequent, baths. Now is the time to act, to make my escape and take my chances under the uncaring wheels of the Cairo traffic. I'll follow the Nile, get out into the fields along the river. I'll catch cats and rats and smaller dogs and scavenge food from the farms and take my chances with the farmers' guns.

I turn around and peer at my lead secured to an eyelet melted by some magic into the truck's metal side. How I'd escaped last time had mystified my handlers, especially as the lead had been undamaged. They'd scratched their heads and, after blaming Ragab, had eventually decided one of the crewmen must have released me out of mischief.

So, I still have the same old metal lead but can I pull the trick with my tongue whilst in a moving truck without any light? The boat had been docked and the rear deck always well lit but even there the task had been a nightmare. Plus, my tongue is still swollen, though the Vet's potions have helped.

A few fumbled, desperate attempts to open the catch has me whimpering in pain and I taste blood on my lacerated tongue. Eventually I give up and sit back on my haunches.

My only hope now is to break away from whoever holds my lead, biting their hand so they let go and I can dash into the embracing anonymity of the Cairo night.

I hope that handler will be Mazan. They're all dopes but Amr is the nicest. Ragab is little more than a boy. Mazan... Mazan I don't trust though I still haven't quite worked out why. Yeah, let's hope it's Mazan I get to bite.

This is not a good district we're driving through. Footpaths that provide at least some guidelines for the mad traffic have long since disappeared, as have parked cars and even motorcycles. Shops have given way to stalls. Even the tuc-tucs have vanished, too afraid to venture here.

Then even the stalls are left behind and we're into a district of high enclosing walls. Above some of these, tall spindly metal structures tower above piles of crushed metal. It's like the legendary elephants' graveyard, except for cars.

Our truck veers to the right and stops before a barred metal gate adorned with loops of the artificial metal thorns that are so popular at the police base. Our truck gives its little squeal and a light comes on in a cabin behind the gate. A guy in a filthy gallibaya comes out. He's got a shotgun and is peering into our lights. Mazan steps out of the cab and the man waves to him then unlocks the gate. They shake hands. Mazan says something and they both laugh.

The Vet's place is bright and shiny and deep inside a place full of policemen. Wherever I am now it's nothing like that.

There's suddenly a roaring in the air. I glance up in alarm and then flatten myself against the cold metal as one of those terrible metal birds roars directly over my head, a hundred shining eyes down each of its sides. It disappears below the level of the walls and a few seconds later I hear a terrible screech. Almost immediately its roar rises to become earth-shattering before fading into the distance.

So, this is where those things nest! Are they the new gods? Are my handlers going to feed me to one of them? Has my act of bravery made me worthy of sacrifice to these awful beings?

The unfairness of it all clutches at my heart. My mind is made up. Whoever takes my lead is going to lose a hand.

Amr and Ragab have also got out and joined the other two. They're laughing their traitorous heads off, greatly enjoying themselves. They're not fools after all. They're evil duplicitous villains. How could I have been so taken in? Some water, a few walks, some crappy food have lulled me into passivity.

They all come around the back of the truck and stare at me.

"It's your lucky day, mighty Cheops," says Mazan.

"We're going to make a man out of you," says Ragab.

"What the fuck are you talking about, you dolt?" snorts Amr. "He's a fucking dog."

Ragab waves a hand. "He'll be a man-dog. Look, you know what I mean."

"You're not even a man-man," says Amr and Mazan laughs.

Ragab reaches for my lead and my natural reaction is to draw my lips back and snarl but I force myself to remain calm. I learned very early on that snarling at my handlers never ever ends well and, anyway, why give them any warning?

"He's not happy," says Amr. "Something has spooked him. Look, his hackles are up! We'd better take care in case he tries to bolt."

"Doesn't know what's good for him," grumbles Mazan as he lowers the tail-gate. He and Amr climb in the back and put their big heavy arms around me while Ragab unclips the lead then grabs my collar. Mazan, demonstrating unsuspected depths of intelligence, clamps a hand over my muzzle so I can't open my mouth and bite his fucking head off.

I'm a big dog but these guys are strong and, for once, determined. The bastards carry me off the truck and towards the gate. Alarmed, I struggle but the big arm squeezes my chest and Ragab pulls hard on my collar so I can't breathe.

"Easy, boy!" says Amr.

The men stop at the gate. Amr begins to count. "One, two, three... now!"

Suddenly I'm flying through the air sideways. The ground hits my legs at an angle, sweeping them from under me and I thud to the ground. I hear the rattle as the gate is closed behind me.

"You're on your own now, boy," yells Mazan.

"Enjoy!" shouts Amr.

"Don't do what I wouldn't do," says Ragab.

"What the fuck does that mean?" asks Amr. "You wouldn't do this anyway, would you?"

"I wouldn't put it past him," says Mazan.

"You're sure he can't get out?" Amr is addressing this to the man from the cabin.

"People round here would steal your shit if you let them," says the man, who has a wheezy voice. "Believe me, nobody can get in so that mutt is certainly not going to get out."

"I owe you, Uncle," says Mazan.

The wheezy man spits. Even in the poor light I can see the big gobbet kick up a respectable cloud of dust. "Just tell your mother to stop breaking my balls about visiting Grandma. I'd see her more often but you know what she's like."

Mazan nods. "Ball-breaking runs in the family. I don't blame you."

I have too much on my mind to listen to this bullshit and I know how it'll go anyway. They'll all start whining about women. In my day men and women were more equal. When a man and wife divorced the woman took back all she had contributed to the marriage. Nowadays the man seems to own everything including the wife. That's bound to force women to fight back by other means.

I'm beginning to realise that whatever is going on here it isn't about castration. The panting in my chest subsides and I no longer have to loll out my big stupid tongue to cool down. This certainly isn't the Vet's and my eyes have adjusted well enough to see that the compound I'm in isn't even that big. There's no room for a big metal bird that would tear me to shreds.

So, what am I doing here?

I tentatively sniff at the air. The crushed cars have spilled their innards and I smell their blood. Someone has been burning something and the air is harsh and bitter. I sniff carefully and there is something else, something both earthy and fleshy, something...

There's a low growl and my hairy, dangling doggy scrotum shrivels to the size of a couple of raisins. Horror seizes me like the wrath of Seth.

I go down on my belly, still my breathing and try to be as invisible as possible, praying the metal bird will swoop down after all, its grisly claws grasping me, tearing me open and spilling my guts, but at least getting me the hell out of here.

I'm shivering like I've got the plague and trying so hard not to whimper, to betray my position to the thing I hear padding towards me. It's not hiding its breathing. It even gives a little yelp.

This place doesn't have any lights but the truck's headlights are shining through, the shadows of the mesh fence criss-crossing the hulking debris. The thing approaching casts a long shadow, making it look big, wolf-big.

I hope against hope it's going to attack and kill me, but I know that's wishful thinking. As it gets within a few body lengths it lowers itself and slinks towards me. It gives another yelp.

The urge to run is overpowering but I'd be charging around in this dark little enclosure cutting myself and banging my brains out on all the metal.

Even so, it's a tempting prospect, better than the stomach-emptying alternative that is now almost within reach. Just as I think this, her slink turns to a lunge and her teeth close on my front leg.

It's not a bite, it's a nip, but she darts back in case I go for her.

If anything, she's bigger than I am. I'm not sure she's a German Shepherd but she's not far off. She has the same short but thick heat-trapping hair. She must know every tiny patch of shade in this damned place.

She's looking at me and she gives another yelp. I give her a meaty snarl and her ears prick up and she shuffles back with yelps that are beginning to sound more like the bleats of sheep.

She darts in and nips my flank.

I rack my brains trying to remember about dogs, trying to work out what signals I should be sending. Our desert hunting dogs that brought down wild sheep and goats, and even the occasional lion, were complete and utter bastards. We'd allow the better ones to breed and sometimes I'd watch. With all the snarling and biting and yelping there wasn't much difference between fighting and fucking. It makes me think that in these circumstances a snarl might be a come-on.

She steps forward and barks in my face. Those are big teeth, I think. This is going to be some fight!

She moves round me and I feel her breath near my bottom as she sniffs. I thrust a back leg at her and she dodges away.

She comes back around in front of me, turns and squats and her backside fills my sight. She lifts her tail and a rainbow of fragrances wafts over me. I don't have the words to describe them and can only liken it to something I had seen. It was like entering Khufu's burial chamber for the first time, before it was robbed of its grave goods. You huffed and puffed your way up through the Grand Gallery, so bare and austere and forbidding, and then your eyes met the gold and the silver and the lapis, the jasper and turquoise and carnelian and feldspar. All used without care of expense in ankhs and collars and amulets, seats and beds and vessels, swords and spears, statues and stellae, canopic jars and censers and funerary masks. A brilliant, coruscating universe of beauty in the flickering candle flame.

Overwhelmed and drowning, I feel with leaden dismay the blood forcing its way into my loins.

I snarl again but more weakly than I'd intended. She steps away quickly but then looks back. For a second our eyes meet, hers as empty of mind as the Sinai is of water. Then she shuffles back and thrusts her bottom into my face.

My mind becomes as empty as hers. The smell of her, of her lubrication and of worse, lifts me up like a rat caught in a wind devil, swirling it round, using it as it wished. I hear a dog barking with loud, ferocious snarls, all of them erupting from my own mouth. I come off my belly and rear up over her, falling forward, crushing her under my weight, sinking my teeth deep into the scruff of her neck. She howls in all shades of agony. Her jaws snap at me but she is trapped.

My cock rears up like a startled cobra. There is so much blood in it I feel it will explode and me along with it. It hurts more than I can say.

Somewhere deep within this dog's body, in some tiny crevice, in some lost and forgotten chamber, a dying remnant of my humanity is faintly crying: Nooooo!

My cock is a spear and she is the enemy lusting for my blood. I thrust savagely and feel my spear miss, sliding harmlessly between her legs. Again and again I thrust, mashing the angry, venom-spitting head against her thigh, her backside, her tail, the ground.

I snarl my rage, stabbing, stabbing and then I enter her, her flesh yielding to my savage weapon. Every muscle in my body is about to burst, my teeth are breaking, my spine is snapping.

And maybe it does all break because the next thing I know I'm flat on the ground, gasping for breath. I can just make out the bitch loping away into the darkness between two piles of cars.

Behind me I hear clapping and whistling.

Please take me now! I think. Great God Osiris, you have brought me as low as any creature can get. I thought myself a god and I see now that was blasphemy. You have punished me, cast me down deeper than the deepest well, ripped my pride from me like the skin from the back of a whipped slave. Kill me now and scatter my ashes to the four winds so the world will forget me and I will forget myself!

I wait.

No such luck!

Ancient Days 2560 BC

The tent city, bigger than many towns, sprawled over the dunes like a dust storm. Built by countless slaves and servants over many weeks, it was stocked with all the accoutrements of royal life. In the centre, the royal tent, larger, grander, more garishly decorated, rose high above all. A pillar of black smoke rising from the hole in its apex tilted over as it slowly dissipated. Long pennants on poles the height of five men billowed slowly in the weak desert wind like fronds of weed in water.

Around the Royal Tent a wide space had been left where barbecue pits had been dug and filled with dried dung and reeds. A trail of servants, like ants servicing their queen, continually fed these hungry fires, flames flickering up to singe the flesh of the creatures slaughtered by the brave hunters. In pride of place, and on either side of the royal entrance to the tent, impaled from mouth to anus and revolving slowly in the flames, were the two lions. Their legs were nailed to their sides and all the skin had been flensed from their red, blue-veined flesh. Their pelts were staked out on a frame topped by the ruffles of their manes.

The smell of the fat bubbling out of the blackening flesh made even my jaded mouth water. My work in Peseshet's clinics over the last year had given me some insight into how the common people actually ate. Most made do with vegetables, with lettuce and lentils and chickpeas, with broad beans and onions and cucumber and bread. Fish and fowl were often the only meats except for feast days when a precious sheep or ox might be slaughtered. The rarity of animal fats in their diet made the people lust for it. In Memphis, stalls that barbecued meat were guarded by heavy-knuckled men.

Earlier, as my servants had bathed me, and though usually respectful of my brooding silences, they had been unable to still their idle tongues. Had the King really slain both lions with a single shot from his mighty bow? Had he really held his ground before the charging beasts with just a brave smile and his godhood to protect him?

I had not bothered to answer but instead just listened to their excited chatter. Neferhotep would have set this rumour rolling, leaving pigeon-brained servants to do the rest.

Now shaved, perfumed, be-wigged, I made my way between the two revolving lions, the blast of hot air from the fires not unwelcome in the cool desert night. The sail-sized tent flaps, embroidered to show hunting scenes from Khufu's blessed life, though soon to be replaced by those from the inestimable Djedefre, had been thrown back. So many oil lamps filled the huge tent that the difference from the darkness of the night made my eyes water. I stopped to let my vision clear and slowly the scene within swam into focus.

On the other side of the tent and facing into the room, Djedefre sat on a huge black granite throne. Carved into the backrest and looming out over the top of the King's head were the heads of a cobra and vulture. The armrests had been carved to resemble the paws of a great cat. The King's arms looked puny upon them.

The weighty throne appeared absurd in the midst of this ephemeral desert encampment but at the same time it was powerfully emblematic of the solidity of the regime. The royal family would always be there whatever horrors the desert or the Nile threw at Egypt.

To the right were tiered tables of food. Around the tables were tottering mountains of flatbreads flavoured with dates and cumin and sesame seeds. On some tables watermelons, pomegranates, figs and dates were opened up like the juiciest of wantons. On others, cakes of every flavour leaked their sweet juices onto the embroidered linens.

In pride of place on the lowest and nearest tier were the heads of ten wild bulls, their short horns pointing up like the sign of the cuckold. Where these bulls had come from was a mystery to which only Neferhotep would hold the key. My bathing had taken me too long and I realised the feast must have been well underway because people had been helping themselves to the bulls' heads. Eyes had been plucked out by clumsy drunken fingers. A cord holds the eye into the skull and needs to be pulled quickly and firmly whilst the eye is cradled in the palm. Done the right way the cord will part, otherwise it holds and the hand compresses the eyeball, bursting it. Several of the bulls had eyes like that, the deflated orbs leaking jelly and hanging from the gaping sockets.

The sweet gamey meat of the cheeks had been a favourite target, leaving gaps revealing the teeth. The main treasures, however, were the tongues. These had been severed and cooked separately and I noticed them all on a spit before the King. A complete waste, for Djedefre had a weak stomach and could barely tolerate even the white meat of fowl.

Already the guests were raucous from the beer and wine carried around on silver trays by servant women wearing only loincloths. The only other women were the dancers and musicians. The naked dancers swayed in the centre, long purple wigs almost down to their knees. Weights on the ends accentuated the gyrations of their broad hips, occasionally revealing thick, comely thighs glistening with oil. Chains of cowrie shells looped down over their hips, each centrepiece a large vulva-shaped shell almost hiding the dancer's own gentle folds. Blue tattoos on their thighs, swirling copulating snakes or the tracks of shooting stars, led the observer's eye ineluctably upwards towards the source of creation.

The musicians were also naked but sitting. Their lyres and kinnors played melodies that rose and fell like the Nile, castanets and drums coming in like the Great Cataract tearing and ravaging the sacred waters, only for the rising sound to herald life returning after the flood.

As soon as I'd entered, one of Neferhotep's servants had come to me, waiting for me to end my survey of the room. I turned and nodded and he led me towards my allotted cushions. Once I knew where I was supposed to sit, I naturally turned away. Over to my right I saw Hapiwer sitting upright on his pillows whilst everyone else was lounging contentedly. The man thrummed with energy, and I imagined he always had difficulty relaxing. The earthenware cup before him held either watermelon juice or watered-down wine.

Hapiwer was alone, an eddy that had broken away and was moving against the flow. In the myth of the hunt Neferhotep was creating there was no room for Hapiwer's selflessness and heroism.

As I approached, he looked up and I was taken aback to see the ugly scar. I thought I'd done an elegant job but the bruised and lacerated skin had swollen to an angry purple and I feared it would tear around my tight stitches.

I turned to the servant. "Fetch honey, frankincense and acacia oil!" The servant, a cleric steeped in the labyrinthine royal protocols but little else, looked at a complete loss. "Immediately!" I said levelly, and he scurried away.

I turned back to Hapiwer. "They will prevent the wound mortifying." Even so, I wished Peseshet was here.

Hapiwer nodded. "I wish Peseshet was here."

I stepped back in surprise. Had he read my mind? Had I forgotten myself and spoken my thoughts out loud? Was I going mad?

Hapiwer seemed confused at my reaction. "My wife, Peseshet, is a physician. She attends your wives and children. I'm sorry if I offended you. I'm sure the remedies you suggest will be just as good."

Recovering, I waved this idly away, searching quickly for something to explain myself. I went for the obvious. "I thought you said Persenet." Persenet was one of my six first wives, the mother of my son Nikaure. Peseshet had attended his birth and I had become confused myself by the similarity of the names. Intrigued as usual by Peseshet, I had found myself addressing my wife by that name. Swollen and in agony from having the robust Nikaure nestling in her guts, my wife had taken offence and had not spoken to me for weeks. She had set tongues wagging in the harem and for a while made Peseshet's life difficult with my other wives.

Now Hapiwer was the shocked one. "Forgive me Your Highness. No, no, I certainly was not referring to your Princess." Consumed by his own mortification, I let him ramble on apologetically. It gave me a chance to look at him directly, to study him, to understand why Peseshet had married him. And to speculate on why she had never mentioned him to me, or, more intriguingly, why she had never told him of our work together in the clinic. Though I'd heard she was married, I realised I had been careful to avoid thinking about it.

Taller than me, less padded around the middle, more happy, more joyful. What could she possibly see in him?

It was at that moment that I realised I was jealous of this man whom she took to her bed. A commoner, little better than a wine merchant, his arse ravaged by every stinging insect in the foetid Delta. Why did I care? I was drowning in comely bedfellows and hardly needed another.

"How did you meet?" I found myself asking. "Was your marriage arranged?"

Glad to be rescued from his roiling embarrassment, he was eager to reply. "No, Your Royal Highness. We have known each other since we were children. Peseshet was... there is no other way of saying this, your Royal Highness... she was the daughter of a slave captured during your father's wars with the desert dwellers to the north and east."

I remembered that time well for I had cherished my father's absences. The war column had returned to Memphis trailing thousands of proud but beaten people, mostly weeping children and grieving women roped together like cattle. Khufu didn't so much capture other lands as crush them.

"Hardly propitious beginnings for a young Peseshet, yet she has risen so far."

"She was always so clever," said Hapiwer proudly. "So full of life, so full of questions. My father grew to love her like his own daughter and, when her mother died of the bloody flux, he both freed and adopted her."

I could not help the green serpent of jealousy from striking again. "So, you married your sister?"

Siblings marrying might be almost unheard of amongst commoners but was hardly without precedent amongst the royals. Indeed, my mother, Henutsen, was the daughter of Sneferu, Khufu's father, and his wife Annara. So, father had married his half-sister, as indeed had I.

Thus, as the product of an incestuous union myself, I was hardly in a position to object. However, Hapiwer had both the good grace and good sense not to be as ill-tempered as me. "We are not blood, your Royal Highness, and Neferhotep himself gave us licence to marry, though it cost my father a large farm in the Delta to pay the legal fees."

Perhaps lawyers really had been involved, but it was more likely this was simply a euphemism for filling Neferhotep's capacious pockets.

"Your father was Commissioner for Wine, yet Peseshet is a physician."

Hapiwer looked uneasy but most people did when they talked to me or, to be more honest, when I talked to them. I asked too many awkward questions and some feared I was trying to trap them. "Peseshet was always interested in healing. Our neighbour was called Rennen and he was a sau and High Priest of the Temple of Sekhmet." Sau were physicians of the highest quality, as opposed to the snnw who attended to the common people and were without benefit of the magic afforded by Sekhmet. "Peseshet followed him round like a puppy. Out of respect for my father, Rennen indulged her but soon saw her worth. Rennen was without issue so she followed him as sau. Indeed, she attended to him in his final illness."

"But she rose to become High Priestess and Chief Physician? I can't see the other sau liking that." Professions being passed from father to son, or even to daughter, were like the bamboo frames supporting the tent that was Egyptian society.

Hapiwer smiled ruefully.

"Let me guess," I said. "More farms."

Just then a servant came by with a bowl containing a yellow paste and, next to it, a vegetable root shaped like a man with legs entwined as though from the effects of a full bladder. This signified that the paste was mandrake, the roots and leaves pounded with oil and honey to subdue its bitterness.

In a synchrony that we could not have achieved if we'd planned it, both of us waved our hands in dismissal. Embarrassed, I recognised Peseshet's handiwork. We'd both been on the receiving end of her lecture on mandrake. She acknowledged the symptoms may be pleasant, euphoric even, with some even saying it allowed them to converse with the gods. However, the drug also brought vomiting and diarrhoea, and she had been at several feasts where people had died, their lips blue, their faces pale. It was as though they had just stopped breathing. She felt that the roots, so often taking human shape, were an incarnation of the chaos god Seth, the mutilator of his brother Osiris. If you took the mandrake then Seth fought Shu, the god of the air, driving sweet air from the person's lungs.

Looking round I saw the servants with vomit bowls standing ready at the sides of the tent. Beer and wine were the usual culprits, but with mandrake circulating as well the servants would have their work cut out this evening.

The salve I had ordered arrived and I applied it to Hapiwer's wound. The noise around us was rising and the fine efforts of the musicians were for naught. The audience seemed more interested in their own drunken jests than in the beautiful dancers. Up on his black throne Djedefre was having trouble staying awake, his head drooping like an old man in the sun then starting upright. The little man had had a busy day.

Hapiwer isolated, his unselfish act being determinedly forgotten, would have been a tempting target for me to sit with all evening, if only to annoy Neferhotep. Even so, I found I did not have the stomach for it. I could not rid myself of the thought of Hapiwer's thin hands caressing Peseshet's body. I looked around at the dismal guests, trying to identify the least boring, when I realised that Neferhotep's factotum was standing by my side waiting patiently for me to notice his presence. Khaba was stooped, his eyes sunken and black with the joy of having the High Lord as his master.

I nodded for him to speak. Khaba raised his hands above his head. "The High Lord Treasurer sends his most fulsome compliments and prays you have more sons than all the stars in the sky. He would consider it the highest of honours if your Royal Highness would meet with him and kindly bestow your advice."

That sounded hopeful, if only in the sense that it seemed unlikely he'd be pulling my tongue out with pincers. Though hurling me into that temple pond as a child had been the low point, our relationship had shown little signs of warming since.

"About what?" I asked, immediately cursing my naivety for that was like asking a mouse to speculate on the workings of the gods. Poor Khaba couldn't even respond and he rolled his eyes as though seeking new words to coin for the occasion.

"Never mind! Does he want to talk now?"

Khaba bowed. Though he would have access to better food than any but the highest-ranking royal servants, he had lost considerable weight over the time I'd known him.

"Then take me to him!" I followed Khaba's spindly figure past the alluring thighs of the dancers, one of whose cowrie shells had been artfully lodged to form white petals within red. It was an arresting sight but I barely noticed. Meeting Neferhotep was never joyful.

Khaba led me back out through the main entrance and past the fire-pits and the smell of roasting meat. Neferhotep had a tent looking onto the cleared space. It was guarded by ten soldiers in full battle gear who stepped quickly aside as we approached. Khaba pulled back the flap and I walked into a burst of colour. Riotously woven wall-hangings vied with boldly painted wooden statues of blank-eyed gods. Amongst this stormy sea of colour stood Neferhotep. He was bare to the waist and, though his kilt was thickly pleated, it was the plainest of whites, almost willing you to underestimate his wealth. Neferhotep was never less than a danger, even to me.

Especially to me.

The High Lord was consulting a papyrus whilst speaking to an older man. Shaven-headed, with a floor-length white tunic, shoulders draped in leopard skin, the man was clearly a priest. As with everyone dealing with Neferhotep, white showed around his eyes. Priests were proud and haughty and it was good to see one so evidently fearful.

Neferhotep thrust the papyrus into the priest's chest. "No!" he said. I'd seen spitting cobras communicate in a more friendly manner.

"But they will starve, High Lord Treasurer."

"Tell them to use the grain that would have been their profits. They should have stuck to their end of the bargain."

"The marble was flawed and many more blocks had to be cut to find ones that were suitable. It is not the fault of our workmen."

"Then it is your fault for not taking this into account before you gave me the estimate. The King paid in good faith. Why aren't you cutting your own throat for the shame? You have betrayed Sobek and you have betrayed the God-King. If the temple isn't finished, I will feed you to your own crocodiles. Then I'll collect and burn their shit until it is powder and I will cast it to the four winds. No eternity gambolling through the Field of Reeds for you. Go!"

The idea of Neferhotep himself collecting up the crocodile shit was amusing, and I must have been smiling because the priest gave me an aggrieved look as he passed by on his way to the exit. One way or another the damned temple would be built, which was a shame as there were already far too many temples to disgusting Sobek, the crocodile god, as far as I was concerned.

"Please take a seat, your Royal Highness." He clicked his fingers and by the time I had sat down on a spindly-looking but rather firm chair, servants were all around me offering fruit and cheese and beer and wine. I waved them away.

Neferhotep grasped the back of another seat and brought it over to be opposite me. He lifted it easily and I wondered what sort of tree produced wood that was both strong and light. Whatever it was, it must have cost a fortune to bring from some faraway land.

We regarded each other in silence, me too proud to ask why I had been summoned, he too busy appraising me like a piece of prime beef, freshly slaughtered, butchered and laid out for discerning inspection.

"I may have underestimated you," Neferhotep said, leaning back in his chair, more relaxed than I had ever seen him. So strange was this that it had quite the opposite effect on me.

I would like to say my mind teemed with responses, sarcastic or serious, insightful or insolent, but it was as blank and empty as the sky in high summer.

"What you did to that dreadful little wine peddler and the chickpea counter. It was surprising but in a good way."

"Flesh wounds. I tidied them up, that's all."

He waved a finger at me. "But you are royalty, not a physician. To be frank, your brothers and sisters can't even dress themselves unaided yet you showed expertise and you acted calmly even after the alarm of the lion attack."

I smiled. "The attack so ably thwarted by the arrow of the God-King, or so it is said."

Neferhotep bowed his head, accepting the compliment.

"Why are you talking to me like this?"

"Like what Your Royal Highness?"

"So frankly, so carelessly. What you've just said about my royal siblings was deeply disrespectful."

He nodded. "Indeed, but that was but a wasp's nest compared to the pyramid of your own derision."

A good High Lord Treasurer knows everything. The Kingdom was like the priest's marble quarry. Appearing solid, eternal and strong, it was riven with exploitable flaws, lines of fragility along which information flowed. And at every weak point could be found Neferhotep's spies. Every village, every whorehouse, every tavern would have one. Hovels would be exempt, unless a trouble-maker lived there, but as the houses grew in size so would the number of spies until, in palaces like mine, most would be working, however indirectly, for this man.

Thus, there was little point in denying my indiscretions. When I didn't respond I thought I saw, or perhaps wished to see, a flicker of disappointment cross the hard leather of his face. Perhaps he would have liked to see me rage or weep, to deny or insult. Perhaps he would have enjoyed smacking me down, throwing back in my face some action or careless word. There were so many to choose from I doubt I would remember half of them myself.

Instead I raised my arms from my sides in what I hoped would be exasperation but probably looked more like surrender. "Why am I here?"

"I wanted to talk to you about the King."

"What about him?"

"Do you think he looks well?"

"Djedefre has never looked well but he keeps going. He suffered from every childhood illness imaginable. He'd break a toe just looking at a marble step. Has something happened?"

It is difficult to shrug and still look elegant but Neferhotep carried it off easily. "The cares of state hang heavy on shoulders that were never robust. I worry for him."

It was almost as though I was being sounded out, though for what was difficult to say, unless...

I sat bolt upright. "Has Djedefre nominated me as his successor? Surely not?" Kawab, our eldest brother, would have been the obvious choice but was even now dry as dust and wrapped in linen deep inside a mastaba in the necropolis at Giza. Horbaef, the next in line, had joined him in the Field of Reeds during childhood. Djedefre's own sons were too young to be made king but I had always assumed Queen Meritities, his mother, would be regent until one or other came of age.

I'd hardly known my own mother. Khufu had seen to that, the evil, spiteful old bastard. I had been delivered straight from her womb into the warm, encompassing arms of my wet nurse. Not being Queen Meritities' own son, I was hardly high in her estimation.

Neferhotep had remained silent as I made these well-worn calculations. He was looking at me expectantly. Clearly, I was missing something.

"Is Meritities ill?" Neferhotep gave a rare smile and I felt the whole of Egypt move beneath my feet. There had always been a possibility, albeit remote, that circumstances might conspire to make me king. I suddenly realised I had always shied away even from the thought, happy with my drink and my concubines and a life never sullied by hard work, other than the dreadful burden of keeping my wives happy.

Also, showing even the slightest interest in being king could get you very quickly killed in this brutally hierarchical world.

I swallowed and I could see his eyes follow the dip and bob of the man's lump in my throat. "You don't want to be king, do you?" he said more gently than anything he had ever said to me before.

"All that power, all that responsibility..."

"Our long history shows that Egypt is not best served by kings who wield their power with relish, who provoke unnecessary wars and give us cruel new laws conjured at a whim. Some kings become drunk on their divinity and offend the old gods, almost damming the flood with their own hands and bringing hunger and death to their people."

"But me? I'm not sure I even..."

"You would make a fine king. With justice and mercy, you would maintain the universal equilibrium, not unbalance it to let in the god of chaos. But..."

"But?"

"...you would need help. The humbler kings always do."

Humble I wasn't but that was not the point here. Neferhotep was securing his position in a royal world more fluid than I had imagined and staking his future on me, of all people.

Neferhotep on my side. I was disturbed at how warmed and comforted this made me feel. That I responded so to the reassurances of such a monster showed how isolated and abandoned I had become.

Neferhotep's vulture eyes looked deep into mine, awaiting the answer to a question he was too shrewd ever to put into words.

Modern Day

Home sweet home: a cage barely three times my length. Around me I can hear the slow, heavy breathing of mutts lost in the land of sleep. What simple dreams lubricate their torpid minds, I wonder? Do dog-gods come to warn them of things undone? Of bones mislaid, of a claw unbitten, of a nut sack ungroomed?

How I envy them! I doubt regret is an emotion that usually finds much purchase in the mind of a dog. The past is the past, only humans pick away at the bones of bygone events as though they could somehow be fixed: wrongs undone, horrors unseen.

All these stupid bastards have to worry about is when the next meal is coming. I, on the other hand, have the leisure and brain power to dwell morbidly on the events of the previous evening and, try as I might to resist, that's all I can do.

I have the mind of a man trapped in the body of a beast, I keep telling myself. The beast reacts to stimuli. It always has, it always will. My mind, protesting, is taken along for the ride, a reluctant passenger on a chariot whose reins have been seized by a slavering lunatic.

Monthu has been moved into the cage next to mine. We're heroes but I'm the only creature here who even knows what that means. Monthu is awake and licking himself as usual. Earlier, he'd come up to the mesh that separates us and pressed his nose against it. I've been around dogs long enough to know I was supposed to do the same so we could smell each other. If there hadn't been the mesh to stop him, he'd have circled round to stick his nose in my bottom to get a really good whiff. If I'd been a proper dog, I'd have done the same, eager to check out his age, health, what he'd eaten recently, his state of arousal and whether he was getting enough water. One good sniff and I would have gained more information than Peseshet from a patient after hours of coaxing.

But I didn't sniff and that unbalanced Monthu's exquisitely refined sense of etiquette. Offended, he had given a low snarl (too low to excite our guard so dear old Monthu isn't completely stupid) and turned away.

Clearly, we will never be friends but I'll just have to contain my disappointment. It's actually kind of a shame because we are so similar, though I suspect Monthu has a little more of the ancient type of dog in him. He has long, upright, pointed ears and a less muscled frame than mine. His hair is thick but shorter than mine, and at first glance you'd think it might just be brown skin. He'd be faster than me but, if I could summon up the savagery, I'm pretty sure I could take him in a fight.

Hang on a minute! Is there something driving me to establish a pecking order? Is this me thinking or is my dogishness surfacing again? Perhaps the dreadful sex of last night was just the start and now my doggy nature will assert itself more frequently and more fiercely. The idea is so shocking and so horrible that a bolus of piss shoots from my dick and right through the mesh into Monthu's domain.

This doesn't go down well. Years of training disappear like larks' tongues at a feast and Monthu is head butting the mesh, snarling and barking. That's enough to set off the other dogs and soon fat old Amsu comes waddling out, smashing his thick wooden baton against the cages. "That's it, I'm cutting all your balls off myself. With a rusty fucking razor blade."

Dogs shrink back but keep barking. These eruptions happen a couple of times a night and I think Amsu secretly enjoys stomping around and yelling for all he's worth. Gets all the frustrations of his miserable life out in manageable bursts of rage.

If I wasn't so out of sorts I'd be barking as well. I hate to admit it, but I occasionally like a good bark. Not now, though. I lie down on my belly, ignoring the hell breaking loose around me, lower my head onto my paws and try to think things through. Was last night a one-off or just the start of the unstoppable rise of the hound?

It isn't as though my reawakening had been instantaneous. I hadn't just woken to find myself in the body of a dog. At first, I had just been a dog with strange and vivid dreams. I would go about my doggy business, play-fighting with others in my litter, pissing where and when I wanted. It took perhaps a year before I began to wonder what the fuck I was doing. It was like waking from a night where the wines had been too generous in their variety. At first you don't know who you are or where you are. Layers are then slowly stripped away to reveal a world you'd quite forgotten. Over time it all started to come back.

Since then I have grimly tried to keep control but at times it has been a close-run thing. A glimpse of a cat can send me leaping forward, only to choke on the end of my lead. Up to now I've been able to put this down to aberrations, instantaneous instinctual reactions that no dog could resist.

Last night had been different. I had lost control completely, had yielded to innate ferocity and not just for an instant. The act of love can be a little ferocious, at least if you do it right, and for a split second, as your seed surges, you do lose control. Last night I had lost control when I smelled her, a bitch in heat, and I'd been lost until orgasm had freed me like a bird from a cage.

Even now I could still smell her on me and it made me, made me, think of her and of my degradation.

If only I could stop.

Suddenly the thought of 'the snip' doesn't sound quite so bad. I begin to wonder if there is a way to manipulate my handlers into getting it done. I could stop being so well-behaved because whenever I do something they don't like then that's when the subject comes up.

I mean, it's not like I'm ever going to get the chance to make love to an actual woman ever again and, even if I did, I don't think I could handle the sight of my hairy prick doing its business. So yes, getting castrated would be an act of pure desperation but if I can't quieten these urges, I think they'll drive me crazy.

I plot my moves in a hazy half-awake, half-asleep way until the sun emerges from its journey through the underworld and the world around me is reborn. The dogs yawn, Monthu farts and Amsu starts preparing our food. I hear water sloshing into dishes and the grinding sound as he opens the metal containers our food arrives in. Every action makes Amsu grunt. Then comes the rattle as lumps of dried whatever are tipped into our dishes.

Monthu and I are the heroes so we get fed first. Amsu approaches, two dishes of food shaking in his plump, outstretched hands. He grunts as he kneels and slides a dish through a little rectangular slot in the bottom of my cage door. I get served first so that means I'm now a bigger deal than Monthu. I only hope he has brains enough to appreciate the slight.

When I had a human tongue, I enjoyed the taste of food. Now that I have a doggy tongue, do I savour doggy food? Not even close. Pass down any main street, now or four thousand years ago, and the flayed carcases of cows or sheep or goats hang like red dripping flags. Flags that never billow in the desert wind that embeds its sand grains into the fly-wrapped flesh. I'm not sure if I've mentioned this before, but Egypt can be quite hot and that's why customers buy their meat early before the flies and the heat have had their way with it. I'm guessing that only after the last bleary-eyed, wine-marinated customer has bought the final morsel of non-pustular meat - that only then are the carcases chopped up and made into food for dogs.

It tastes as bad as it sounds but a dog's appetites are strong. I don't quite lose control the way I did last night, but I don't stop myself either, the empty ache in my belly being too sore, too in need of filling. I slurp down the rancid meat and crunch up the dried chunks. I cannot even begin to work out what these contain but they give me the only pleasure in the whole experience. Dogs like crunching: it's soothing because that's what dogs are supposed to do. It also sends little shivers of pleasure through my jaw, making me crunch harder and harder. Sometimes as a treat, we all get a bone chucked into our cage and we leap on it, the snapping of bones like the crackle of gunfire on the shooting range at the training centre.

The human in me also relishes the crunching because eating involved caution in those long-ago days. Bread was what we all ate, even a god-king like myself. Sand got in the bread and wore our teeth down, making them sore all the time. The stones used to grind the grain would also shed larger pieces of grit. One incautious chomp and you'd lose a big chunk of tooth, setting yourself up for months of agony.

The hard stuff may be crap but it's not gritty and, even if it were, my big doggy teeth would make short work of it. So, I crunch the bones as joyfully as the rest, the splinters only tickling my rock-hard gums.

Amsu brings a dish of water next and I lap it up using my ridiculously long tongue. I swear, I could lick my own eyeballs if I tried.

Replete, I slope over to my sand-filled tray and have a big doggy dump, only too aware that no servant will whip it away before the stench hits me. I walk back to the other side of the cage, as far away as I can get.

I blink at the rising sun, which is still a ball you can look at, the haze on the horizon blunting the sharpness of its rays. Our cages are in an open-sided building and soon the sun will rise above the roofline and we'll be in the shade and left to our thoughts. When not on the river cruises, my handlers work five days on then disappear for two days off, leaving me moping in captivity.

And right there is the big mystery I can't fathom and it's all to do with the Nile. In my day the Nile was the real ruler of Egypt; millions living or dying at its lordly whim. Its floods would drown thousands, its droughts and famines killing many more. All lives, even mine, were governed by it. When the yearly flood retreated all the people followed it down to its banks to plant seed. They would weed and water and tend these crops for six months and then harvest them quickly just before the waters returned. Only then could they relax.

So, this five days on, two days off seems like an aberration because they do it all year round. I'm too ashamed to say how many trips it took me along the river on those boats before I realised the obvious. Somehow, they have tamed the Nile, for it is supremely well-behaved throughout the year. Once it was fearsome, washing all before it, the buildings and wailing people, but now there are long sections where it doesn't flow at all. Instead it lies calm, the buildings and vegetation of the banks perfectly reflected in its serene waters.

How did they do that? Maybe this Sisi God-King is infinitely more powerful than he looks, or the gods have got far more amenable to his arguments. Sometimes, and let's whisper this, I used to suspect that despite all the temples built in their honour, the other gods paid very little attention to the God-King's requests.

So, I hunker down for the long weekend wait. Amsu is supposed to take us out individually for walks in an enclosure on the south side of the base, but he never does. Even he's not stupid enough to let us all out at once. The bestial need to establish a pecking order, stymied when we're all cooped up in our cages, would overcome the other dogs' training and they'd be at each other's throats like a crocodile at a tethered goat.

The sun rises and brings with it the stink from our litter trays. Amsu, the mighty task of putting out twenty dishes struggled with and heroically overcome, is sitting at his table, feet up and snoring. I suspect even Monthu can dimly sense in his empty, echoing mind that we're in for a couple of days of boredom.

That's why I'm surprised when I hear steps, though I'm too lost in feeling sorry for myself to notice as quickly as Monthu. His long pointy ears become even more erect and he growls and gets to his feet. All the other dogs follow and a few begin to bark. If in doubt then bark being the hound motto.

There's a knock at Amsu's door and he stumbles to his feet, buttoning up his tunic and straightening out its wrinkles. I can't see the door or who he opens it to but I recognise the voice.

"Sorry to interrupt your alone time with your precious dogs, Amsu, but I'm taking mine for a trip," Ragab is saying with a laugh.

Amsu is no doubt scratching his balls as he always does when puzzled. "Where are you taking him? I got no orders."

"No orders. It's for his pleasure."

Amsu gives a curt laugh. "Seeing as what your last favour did for him, I'm not sure that's a great idea. Ever since you put him with that bitch, I've never seen a more miserable specimen. Was she ugly as fuck or something?"

"It'd take a connoisseur like you to answer that question, Amsu. And anyway, that was a one-off. We don't want to spoil him. I'm just taking him to meet the family and then for a nice long walk."

I produce a very undoggy-like sigh of relief. I know for a fact I wouldn't survive another one of those trysts. Shame would kill me more effectively than an executioner's blade.

"You're welcome to him," says Amsu and appears at the entrance to our enclosure. Ragab follows and I go through the charade of standing on my hind legs, forepaws against the mesh, tongue lolling out. It's what they expect.

"Good to see you too, boy." Ragab is giving me a big smile. "Was she nice, boy? Are you in love?"

Both men laugh and it's all I can do to stop myself barking at the bastards. Amsu unlocks the door and Ragab snaps the lead on my collar. He makes a face. "Don't you ever clean out their trays, Amsu?"

"I was just about to," says Amsu irritably. We troop back to his office and then out of the door and onto an avenue that leads to the main gate. Our truck, dust-caked enough that it doesn't even shine in the sunlight, is waiting.

"Where are your pals?"

Ragab shrugs. "Amr will be deep in his wife. Mazan deep in whatever the fuck gives him comfort."

Amsu nods. "He's a funny one. Do you think he's..."

Ragab waves a finger in admonishment. This is a touchy subject nowadays. In my day, men in the army did nothing but have sex with each other when they were stationed far from their women. Nobody cared then but they certainly do now.

Ragab ties me up in the back of the truck, gives Amsu an airy wave and then we're off. Thick steel poles retract into the road as we approach the gate and we're through into the mayhem of the Cairo traffic.

It takes us about an hour and, as the time passes, the housing becomes older, more densely packed and unquestionably poorer. Dress becomes more traditional, the women wearing fewer trousers but with more scarves to hide their lustrous hair. We drive through narrower streets, all without pavements. Men and women, unconcerned by our fast-moving metal beast, step into our path to get around a parked car or motorbike. I admire their nerve, their resolute belief that Ragab will apply his brake rather than crunch their bones under his wheels. Dogs, of course, do not merit that sort of consideration.

We pull into a side street so narrow that when Ragab parks he blocks it almost completely. Indeed, if he wasn't so skinny, Ragab wouldn't have been able to open the door and squeeze along the length of the truck to let me out. As he unclips me, I notice people coming down the street and giving little inconvenienced grimaces when they see the police truck, but then turning back to find an alternative route.

All except for one fat old lady who sizes up the gap between truck and wall and finds it wanting. "Move your truck!" she says. It seems some old women are fearless even now.

"Police business," says Ragab dismissively.

"Lazy little shit more like."

I guess old women get away with this because a policeman giving them a hard time is never going to look good. Despite the myriad depredations of their lives, Egyptians are a kind, hospitable people and passers-by are likely to side with an old woman even against a policeman, especially a lone one. I notice the grim little twist to Ragab's lips. He has already lost but is too stupid and stubborn to back down.

"I'll tell your mother!" says the old lady.

Ragab stops grimacing and takes a better look at her. "Mrs Elliathy! I didn't recognise you. I thought you moved away." We both squeeze back along the gap between truck and wall so we are standing by her. She's short and has a mole as big as a blueberry on the side of her nose.

"I'm visiting my sister but some thoughtless idiot has blocked my way with a big truck."

"I can't park anywhere around here without blocking something, Mrs Elliathy. You know what these little streets are like."

"A rat warren," Mrs Elliathy agrees, though not mollified. She's distracted by the sight of me. "That's a fine-looking dog." But she doesn't sound entirely convinced for I am a dog and so unclean to most.

"Oh yes, but he's also a big hero. This is the dog who bit off the... who attacked the terrorist trying to blow up the Nile cruiser last week. He is my dog." I'm almost touched by the way he says it so proudly.

Mrs Elliathy is impressed, nodding her head appreciatively. Though she's short I still have to look up at her. Above and behind her on the roof, dusty sparrows are looking down on all of us. "So, this is Monthu," she says.

I give a growl and she jerks back the hand she had been stretching out to stroke me.

"Cheops!" shouts Ragab and slaps me hard on the top of my nose, the same sad old recourse. It may be old but it still hurts.

"Sorry, Mrs Elliathy. He was injured and it's put him in a bad mood. Normally he's much better behaved."

"Poor boy. You shouldn't hit him so hard."

Something heavy lands on my back and my legs almost buckle. A hand pulls at my tail. Before I can react, Ragab pulls the lead so tight my neck stretches. He pokes a warning forefinger like the barrel of a gun between my eyes. "Stay!" he says fiercely.

With the thing on my back pulling me down and the lead pulling my head up, and the grip on my tail pulling me to the side, there's not much else I can do anyway. I feel something crawling up my back and grabbing my ears.

"Such a big dog, Father," says a childish voice from behind me.

"Cheops, I am Kiya. You will be my special friend." This second voice is a little girl's.

I rapidly suppress my doggy outrage and, as Ragab slowly relaxes his grip on my lead, I lower myself to my belly. The kids crawl all over me and I let them, Ragab's finger still pointing at me.

"At least he's good with children," says Mrs Elliathy.

I'm definitely not but I'm also not stupid.

"Stop pulling his ears, Aleko! Just stroke him gently! Kiya, let go of his tail!" Ragab may be at the bottom of the pecking order at work but here he's top dog. The kids do let go and come around to stand by Ragab. They're looking at me in wonder. Aleko is the boy and the older of the two, Kiya his younger sister. I'd seen them once when Ragab brought them to the training ground where they'd peered at me in my cage. I'd liked the awe and wonder in their eyes, a comforting echo of old times.

Aleko is skinny like his father and claps me none too gently on the head. He can't be more than five years old and wears what had once been a white tunic. Kiya's tunic is even grubbier but I can just make out some pretty stitching underneath the dust. Her big brown eyes are moon-sized in her round little face.

"Mrs Elliathy, what a pleasure!" Two older people have appeared. As a rule of thumb, if there are more than four people around me then sooner or later someone is going to step on my paw. I tuck my legs and tail under my body as best I can.

"I had not realised your son was such a hero, Mrs Halim."

It's clear Ragab takes after his father: both have the thinness that hovers on the borderline between lithe fitness and a wasting disease. Mr Halim is more stooped and hollow-chested and does not look well. His wife is sheltering under a fan to keep off the sun. It's working because her complexion is paler than anyone else's in this little group.

"He was always my little hero," says Mrs. Halim proudly, and she pinches Ragab's cheek to his evident annoyance.

"Where is Walidah?" he asks.

"Shopping," says Mrs. Halim a little too quickly. "She says she will be here when you come back." Exquisitely attuned to the slightest movement, I pick up the tiny narrowing of Mrs Elliathy's eyes.

"Speaking of which, let's get going."

There's a general milling around and confusion but, wonder of wonders, I don't get trodden on. I'm put in the back of the truck, which raises the question of why I was taken out in the first place. From the way they move around, all getting in each-others way in trying to get the kids into the front of the truck, I'm guessing this isn't the most organised family in the land. Even after the kids are in the truck, it takes a minute or two for the older people to realise they are in the way, turn around and head back up the narrow street. We follow slowly in the truck until the three older people come to a doorway and disappear into it, Mrs Halim and Mrs Elliathy in earnest conversation.

We drive south past the pyramids of Giza and I force myself to look at the desecrated remains and wonder once again whose pyramid the third and much smaller one is. Was it for one of my sons? Anhkmare or Menkaure perhaps: they were the oldest. I had so many children, but I am ashamed to say that not for one of them did I show the affection that I just witnessed in Ragab's eyes.

God-kings, even those in waiting, don't show affection for that's a sign of weakness, of vulnerability. I never laughed with my children the way Ragab is laughing. Instead I would command and admonish as they cowered in fear before me, just as I cowered before Khufu.

For the first time I begin to wonder whether some of the things I hate about my father are simply reflections of myself.

Just for a second, through a gap in the buildings, I catch sight of the decrepit Sphinx, its disfigured face a brutal reminder of my hubris.

But I can't bear to think of that right now. Instead, as we head south along the Nile towards nearby Memphis, I can feel the shifting sands of time slip away beneath me for other reasons. Cairo, that vast abomination, had not even existed in my day. Memphis, on the other hand, was the centre of the universe. From there we governed nearly all of the known world. During my thousands of years in the darkness, the sands had reclaimed the palaces and gardens and temples. So much has changed that I recognise nothing until we come to the old pyramid of Djoser. Djoser, or at least his chief architect Imhotep, had the bright idea of taking the simple old slab-like mastaba tombs and putting in tapering layer upon layer on top. Djoser had five stepped layers to his pyramid. For this brilliant idea they later made him a god. Khufu, the show-off, had two hundred and ten layers to his.

Ragab pulls up by the side of the road. Behind us the palm-lined banks of the Nile, before us the forbidding Western Desert. That, at least, hasn't changed since my day. Ragab helps the kids out, unclips me from the truck and then takes the lead off altogether. I leap down onto the ground and the kids manhandle me again.

I'm quite touched because neither now, nor back at their house, has anyone suggested they should wash their hands after touching me. Muslims regard dogs as unclean and, though they stroke and pat, they usually wash their hands afterwards.

Ragab has a hard little ball that he throws with all his might and I'm off. The sand isn't firm but I can still run like the wind because dogs have four legs and that's what they do. My tongue lolls out automatically as it's the only way I can hope to keep cool. The desert blurs by and so does the ball that's rolled to a halt. For a split second I just want to keep running, to lose myself in the desert, to leave behind the mouldy food and the stamping feet. Just to keep running and running forever.

However, I shorten my stride and come to a halt. I've hunted in the Western Desert and know its nature only too well. It's littered with the desiccated remains of animals that had broken free.

I turn back. The kids are pointing excitedly at the ball. "Silly dog!" says Kiya delightedly. "He can't find his ball."

Aleko is already running forward and he gets to the ball before I do. He throws it as hard as he can but manages to propel it barely two man-lengths. It's embarrassing and I can't bring myself to trot over to it. He looks at me uncertainly.

Ragab arrives and shows Aleko how to throw and soon they are all taking turns. I dash around snatching it up, exulting in the power of my hard-muscled body. My failure with the first throw has given Kiya even more confidence. Whenever I get close, she grabs my ears. It's not too unpleasant.

They walk and throw, walk and throw and we wend our way through fallen columns lying beached in the sand, marking where temples had once stood.

Finally, the family retreats to the truck where Ragab has secreted food and drink. As they eat, I'm allowed to nose around mastaba tombs that were ancient even in my day. Here were buried the generals, the administrators and all the sacred animals. Did their mummies fare better than mine? Each tomb I inspect has a makeshift tunnel where robbers have burrowed in like rats. Some of these holes are big enough for me to shuffle into. The tombs are all empty and smell of piss.

Does a single mummy reside in its tomb anywhere in this new Egypt? Without the dead to intercede with the gods on behalf of the living then what must have happened to this world? Egypt is full of soldiers and police with guns, perhaps to keep a lid on the chaos unleashed by man no longer talking to the gods.

Ragab is calling my name so I lope back to the truck. The kids seem to have got most of their food smeared over their faces. Kiya offers me a brown morsel but Ragab knocks it back. "Chocolate is bad for dogs," he says. Reluctantly she drops it in the sand. I sniff at it. It smells good. I'm contemplating taking a cautious lick when Ragab reattaches my lead and bangs the side of the truck, my signal to leap in the back.

It is early afternoon and the sun, as ever, is unrelenting. At least with all this fur I don't sunburn but the heat does build up, so when the truck starts and we head off, the air rushing over me is most welcome.

We head back into the city and end up once again blocking the narrow alley. This time, to my surprise, Ragab unclips me and we all edge further down the alley and to the right where a doorway opens into a dwelling. There are stairs and we start climbing, the kids dashing on ahead. The smells are legion: spices, sweat, metal and lots and lots of people. We climb up several storeys, passing four or five doors on each landing. Outside each are shoes and bicycles and sweet-smelling bags of rotting food. I can hear people talking and shouting and even snoring. There are also higher, tinier sounds as though people were conversing in a tunnel.

On the third floor Ragab takes out a key and we enter a place that smells of food and spices. Ragab's parents come out in the hall when they hear the door open. They smile and hug the kids and ask questions about the day.

"Is Walidah back?" asks Ragab.

"Not yet," says the mother. "She says the shops are busy." The wrinkles around her eyes get momentarily deeper.

Ragab, the dolt, buys this completely and leans down to unclip my lead. He's a simple soul, and I know that for most simple souls life will ultimately disappoint. I was always a connoisseur of palace intrigues and Neferhotep would often chide me for what he regarded as a womanly predilection for gossip and scandal. Womanly or not, I have a sinking feeling.

They all go into another room and leave me to my own devices. I'm certainly curious to see how these people live. It would seem that at least six of them live here so presumably there must be at least a dozen rooms. I can tell this place isn't big so the rooms must be tiny. As the children excitedly talk about their day I mooch around and am surprised to find only a kitchen, a bathroom, a hall, a wash room, a meeting room and two bedrooms. The beds are massive, almost filling the space. It dawns on me that these people must sleep together like animals.

That's something we never did. Sleep was personal and everyone slept alone so that their dreams were never contaminated, for these were the only times when ancestors and the gods could speak. I realise with a shock that in all the conversations of my handlers, of the endless talk of women, of sport, of Sisi and the Muslim Brotherhood, of prices and cars and guns, of their superiors and their wives and their children, I could not recall a single mention of a dream. Perhaps they no longer have them. Without the guidance of their dreams these people must be as lost as me.

I stop what I was doing (huffing the sheets of the bed which had clearly recently contained the time-raddled bodies of Ragab's parents) and blink. Without the messages of dreams how could you live your life? It would be like losing a sense: not as bad as sight but worse than smell. A world where the future was as blank as the Sinai sands.

No wonder they're all so messed up! They have absolutely no idea what is going to happen next, or whether the gods favour them or not.

I pad into the meeting room and regard the poor, sad creatures. There is a big divan and I can smell that this is where the children sleep. Like the beds it almost fills this little room. The walls are blank except for their squiggly writing which, despite my best efforts, I have never been able to decipher. I do know the text usually has something to do with their single god. A threadbare but highly intricate carpet almost covers the hard concrete floor. Cushions against the walls are where people sit if they can't find space on the divan. The walls above the cushions are smeared with crescents of oil from their hair. The square of a single small window is filled with the view of the faded white wall of the adjacent building.

"The poor dog looks hungry," says Ragab's mother, a delightful misinterpretation of what I was actually feeling. I am feeling a bit peckish even for the tinned crap. I follow her into the little kitchen. Instead of opening a tin, she takes the lid off a pot and I'm drowning in the smell of cooked fowl. Surely she's not...

But she is, and a bowl of fowl stewed with aubergines is suddenly at my feet. Saliva gushes into my mouth and Ra himself couldn't stop me as I dive in. The cook on the boat brought me morsels but this is a whole human meal just for me. Though the wolf in me wants to gulp it all down, I have just enough self-control to take my time and savour it for once.

"He's a delicate eater," says the grandmother and I can hear the puzzlement in her voice. I should be more careful, more dog-like, but I don't know if this chance will ever come again.

Taste, like my sight and hearing, is different. Humans can find sour things pleasant, like lemons and limes, tamarind and vinegar: not so much by themselves, rather as flavourings to temper sweetness. To a dog's tongue, sour is amplified and anything that smacks of it is distasteful. Sweetness is far more enticing.

The spices in her food are not to my taste, though the aubergine is sweet and oily. The fowl has me deeply puzzled as it's nothing like the gamebirds of my day. The meat of the breast is thicker and the bird must have been far plumper than any Fourth Dynasty birds, but the taste is as weak as a widow's beer. In my day gamebirds fought and ran and fucked their way through life and were skinnier, gamier and you felt like you were eating meat. This has little more taste than bread. Is it my new doggy taste or have birds changed over the millennia?

My gourmet meditations are interrupted by the front door opening and shouts from the kids at the appearance of their mother. To my surprise she's tall, taller than most men and, though she looks stressed and harried, she moves in a willowy way that is immediately beguiling. What is she doing with a scrawny little piece of nonsense like Ragab, I wonder?

Ragab immediately comes to her and she lets him kiss her on the cheek. "Mrs Guirguis would not stop talking," she is saying. "If I had heard one more thing about her son, the doctor, I would have screamed." By now the kids have got to her and are hanging on to her legs. She bends and kisses them gently on their foreheads and I see her rather insignificant chest swell with pride and love. It is a wonder her children have grown up to be so healthy.

Ragab starts to pull at her and she, kids in tow, follows. "And this is Cheops, the Wonder Dog." The room is small so I'm crowded in. Walidah has jade-green eyes and a slight hook to her nose which is far from unbecoming. "He's bigger than I expected. I thought you were joking."

Ragab's chest also puffs with pride and I even catch the gleam of water in his eye. She is far better looking than he is and he must work hard to please her.

"Can I stroke him?"

"Put your finger out like this," says Ragab and puts his forefinger just under my nose. It smells of tobacco and dust and a poor man's diet.

Walidah steps forward and a long slender finger is held out. I think I know what to expect but, even so, I am taken by surprise. I can smell another man and the odour is so powerful he must have licked this very finger not half an hour ago.

The thing I hadn't expected was that that man would be Mazan.

Ancient Days 2559 BC

The monster had awoken, bellowing its jealousy and rage. All of Egypt had fled for shelter like rabbits before a rampaging lion as the desert sought to reclaim the Nile. Everyone felt its hot breath on their necks, each grain of sand a stinging insect.

For three days even Ra was overcome and was, at best, just a red faded disc as dust clouds covered it with ghostly veils. Grapes hung punctured and deflated on their stalks, and wheat was cut down as though Seth himself had swung his monstrous scythe.

When you can't leave it, even a luxuriously appointed palace can quickly become a prison. I was growing bored of my concubines and sated with the wine. Worry gnawed at me, like an army undermining a city's walls. I had never seen a sandstorm like this, had never seen the world so out of kilter. It was the king's duty to bargain and deal and sacrifice to the gods to maintain the cosmic balance. What the hell had Djedefre been doing?

I was in the coupling room, lolling on its wool-stuffed pillows, drunk and idly stroking the swelling hip of a Nubian concubine, when I heard Salas's double then single-tap knock. He waited respectfully without entering, for I allow nobody to watch me mating except for slaves. A slave was always useful to provide a towel or wine or to help a more lushly built partner into a more satisfactory position.

"Yes," I said but not loudly as Salas's ear would be closely pressed to the door.

Salas came in slowly, eyes averted. The concubine turned over so she was facing me, her heavy lips forming a pout. As she turned, her breasts, magnificent enough to suckle a tribe, swung over then collapsed down in front of me. Absently, I brought up a finger and drew it gently over the uneven surface of a wide black aureole.

Salas cleared his throat.

"What?"

"The Lord Neferhotep begs your attendance at the Palace of Queen Meritities."

Befuddled by drink and satiation, I blinked at him in surprise. "Why?"

I might as well have asked a dung beetle but Salas, though ignorant, was not stupid. "The messenger was very frightened," he said simply.

"By the sand storm?" The Queen's palace was a good five minutes' walk along the avenue connecting all the palaces. It was surprising the messenger had made it without being flayed.

"By more than that, Master. Much more than that."

That was sobering. Something dreadful must have crystallised out of the chaos of the storm. I shrugged on a tunic and Salas held open the door as I slipped my feet into sandals. Four armed guards who were not my own were awaiting me. The gusts of wind across the roof felt like the slow beating of leathery wings as we made our way down the twisting passageways.

Had I done something untoward? I thought I had been careful to hold my tongue of late, though when drunk one could never be sure. Some of my wives were loud and argued with the wives of other royals. However, even if one of them had been objectionable to Meritities herself, it would have hardly merited such a peremptory summons.

When we got to the main entrance my dismay increased when I found twenty soldiers sheltering there. They were in full armour, perhaps ready to lead me to my execution. What in Osiris's name had I done?

Out in the open the flying sand was horizontal. I turned to Salas. "Fetch me leathers!" I cursed myself for not thinking of this before I left my rooms.

"There is a chair, your Royal Highness." Salas pointed at a soldier who had stepped out into the sandy blast and was signalling frantically. Out of the gloom a straight-sided shape rocked into view, carried by ten slaves wrapped in the coarsest cloth, scarves round their heads leaving only slits for their eyes.

Without asking, the soldiers lined up to form a windbreak so I could walk to the sedan chair with minimum discomfort. Even in the gloom of the interior I could make out the sigils and cartouches of Meritities carved and painted on the sides. I eased my buttocks down on the thickly stuffed pillows and the chair rose immediately.

As we moved out of the shelter of the palace, sand burst in through one window of the chair and hit the insides with impacts so numerous it sounded like the hissing of a snake. I leaned back out of the blast and we headed into the red gloom.

Just then a fierce gust caught us, tipping the chair and sending me crashing into the side. A forest of leather-clad arms seemed to sprout from the leeward side and pushed the chair back upright. The soldiers' arms stayed there as the speed of the sedan picked up, moving well beyond the point of elegance and ease. The jolts sent my spine spearing up into the base of my brain, or so it felt. Speed rather than comfort was the order of the day.

This was, in its way, good news. If they had been intending to execute me, they'd have dragged me naked through the scouring sand. Wherever I was going it was not to my death.

Not yet, anyway.

Seth was the god of the desert, as he was for all things evil, and at times like this one could hear his voice roaring for our blood. The wind suddenly fell as Seth took in a deep breath to blow even harder and, just for an instant, I could see over the balustrade to my left and all the way down to the Nile. Blown sand had stuck to the reeds, bending them down as though fingers of the desert were strangling the long slender throat of the river. Then Seth found his breath again and my chair bucked to the right, knocking me off my seat and onto the floor.

The entrance to palace of Meritities was to leeward and as we entered its shelter the noise of the wind cut out and I sighed with relief.

I felt the chair descend and the door was pulled open. A tall servant grasped my hand and helped me out. The softness of his flesh and the gentleness of his touch made me look more closely. He was a eunuch and I saw tears making tracks through the smear of sand that had adhered to his face while he had waited.

As we hurried into the palace, oil lamps revealed other servants, heads bowed, the air seeming to waver with their ululations. A clattering noise behind me made me turn and, to my surprise, I found all the soldiers had followed me into the palace.

The Royal Palaces were sprawling single-floor affairs but that of Meritities had been built over a natural mound and so contained the rarity of wide marble steps leading upward. Egyptians were enamoured of bright colours, especially reds and blues but the Queen was even more seduced than most: every wall and ceiling was hung with billowing embroidered cloth portraying the brutal history of the gods.

The further we penetrated into the palace, the louder rose the ululation, and I prepared my face as best I could, for clearly death had arrived for someone. Most likely it was Meritities herself and that presented a big problem.

Henutsen, my own mother, had been exiled to the Delta where she had died from the fever, the long-standing victim of palace intrigue by Khufu's other more senior wives, Meritities among them. If Meritities was dead it would be difficult for me to weep for her, though at times of sudden change like this my life could depend on it.

The nearer we got to her private rooms, the drier my eyes seemed to become. I scraped my nails over my own flesh but they had been cut only this morning. I tried to bite my own cheek but my mouth was as dry as a worm in the sun. Ahead of me a group of senior officials wearing the full insignias of their offices were clustered around a doorway, wailing. In desperation I surreptitiously reached under my kilt and squeezed my testicles, but in my haste I did so more firmly than I had intended. I yelled and my shocked legs gave way. Before I had pitched forward to the marble floor, a multitude of slave hands had broken my fall. They tried to straighten me out but my pain was too great.

I looked up at the hovering officials who had turned at my shout. "The Queen," I wailed plaintively. "Is she dead?"

As one, they all looked away, shamed by the magnificence of my grief. I looked up through a Great Cataract of tears as a tall figure emerged from the bedroom. I felt the figure's hand on my shoulder and recognised the desert dryness of Neferhotep's voice. "The Queen has indeed gone to the Field of Reeds. I am sorry, Great Khafre."

Great Khafre! What the hell?

While I had been distracted, the officials had all sunk to their knees. With Neferhotep's assistance I shuffled into the room. The first, and for a while the only thing I could see, was Peseshet leaning towards something on the grand bed. She was dressed in full High Priestess regalia, with a hat like the mane of a lion but of pure gold with horizontal blue stripes. The sleeves and the bottom of her white tunic had similar trim, and she wore over her shoulders a circle of spun gold cloth.

I had not seen her for some time. This unexpected meeting made me suddenly aware of something I had not previously admitted. When Peseshet was in a room, I no longer felt alone.

As she heard me enter, she turned and then she too fell to her knees. My view now unobstructed, I could see Meritities laid out on her bed, though 'laid out' was a feeble way of putting it. Her arms were drawn up as though she were pulling herself over the lip of a pool, and her knees were curled so much they touched though her feet were wide apart. It was as though she had been caught mid-step while lost in an abandoned dance. She too was in her full regalia but her wig of spun gold was askew and the light blue linen dress too clearly hugged her scrawny legs and thighs. I found myself shuffling forward to get a closer look. Her eyes were wide open, the pupils so large each iris was just a thin circle. Ever morbid, I noticed a trail of vomit from her mouth that disappeared over the side of the bed.

By now my tears had ceased and I was able to stand upright. Every single eye was turned towards me, waiting.

I turned to Neferhotep and even his fearless gaze dropped. "How did this happen?" I asked.

The High Lord lifted his eyes to find Peseshet. "Chief Physician?"

Even doughty Peseshet looked as though she would cry. "It would appear it was apoplexy, brought on by a broken heart."

Broken heart? Who had the old boot fallen in love with now? "Has the King been told of his mother's death?" I asked.

All eyes dipped again. Were they too afraid? "Am I to tell him myself?" I asked.

"Great Khafre," said Neferhotep and only then did he raise his eyes to find mine. "The Great God-King Djedefre is dead."

Later, at his mortuary temple, I came to ensure that Djedefre, my favourite amongst my difficult family, would be properly prepared for his journey to the Field of Reeds. Exquisitely conscious of my presence, and after numerous apologies, the priest brought the stone hammer sharply down on Djedefre's knee with a snap like a clicked finger. Perhaps to spare me, he left little delay, quickly smashing my brother's other knee, then both his hip joints. Thankfully, whatever dreadful spasm had shaken his body had left his arms crossed across his chest, close enough to bind them more or less together, as was the custom. At least these did not have to be broken as well.

Under Peseshet's direction and as gently and respectfully as he could, the priest straightened my brother's legs. In the last spasm before death had claimed him, they had bent and then splayed so he looked like a frog that had died on its back. He would never have fitted in his lovingly crafted sarcophagus. The limbs of Meritities had been much easier to rearrange.

"This is so... I am sorry Your Majesty. We must do more. Perhaps you would be better not to see what happens next."

As Peseshet said this I got the impression she was fighting herself, fighting the human need to reach out and place a comforting hand on my arm. I smiled but shook my head.

She continued, clearly hating every word. "Your final act, after the King has been mummified and before he is placed within his tomb, is to open his mouth so he can eat and drink and breath in the afterlife. However, you must also open the mouth to allow the Ba, your brother's personality, to be released so it can unite with his Ka, his soul. The Ba can only be released after mummification and must be contained before then. This means..."

We both stared silently at Djedefre's mouth, wide open in a scream of pain.

"Just do it!" I said. The priest reached for the hammer but I held up a hand and he froze. I turned to Peseshet. "Not him. You. Be as gentle as you can!"

She bowed. "Of course."

The preparation area was as full of priests as it had been for Khufu's mummification. Death drew them out of their temples and their bawdy houses, from their men and their women, their girls and their boys. I hated them all except for Peseshet. She was the only one who seemed genuinely upset by my brother's death. She had been my brother's physician too and she had failed him. Perhaps she feared I would put her to death, as indeed I now could.

Impulsively I found myself blurting: "It was not your fault."

She shook her bowed head sadly. "Your brother was a young man. He should not have died."

"Did he die because of that?" I pointed a jewelled fingernail at the base of Djedefre's neck and at a small, congealed globule of blood like a little red pearl.

For an instant she seemed surprised I had noticed this, but my eyes are sharp. "Perhaps an insect has bitten him. Sometimes, very rarely, that can be fatal. He was hardly very healthy to begin with."

"It's not red or swollen like an insect bite. When I get bitten it swells up like my father's pyramid."

She opened her hands, palm up, a gesture of surrender. "Indeed, perhaps in his final death throes he simply bumped against something sharp and that is what left this mark. I will inspect his organs when I remove them. Perhaps they will yield some other clue."

Perhaps. More likely this was the work of Seth, taking the shape of some infernal insect and doing his worst, mortally injuring the King and upsetting the eternal balance so he could unleash the sandstorm that had wrecked the country. The crops were flattened under sand. It would be a dreadful harvest.

She was waiting. "Continue!" I said.

She turned and walked towards a bench heavy with implements. Her long tunic, weighted at the hem, swayed over her shapely hips.

She returned with another stone hammer, this one smaller and tied to its handle with a delicate tracery of fine leather cords. Bending down she felt the side of my brother's jaw and then, with a single tap, she broke it. That side of his face slumped, skewing his last horrified roar. She moved around the other side and did the same, loosening his whole jaw. A priest had a bandage ready and Peseshet secured it around the jaw and over the top of Djedefre's head. She made a knot and pulled it tight, closing his mouth. I was surprised to see clear fluid spill out. His mouth had been full of saliva.

Djedefre had never wronged me and I would not relish seeing his viscera removed so I turned and left the room. My guards, who had frozen themselves into immobility, came to life and made a wedged formation, pushing aside anyone careless enough to get in my way.

I still thought of this as Djedefre's palace. Far larger than mine, a man would take half an hour to walk around it. It nestled against the boundary of the temple to Osiris, whose hypostyle columns soared far above, dwarfing the rambling structures of the palace just as the gods dwarfed men. The temple had been built by Djoser of the Third Dynasty over a hundred years ago, serving as a salutary reminder that though we, his successors, might be god-kings, there were those who had been mightier.

Over a thousand people lived and worked in the palace and a third of these were Djedefre's family and personal servants. On his death they had simply melted away, their tumult and anger contained by Neferhotep, so I could maintain my serenity and concentrate on keeping the cosmos in balance.

And, of course, it was Neferhotep who orchestrated the tumult of my own family and servants moving into the King's palace.

Godhood had fallen on me from an empty sky. One minute I was the dissolute Khafre, wasting away my hours, disrespecting everything, believing nothing, and then suddenly the fate of Egypt rested in my pillow-soft hands.

Neferhotep had explained it all. He had come to me, an event which alone showed how much the world had turned. There was a room in my old palace set aside for meetings with officials and that is where we had talked. Djedefre's succession had been clear for he had been aware he might die young. He had nominated Meritities as Regent until Setka, his eldest, was of age. Setka was yet but eight years old so the period of regency would be long. The death of Meritities left the realm without either an adult successor or a regent, Djedefre's wives being held too young and foolish for such a task.

Thus, the line of succession shifted to Djedefre's oldest sibling and I found myself thrust unwillingly into godhood.

Did godhood feel different? Not so far. The most miraculous change to date was Neferhotep's sudden subservience and respect. When he bowed and kissed my feet I almost swooned. I found myself looking down on his bald, gleaming head. It reminded me of an ostrich egg and it made me realise that even Neferhotep was fragile, in his own way.

We sat late into the night as he explained my duties, reassuring me that he would be by my side constantly, that he would make sure I always knew what to do and when to do it. He told me of the exchequer and the depth of our debts. He told me secrets of the neighbouring states, their strengths, their weaknesses. Of tempting targets, of mines and harvests, of jewels and gold and treasure in these kingdoms. Of how the Egyptian state kept afloat on the income from war and plunder.

He told me of the official spy networks and the mood of the people, of the plots and politicking of the High Administration. He talked of the coming flood and the estimates of the harvest into which the sandstorm had already been factored. He told me how many would die from starvation, and described how troops would need to be reassigned to counter the brigandage of poor people driven to desperate measures to fend off starvation.

Neferhotep opened my eyes to all that I, in my princely self-absorption, had missed. Dazed, my back broken by the weight of this new knowledge, I finally held up my hand and, miracle of miracles, Neferhotep fell silent.

"It is too much."

He shook his head. "Never while I am here, my King. I will help and advise in any way I can, to take off your shoulders the wearying load of the affairs of state, to free you for your duties as a god."

I nodded in gratitude. Now that he had explained everything, I almost began to feel sympathy for him. I began to understand how a man with so many responsibilities to master would have so little time for mercy.

My eyelids were drooping as sunrise approached. "You are tired, my King. I will leave you to sleep. Your meeting with the council of High Priests is not until noon tomorrow. They can advise you on your duties in the temples."

He made as though to leave but then stopped and placed a finger against his lower lip as though struck by a thought.

"Go on!" I said, for everyone now waited for permission to speak.

"I have told you of all the duties, of all the burdens of state. The High Priests will do the same for your religious tasks. We are all asking so much of you, never considering what we might give in return."

"What do you mean?"

"What can we... what can I do for you? Is there anything you want? Is there something you crave that has been denied you? I would do anything, anything, to please you. You must be at ease when you speak with the gods as the fate of Egypt rests on your happiness. Nothing else matters."

I did not understand at first. Already I was getting used to everyone waiting for me, so I took my time before answering. As a royal, once I had grown out of the control of tutors and nurses and nannies, I had got and done almost everything I wanted. Did I want more concubines? Hardly.

I had lost track of those I already had. Even if I returned to one, I rarely recognised her face or her body.

Fewer wives would have been good but now that I was King that was out of the question. The more descendants, the better. As soon as a wife gave birth the child would be snatched away to the breast of a wet-nurse so the wife could be fertile again as quickly as possible. More so now, the harem must produce princes and princesses who could be married off in alliances with rich merchants and the chieftains of surrounding tribes and kingdoms.

"I already have everything. What else could I want?"

Neferhotep's mouth moved, just a little. It wasn't quite a smile but for once he appeared neither angry nor studiedly neutral. "Sometimes, Great Khafre" he said quietly, "the answer to a question can be so large, so obvious, that one cannot see it."

Modern Day

The revelations come thick and fast. I'm on my belly, one forepaw over the other, tongue hanging out, ears as erect as a soldier home on leave. Behind me, Ragab's family is eating and talking away. The revelations aren't coming from them, needless to say, but from the big rectangular eye which has suddenly come to life.

When it happened, I found an earnest young man addressing me directly. I hadn't even seen him enter the room. I checked behind this big eye thing, expecting to find a little doorway to the next apartment, but there was just a blank wall. The family had a good laugh at my confusion. "Silly dog, it's just the TV," Kiya had said.

So, this was TV. My handlers talked of little else but it had never made sense until now.

This was proper magic, up there with the taming of the gun-devils. The guns and the cars of the modern Egyptians had frightened me but, over time, I had come to see them simply as progress. Bows and arrows to guns, sedan chairs to cars. But this... where did this TV come from and what was it showing? Was this the modern equivalent of dreams?

Whoever he is, the man in the dream is definitely looking at me. Even if I move my head, his eyes are always on me. Sound and colour are also not quite right, being slightly distorted and exaggerated just as in a dream.

Suddenly the man is gone and instead I am looking over a busy city. The shift makes me almost swoon and I have to look away, to anchor myself in this human-filled room.

"He doesn't seem to know what to make of it." Walidah's voice is soft and gentle and belies the terrible things she must be doing behind Ragab's back.

Though I'm looking at a city, I can still hear the man talking. Maybe I should listen. Dreams can tell you so much, though whose dream this is I have no means of telling.

"Cairo is a city in fear," he is saying. "People are preparing for the worst."

"God, they talk such terrible rubbish," says Ragab's father, his voice high and a little shaky. He seems much older than his wife. People generally don't introduce themselves to dogs so I don't know what his name is. All the others simply call him Dad.

"There will be a test of the evacuation sirens this Thursday at midday. This will be a practice only and is for citizens to familiarise themselves with the sound. Here is a preview."

The TV makes the rising sound of a cat being slowly disembowelled.

"As if we could get out of this godforsaken city if we tried," says Dad. "Most of the day it's locked solid with traffic."

"There would be plenty of warning," says Ragab. Kiya has just given him a bracelet she has made from thread and brightly coloured beads. It seems effeminate by modern Egyptian standards but he wears it with pride. "Just keep walking west up into the desert. You'd be fine."

"This is making me ill," says Ragab's mother, who also seems likely to remain nameless.

"Never going to happen," says Dad with a sweep of his hand. "Nasser knew what he was doing. Good old German and British engineering." He gives a bitter laugh.

I'm never going to work out what's going on from listening to these idiots, so I concentrate on what the bizarre modern TV dream is telling me. I can swivel my ears to a startling degree so it's easy.

The view shifts, the city tilting and then retreating at a breathtaking rate. My mind reels and it takes quite a spurt of imagination to make out that the city has retreated into barely a dot on what I'm guessing is a chart. A delicate, twisty, serpentine line of green sandwiched between yellow plains can only be the Nile. "Cairo," and here the dot pulses yellow, "is eight hundred kilometres downriver from Aswan." Another dot lights up that's well into Nubia.

"Classic tactic," says Dad raising his voice above the TV, "Focus on an imaginary threat to take people's mind off their real troubles. I thought Sisi would know better. I thought Egyptians would know better. We've been lied to for generations."

"It is best not to say such things, Dad," says Walidah gently.

"I will say what I wish in my own house," says Dad, but there's no anger in his voice at her suggestion. I'm pretty sure Ragab is the only adult in the house who doesn't know what's going on, but even Dad finds it difficult to be angry with Walidah and her evident gentleness.

In the family silence that follows, the big revelation arrives. "The Aswan High Dam was constructed in the 1960s to produce hydroelectricity but also, and much more importantly, to control the flow of the Nile so that three whole harvests can be produced every year rather than just one."

Controlling the Nile is as absurd as controlling the sun, and for a second my mind refuses to believe it, but then I remind myself of today's mirror-flat waters which once upon a time carried away men and cattle as easily as dried reeds before a dust storm. A roaring monster had been tamed and used like a wet-nurse slave.

"The Generals are taking this seriously. Threats have been intercepted," says Ragab.

"From whom?" asks Dad.

"I cannot say," says Ragab.

Dad snorts and Ragab colours.

I remembered once, in the twentieth year of Khufu's reign, a great flood. Far earlier than normal, the waters had raged in and then retreated after barely a few days, leaving the fields carpeted by the blackened and bloated bodies of the dead: cattle and humans, dogs and cats, rats and mice. Later that year had come a bumper harvest, the fruits of which people ate with quiet horror.

I look again at Ragab and his family. I think of Amr and Mazan and Amsu. Am I exposed only to the poorest dregs of this civilisation? How could barely toilet-trained people like this tame the mighty Nile?

Meanwhile the TV is showing me something else and it isn't until I see something moving, and realise it is a truck just like ours, that I get the sense of scale. A huge wall stretches all across the width of the Nile and well beyond, a white sword that has severed the river. On this side of the barrier the Nile is weakened, a starving snake slithering through the rocks, but as I watch the view changes and climbs high over the wall. On the other side is an ocean as far as the eye can see.

"Lake Nasser," the voice intones. "The largest man-made lake in the world. Nearly five hundred kilometres long and many kilometres wide, holding back over one hundred and thirty cubic kilometres of water." I have no idea of how much that is, but my eyes are making a compelling case that it has to be one hell of a lot.

"Are we going to drown, Dad?" asks the mother.

Dad, clearly the brains of this outfit, shakes his head with utter certainty, however much or little he actually knows. It's a trick I had to pull off all the time in my past life and I recognise a fellow practitioner. Teachers did that sort of thing with kids and I'm guessing that's what he is. "The dam is bomb-proof. It's not a wall of concrete like they use for dams in the States or China. It's made of a big long mound of rock and clay. You can't punch a hole in it as you could with the Hoover Dam or the one at the Three Gorges. We're fine."

Ragab is respectful even when he demurs. "Munitions have moved on a lot in the last fifty years, Dad. Bunker busting bombs and the like."

Dad waves this away. "It was designed even to withstand a nuclear bomb. Nasser and his Germans knew what they were doing."

It's the first I've heard of a nuclear bomb. I wonder what it smells like.

"But the stakes are so high, Dad. The Nile is basically a river with desert rising steeply either side for most of the way. Those one hundred and thirty cubic kilometres of water would barrel down it. A hundred million people live within a few kilometres of the river. Even if we could get to higher ground before the wave came crashing through it would still wash away all the houses, bridges, roads and factories. Egypt, at least the bits people live in, would be wiped out."

OK, I think, I've had enough of these revelations. Sometimes there's such a thing as too much knowledge. Already I have a headache.

"It will never happen," says Dad dismissively and I pray on Atum's seed that he's right.

As the days pass, I find my mind can't help but keep returning to this new bewildering panorama that the dream machine has provided. The business with Mazan and Walidah had also disturbed me, but now it's a welcome way of getting my mind off the far larger problems that Egypt apparently faces.

I'd always thought Mazan was a homosexual. Mazan is a big man but not a little of this is fat. Despite his size he moves with a certain delicacy that his theatrical hawking and spitting do not quite manage to belie. Sometimes, when Mazan struggles with something heavy, like a box full of flak jackets, in a nevertheless dainty manner, I've seen Amr give Ragab a look and hold his arm out, wrist and hand hanging down limply. At those times Ragab would hold his own hand to his face to stop himself laughing.

I'm just not getting this. Is Mazan's behaviour the camouflage of a devious cuckolder? Surely not, unless Mazan is a great deal smarter than I've given him credit for.

Perhaps Mazan is living a lie even to himself. Perhaps by seducing Walidah and making a cuckold out of Ragab, he's kidding himself into believing he's a tough woman-loving man. And in a way that's actually true because you'd have to be one tough motherfucker to cuckold a man who routinely carries an AK-47, even if he isn't adept at using it.

Mazan's weird cinnamon stink has always made me keep my distance. Now I try to get closer, nuzzling at his hand and crotch like I gave a shit about this epicene dolt. Some days I can smell Walidah on him. Her perfume, yes, but also more intimate smells.

I wish Neferhotep was here with me now. He'd shake down the quivering bastard, find out what his game was, even if he had to reduce Mazan to his individual organs. I would pay good money to watch that.

I've been a real hit with Ragab's kids and he starts to bring me home every weekend. He is a worried man in a listless, unfocused way. Now, when we travel back to his house, he lets me sit in the front of the truck so he can confide in me.

"I am not good enough for her," he moans. "I do not bring home enough money. She should wear the finest clothes, eat the best food. She is so beautiful and I do not deserve her." So far so obvious but then, finally, I get some actual information.

"It was not a love marriage," he sighs. OK, this is hardly a revelation but it's a bit more solid than his usual whiny nonsense. "My father knows her father. He was in my father's debt. Don't tell this to anyone, Cheops," and he even looks around to make sure no urchin is clinging to the sides of the careering truck (hardly beyond the bounds of possibility!).

My life as a dog had been easy, I belatedly realise. The most I've had to worry about was the snip and, after my idyll with the bitch, even that has started to seem like a good idea.

Now I find myself in a world where two of the people closest to me, both possessing automatic weapons, are wandering down a path to disaster in a country where millions could be swept into the Great Green Sea at a moment's notice.

Happy days!

Ancient Days 2559 BC

The columns, wide as two men, tall as thirty, arose above me until lost in darkness. Here and there, Ra's light penetrated through openings in the roof, slanting down in fierce beams dancing with dust motes. Oil lamps placed at the foot of some columns gave weak, flickering illumination as I made my way, one heavy step after another, through the menacing gloom.

The weight of Egypt rested on my weak and shuddering shoulders. Even the High Priest of this temple of Horus had been left outside, safe in the heat and the light and with a crowd of acolytes to keep him company.

I was alone, though a temple as large as this employed over fifty thousand. Some attended to the toilette and dressing of the statues of the gods. Each statue had a man whose only function was to change and launder its loin-cloth. Some priests cared for the sacred texts, whilst butchers attended to the ritual sacrifices and disembowelling and veterinarian priests decoded the patterns of the entrails revealed. Florists decorated the mortuary alcoves where priests and priestesses remembered the rich dead who had paid for their services in perpetuity. Each serviced a hundred or more mummies, all buried in tombs far away in the desert.

Horus, with the body of a man and the head of a falcon, was emblematic of the God-King in life. He was me and I was him, yet still I feared his hooked beak and woke with nightmares of him plucking out my eyes.

A sudden skittering sound made me crouch down, hands over head, eyes tight shut. With walls so thick they strangled all sound from the world of man, this allowed sound from within to echo loudly and endlessly, both from my footfalls and the beating wings of trapped bats and birds. Far above me, something went on a panicky flight through the thicket of lotus stem columns, its echoes sounding as if a flock of birds had been trapped beneath this stone firmament.

I calmed my breathing and stood, unable to resist looking behind me, fully aware that a flashing beak might be the last thing I ever saw. That there was nothing to be seen was of little comfort. A hundred men or monsters might be lurking behind the columns or in their sombre shadows.

I was naked but for a pleated kilt. My feet were unshod and I felt every grain of sand between my feet and the marble. Even looking down was a trial for the wavering light made the designs in the marble, of gods and men and battles, come to life and I feared these ghostly demons would consume my feet, pitching me forward so they could tear at my face and heart.

I rested my forehead on a column and let the carved sandstone rub against my brow. I had been shaved by the priests, carefully and painstakingly over every inch of my body, and there was nothing to stop the sweat that flowed freely.

My stomach hung heavy on my hips, pregnant with fear. How I wished I could have asked Djedefre what I was supposed to do now.

Countless Egyptians might have believed I was a god but I did not. What was I doing here?

Ahead, at the end of the aisle, a large square break in the wall led to the inner chamber. I could see the god himself, taller than three men even without the red and white crown of Egypt that he wore. In one hand was a golden ankh the size of my forearm, in the other a crook which ended in an eye-gouging fork.

I wanted to turn and run but, if I did, I knew I would be dead. Horus would fall upon me from behind, cutting me to pieces, feeding my parts to the crocodiles so my Ka and Ba could never rejoin in the afterlife. Even if I made it out of the temple, Neferhotep would be waiting, keen to offer me a similar fate.

Meanwhile, the god waited for me patiently, as he had waited on all god-kings for centuries before. He had waited for Sneferu and Sekhemet, for Narmer and Djoser. He had waited for Khufu. All men who in their way had been more than men, beings who could withstand the regard of the god.

But then I thought of poor, weak Djedefre. Even he had survived this, so why couldn't I?

Another skittering sound, this time ending with an enraged squawk, sent me down on my knees, my heart hammering in my chest. How could the fate of Egypt rest on shoulders as unworthy as mine?

I stood upright again and forced myself to resume a measured tread towards my destiny. The nearer I got, the more crushing the presence of Horus. His golden kilt, reflecting the flames of the oil lamps, seemed on fire. His black eyes, so large in his small hawk face, regarded me unblinkingly.

I hesitated on the threshold of the chamber. Every wall was minutely carved, giving the place a texture like living skin. In the flickering oil light the carvings writhed with tales of the god, his birth and fight with Seth, of the dismemberment of his father, of the final vanquishing of Seth to the stones and the desert.

Far above me his sharp beak waited as I stepped forward and stood before him, a mouse before the eye of a hawk. I dropped to my knees, lowering my head so my eyes were hidden.

"Great Lord Horus," I began, but my voice came out as though I was being choked. I cleared my throat but then swallowed the phlegm rather than spit it out. Nothing must desecrate this temple, not even a hair.

"Great Lord Horus, I come to offer my most profound respects. I come to you as the King of Egypt. I come to you as the spokesman of the people. I come to you for your kindness."

I waited but there was only the echoing silence of the tomb.

"The river is low," I continued. "The inundation will be weak. The people who love and worship you will starve. I beg of you, Great Horus, to intercede with Anuket, Goddess of the Nile, to swell the bounteous waters so we can fill the bellies of our children."

A perfect delivery: not a stutter, not a stammer. Much better that anything that poor Dj... Dj... Djedefre could have mustered.

I waited in the still air of the looming vault. I feared even the voice of Horus. Would it be ferocious, for a glance at the history of the gods revealed fierceness at every turn? Or would it be the calm and ethereal voice of a being so divorced from humanity that even the concept of kindness and charity would have no meaning. To such an unfathomable deity the people of Egypt would be just ants, a trivial nuisance one could either indulge or annihilate with a single step.

My body thrummed with suspense, stretched like the string of a harp, waiting for the touch of the god on my shoulder. My bowels, ever unreliable, had urgent need to expel their liquid contents.

"My Lord, I beseech you to answer my request," I said, desperate to leave.

Time passed in the silence of the grave, drawing me downwards until I entered a realm where only the god and I remained.

The pressure in my stomach rose until the prospect of soiling the sanctum of the god became alarmingly real. Finally, desperately I raised my head and stared up into the predatory eyes of the hawk god.

Neferhotep had insisted I attend the hearing. I could have refused, thought up a thousand and one excuses, but that would be a cowardice even I could not face. Hapiwer was, after all, just a wine merchant and nothing to me. I found myself looking down from my high dais at the small crowd of nobles and merchants who had come to see justice being done. We were on a small plaza, built below the level of the royal palaces so it was shaded from the low evening sun. Wide marble steps led down to the Nile where many boats of the royal flotilla bobbed gently, tied to the piers with thick hemp ropes. Above us a faint curving wisp of cloud, pink in the dying sun, lay like a sidewinding viper across the sky.

Neferhotep was seated on the dais, though his seat was positioned lower than mine. He was in his finery, his long tunic made of parallel stripes of blue and red and gold from neck to feet. A dark wig hung below his shoulders and a neat rectangular beard, supported by a strap over his head and hidden by the wig, jutted down almost to the level of his nipples. Designed to bolster his authority, to me his outfit was too garish, detracting from his naturally austere and frightening dignity.

The accused, dirty and beaten after a night in the cells, knelt on the marble, his hands tied behind his back and his head down. Noseless Kamwase waited ready, a thick wooden stave held in his hands.

Down at the jetty the side of one boat creaked against another and across the river a pack of wild dogs howled their fury.

Neferhotep began without preamble. "Tomb robbing is an infamy, for it deprives the dead of a beloved object for eternity. To rob the tomb of a king is a crime beyond reason. Repent your sins and tell us where you have hidden the other grave goods you stole."

Hapiwer looked up from his kneeling position, misery incised in deep creases across his face. "I am innocent, my Lord. I opened no tomb, I took nothing."

Neferhotep lifted the object in his hand. I had inspected it earlier. The amulet, suspended by the finest of gold chains, had on its face an image constructed from the tiniest fragments of a variety of coloured gems and precious stones. A dizzying amount of workmanship had gone into it and thus it could only be the treasure of a king.

"Hardly nothing," said Neferhotep. "Though too young ever to have seen it, the royal jeweller testifies this to be the work of his grandfather who described it in considerable detail, saying it was his greatest creation. The image is that of the Hetephernebti, Queen to Djoser. The same God-King Djoser whose stepped pyramid in Saqquara was emptied by jackals such as yourself."

There was a sharp intake of breath from the high-born audience. Even the merchants looked shocked. Before they came, they would have known the matter would be serious, for only regicide or extreme blasphemy merited a High Court trial overseen by the High Lord himself. They had not, however, known the actual charge. The pillaging of Djoser's tomb was held responsible for two poor floods and the famines that had followed. Tens of thousands had died of starvation.

Hapiwer shook his head firmly. "I've never seen that before, I swear by Isis and Osiris, by Horus and by Maat." Neferhotep answered to Maat, the goddess of truth and justice, and appealing to her directly was going above Neferhotep's head, a breach of protocol but probably the least of Hapiwer's problems.

Neferhotep nodded at Kamwase who brought the stave down on Hapiwer's back. I could feel the heavy thump resonate in my own chest. A wail to my left made me turn and a figure I had not noticed before had stood up, her shawl falling from her head to reveal the lovely tear-stained features of Peseshet.

I swallowed hard, sorrow for her and my jealousy towards Hapiwer warring within me.

"What other objects have you hidden?" Neferhotep was asking.

Hapiwer had pitched forward and Kamwase hauled him back to his knees. The wine merchant's chest was heaving and he could not speak but he looked directly up at me, the entreaty on his face like a physical blow. Unable to remain aloof and dignified, I found myself looking away.

Time stretched agonisingly as Neferhotep waited for Hapiwer to regain his breath, all the time Peseshet weeping tears of anguish.

"My Lord Khafre," Hapiwer managed at last. "I swear I know nothing of this. I risked my life for sacred Djedefre. You know that. Why would I do this dreadful thing?"

"You will speak only to me!" Neferhotep signalled again and this time the stave came down at an angle and his upper arm took the full force of the blow, producing a sickening crack. The colour drained from Hapiwer's face, his eyes rolled up and he pitched forward. At a signal from Neferhotep, servants came with jugs and water was hurled in Hapiwer's face. His eyes re-opened but the pupils rolled as though he was lost and unable to focus. Neferhotep would be getting nothing useful out of him for a while.

"My Lord, my Lord," Peseshet had fallen to her knees, her hands clasped in supplication before her, her eyes on Neferhotep. "I implore you to let me speak."

Neferhotep raised a single finger in agreement.

"High Lord Treasurer, my husband speaks the truth. When they searched our house the soldiers claimed they found it in my husband's chest that he keeps in his bedroom. I have many times seen my husband use the chest and I swear there was never an amulet like that."

"Then how did it get there, Chief Physician? Before you answer, remember the soldiers were sent on my instructions."

I held my breath for Peseshet was in dangerous territory. The last thing I wanted to see were her elegant limbs being broken. After a second's hesitation she hung her head. "I do not know, your Lordship," she said simply.

"This greatly saddens me, for your sake. You have rendered great service to the Royal Court and I would show mercy to your husband if I could, but the scales of truth and justice have been so offset that there is but one way to restore equilibrium. However, as a favour to you, we can spare your husband some pain." He pointed at his bodyguard. "Lord Kamwase, act speedily!"

Even as Kamwase leaned down, taking hold of one of Hapiwer's arms, three soldiers ran forward and grasped his other limbs. As they lifted him above their shoulders,

Hapiwer's head lolled back and I prayed that he would never regain full consciousness. Up to now I had ignored the presence of the stake, as wide as a fist and made from a pine tree imported from the highlands of the Amorites on the eastern shores of the Great Green. The stake, taller than a man, tapered over the length of a forearm to a sharp point. The point was sharpened after each execution so fresh new wood was revealed, but along the rest of its length it was covered in blackened, sun-dried blood.

Peseshet fell to her knees, her weeping tearing at my heart. Even the merchants, hardened to public executions, clutched at their tunics, the death of one of their own too close a reminder of their own vulnerability.

The stake was buried deep in the bank above the jetty, a salutary sight for anyone sailing by on the river. The soldiers and Kamwase carried Hapiwer down towards it. They were brawny men but Hapiwer's height made him heavy and his body rolled like a ship on the Great Green as they negotiated the slope. Reaching the stake, they shuffled sideways so that the centre of Hapiwer's spine was above the point.

"Now!" Kamwase shouted and they all pulled, but the suddenness of his command had startled the men on the right for they did not react quickly enough, Hapiwer's body turning as he was brought down. The point penetrated just below his shoulder blade and exited through his armpit. The flesh tore open, his body came free of the stake and Hapiwer tumbled to the ground. I saw the whites of his eyes as his eyelids sprang open and a wail of agony escaped his lips.

Kamwase beckoned angrily at another group of soldiers; with the victim no longer unconscious, the task would be harder.

Eight men now lifted the struggling figure aloft and again they did the awkward sideways shuffle to bring Hapiwer over the stake. Blood was pouring from his massive wound and he was screaming, a sound I knew would cut through my dreams until my own death.

"One... two... three!" This time all the men were ready and they brought their full weight on Hapiwer's limbs. The point tore through his body, emerging just above his belly button. At another shout from Kamwase the men let go and Hapiwer hung there, arms and legs hanging back, his eyes fixed on some point far above, in agony if he moved, in agony if he didn't. His body vibrated and an ululation as though from a mourning woman came from deep within his throat and echoed around the marble steps.

The stake had shattered his spine so his legs hung useless but his arms fluttered up to the bloody point and touched it, as though trimming the wick of a votive candle. The merchants watched aghast, whilst Peseshet hid her head in her robes.

Turning around in his chair, Neferhotep looked up at me with his grey eyes, a single eyebrow raised.

Days later, when Hapiwer's blackened corpse, now more like a spider impaled on a pin than a human being, had fulfilled its salutary function and deterred anyone from robbing the tomb of a king, it was pulled off the stake at sundown and tossed onto a pile of dried reeds doused in mutton fat.

The night was windless and I watched the unwavering column of black smoke rise from his pyre all the way to the stars. In the morning, the ashes would be gathered then scattered onto the Nile, slowly, so that every iota of Hapiwer's body would be separated and then lost when the Nile disgorged into the Great Green. His body would never be brought back together and Hapiwer would never find life in the Field of Reeds.

A fitting end for the robber of a king's tomb.

Modern Day

"It's Iran, obviously." Amr's declaration descends with a thud that's designed to end the discussion, but time has moved on, his acolytes have grown in confidence since they became heroes, and his word is no longer writ.

"Not so sure," Mazan is tweaking his little moustache. Mazan has tired of cinnamon, and whatever cologne he's wearing now smells like an explosion in a fruit seller's cart blended with underlying unnatural tangs. Walidah must have no sense of smell.

And neither must Ragab otherwise he would be alert to his predicament.

"So, who do you think it is?" asks Amr stuffily.

"The Israelis, of course. They have never forgiven us for the wars in the sixties and seventies." There's a smear of hot sauce still on Mazan's cheek. What a charmer!

"They haven't forgiven us because they kicked our asses in both. Seriously?"

Mazan shrugs. "Daesh, then."

"They're Sunnis like us. That doesn't make any sense. No, it's Iran, teamed up with those Syrian bastards. Trust me!" Amr chops the air dismissively.

"My dad thinks it's all bullshit. He says it's Sisi's way of taking our mind off the ending of the bread subsidy." Ragab rarely contributes to any topic beyond football so the others look at him in mild surprise.

I tune out. They're like flies commenting on the health of the horse from the quality of its droppings. There may be truth amongst all the shit but it would take forever to find and, even then, they probably wouldn't recognise it.

Besides, I have other things on my mind, not least that I am flying in a huge metal bird so far above the land that the Nile looks like a twisty blue ribbon fringed with green. I had been dragged up a ramp and right up into the bird's arse. Then they chained me up (good decision!). They're probably afraid I'll lose it, go berserk and start biting the bird's innards. And, for a while after the bird launched itself into the sky with a bowel-loosening roar, that had seemed a highly attractive proposition.

We've been flying, flying for the love of Osiris, for quite a while now. My heart has stopped trying to shake itself to death and I find I can even breathe again. There's enough slack on my lead that I raise myself up on my back legs and put my forepaws on a little window and look out.

Further back in the belly of the beast there's four other dogs and their handlers, including my old chum Monthu. The dogs are in a funk and locked in the if we ignore this maybe it will go away style of thinking. Only Monthu seems undisturbed. Amazingly, I've managed to underestimate his stupidity.

My handlers are so undisturbed by these incredible events that they continue with their witless conversation. "I mean, why would anyone do it?" Ragab is asking. "Why destroy Egypt? We made peace with the Israelis years ago. We're not at war with Iran or Syria. We're not a threat to anyone."

Amr shakes his head. "And that's where you're wrong. Egypt is becoming a big threat to the world order. We are no longer a supplicant nation." He pokes one finger in the air. "We've opened a second Suez Canal that can take the biggest ships in the world and we can tax them to buggery..." A second finger. "We've discovered vast reserves of oil just off the Mediterranean coast, perhaps the biggest reserves in the world..." A third finger and his voice is rising. "Our large population is young while people in the West and China and Japan are old and finally, thanks to Sisi, we're doing something about educating our people..." A fourth finger, badly reset after he caught it in the door of the truck, struggles upward. "And we have got rid of the pernicious pharaohs and are a democracy. For once the country is being ruled by the people."

It's obvious who might want to wash Egypt into the sea. These idiots have forgotten the gods. If you needed a subtext for my whole civilisation it would have been do not fuck with the Gods!

Mazan does not appear to have been listening to Amr's lecture. He glances out of the window. "How long to Aswan?"

So that's where we're going! Nice to know! I've been back and forth between there and Cairo on the boats plenty of times and so I'd figured if we were going back that's how we'd do it. I hadn't seen being shoved into the guts of a metal bird in my future.

"Seat belts on!" a tinny voice says from somewhere.

"There's your answer," says Amr, and he pulls a couple of straps across himself. The bird had made a big enough noise trying to get off the ground, every little bit of its metal trying to shake itself lose. I'm hoping it will land by perching on top of whatever building is our destination.

However, if there is a handy perch then the damned bird misses it and instead lands on its belly with a teeth-shattering shriek. Suddenly a force out of nowhere is pulling me towards the front and I'm choking on the end of my lead like a hanged man. Meanwhile, the bird's heavy but constant whine has turned into a rising roar of hysterical outrage. Garrotted on my lead I can't help but look back towards the men who, to my vast surprise, continue to lounge unconcernedly in their seats.

Some of the other pooches are as alarmed as me and those not being garrotted are barking. Only Monthu is still calm and I realise this must have happened to him before. A human would be looking proud and disdainful at others making fools of themselves but, of course, his eyes are still as blank as the surface of a dune.

The noise is abating and the force dragging me forward vanishes. The dogs are barking wildly and are being slapped by their handlers. I feel the bird turn and finally we come to a stop. The men undo their straps as the bird's arse opens, the ramp dropping away to reveal the flatness of sand extending as far as the eye can see. The desert air rolls in and it's like being licked by a warm, dry tongue.

We walk down the ramp and into the featureless landscape. It's not looking much like Aswan to me yet. That's down in the river valley. We used to call the town Swenett and it's just north of the Great Cataract.

Trucks are waiting, their backs covered with canvas. They look like mobile kennels. We climb into the back of one and are in the shade again.

Police take a long time to do anything and so we sit there waiting as the temperature rises. All we can see is the view afforded by the arched doorway of this man/dog kennel. It's not a view I like to linger on. The desert is a place of death and the dead. In a way it is like the sun. Egyptians fear and respect it, but they do not love it.

Mazan is sitting right beside me and I blink in surprise when his votive device rings. He looks startled, as do we all, for this hardly ever happens. He squints at the front of it then pokes something, hurriedly putting it to his ear. To my surprise I hear Walidah's voice. How in Osiris' name can he hear her when she is at the other end of the Nile? Sure, I'd heard voices coming from these things and figured they came from something similar to their gun demons, but I'd never recognised one before. "Hello, lover," says Walidah.

I look quickly at Ragab but he doesn't react and I remember he doesn't have my acute doggy ears.

"Hallo, Mother," says Mazan.

"Is he there?"

"Of course. Aswan."

"Aswan! The little shit wouldn't even tell me that. The Nubian women are beautiful, my sweet. You must not stray."

"Of course not, Mother. Look, I am at work. I must go."

"Not yet. I am touching mysel—" but Mazan pokes again and the voice disappears.

"You just told your mother we are in Aswan," Amr says heavily. "What part of 'secret assignment' didn't you understand?"

"Nobody gives a crap where we are, apart from the people we love. This secrecy business is total bullshit."

Amr seems disinclined to expend energy pursuing the matter further and who can blame him? He is sweating heavily and my fur coat is roasting me alive. I know how stupid I must look with my tongue hanging out but I doubt I could survive otherwise. Ragab leans over and unscrews a bottle of water. He drips it onto my tongue. I lap at it greedily.

Finally, the truck comes to life and we move off. Other trucks follow, one with a much bigger and mounted version of the guns my handlers carry bringing up the rear.

The road is as dusty as the desert and the two are hardly distinguishable.

This high desert road is on the lip of a long incline and suddenly the Nile appears ahead and down to the right. Though swollen at this point it is still preternaturally calm. In the middle I can just make out Elephantine Island. At the south end is to be found the little step pyramid of Sneferu, dear old dad's father. Every other year we took a pilgrimage upriver to commemorate him here. In those days the river was the opposite of calm and the oarsmen had to sweat their balls off to make any headway even to get to Aswan. There we had to leave the boat because the Great Cataract, a little further upstream, was impassable at any time of year.

Those were miserable times. Dad made all of his children kneel at the pyramid, even from the age of two, our finery trailing in the dust, making us pray for the Ka of an old man most of us had never even met. He was training us so that we in our turn would train our children to pray for him.

Fat chance, old man!

I had hoped we would turn right and head down into Aswan where there is shade and the desert winds don't blow their warm breath. Instead we turn left, heading upriver. I've never been this far south, during this lifetime anyway, and I watch with interest. My handlers are dozing as best they can so I don't bother to hide the frankness of my gaze.

We turn away from the river and into another valley. I notice a jumble of rocks in what is clearly a long-dried river bed. I'm embarrassed to say how long it takes me to work out what this is, but it is little wonder as the explanation is just too incredible. The rocks, I finally realise, are the Great Cataract. These modern Egyptians, these petty, undignified, repressed people have somehow diverted the almighty river Nile to bypass it completely. I blink in wonder.

Then the road turns in a long sweep and I can see the diverted river and then the dam, an almost sheer granite curtain cutting right across it. Sure enough, it is holding back the mighty Nile and, once again, I feel boundless astonishment at what these, my descendants, are capable of. At the same time, I'm appalled. The Nile was wilful, tempestuous and downright dangerous, but she was as much a part of our lives as our hearts and without her we would have died. Taming her, bending her to your ways was like whoring your daughter out: you might make good money but something important would be lost in the bargain.

Heavy military vehicles mounted with more of those long thick guns guard the approach, and I'm not surprised when we pull to a halt and a soldier pokes his gun then his nose into our kennel. Soldier and policemen look at each other wearily, too tired and hot to even exchange insults. I can hear and smell another dog padding round the vehicle.

I hear a muffled "Clear", then the soldier disappears and the truck moves along the road over the dam. "The British built this one," says Amr meditatively. "At least that's what they say. Of course, it was Egyptians who actually built it, the Brits just drew up the plans."

So, there are two dams? Passive learning has its limitations: you get what you're given. My analogy needs modification. They're not just using the Nile as a whore, but they're hiring her out as a wet nurse as well. Up to now I've had many feelings for the Nile. I've appreciated her beauty, been scared by her temper, shocked by the terrible things she'd done. Now, for the first time, I feel sorry for her.

Crossing the dam means swerving around various obstacles. At the other end there's more squat, toad-like military vehicles, their guns trained on the road. We swerve around a final barrier and then we're heading south again. Amr sits up, pointing at one inconspicuous patch of land then another. "Missile battery, ack-ack pit, command post, infirmary, radar station... This is the most highly protected ground installation in the world, especially from air attack."

"That's why I think this is all bullshit," says Mazan grumpily. "And it's not just here they've got all this. They've got missile batteries stationed miles out in every direction. Airliners give this whole area a wide berth as even a sparrow trying to fly through will get a missile up its arse. Nothing with wings can get within fifty kilometres of this place."

Amr waves a finger. "What if they poke out our eyes, attack the radar sites?"

I don't get a chance to check if Mazan buys this because at that moment the truck turns onto a desert road and what can only be the other, much bigger, dam swings massively into view. Even seeing it with my own eyes, the scale is still inconceivable. It's placed across a gorge. These bastards have somehow blocked the whole thing off behind a huge, sweeping mound. It's not a vertical curtain like the other dam, but rather something less steep.

I'm guessing they've used at least twenty times as much material as Khufu did for his show-off fuck-you pyramid. Not only that, but they must have laid the stuff down while the Nile was pushing at their backs really, really hard.

The metal bird, now this. For the first time an uneasy thought worms its unwelcome way into my brain like a cobra into a nursery. Up to now I'd assumed something terrible had gone wrong because our gods seem to have vanished from this modern Egypt. Yet modern men perform miracles like this without their aid. Is it possible that these dopes I've been stuck with are actually the new gods?

I look from one to the other. Ragab is picking his nose, Mazan's thoughts are clearly lost somewhere between Walidah's thighs, and Amr is frowning, no doubt working out the next way to show off his superior knowledge.

No, it's easier to assume that I've just gone completely crazy, that I was never a god-king, that I'm simply the proverbial mad dog.

"Something's wrong with Cheops," says Ragab, flicking some snot out into the desert.

"Pining for that bitch, probably," says Mazan, oblivious to the irony.

"He should have married her," says Amr. "That would have killed the pining stone dead."

They all laugh and I wonder how this day could possibly get any worse.

Ancient Days 2558 BC

I felt as nervous as a boy just before his circumcision and walked endlessly around the courtyard, though it was barely ten paces on a side. In the centre of the courtyard a table held the finest food and drink and around it was strewn cushions stuffed with lambswool from the lands around Tyre.

My skin was almost raw from shaving and I had anointed my penis with the oil from acacia seeds mixed with honey from the bees who feasted on its flowers. Never had it smelled so sweet.

What I was wearing had been a subject of interminable indecision. My robes filled three rooms, my footwear two. In the end I had cast aside the blues and the golds, the ornate and the elaborate, and settled instead for a simple ankle length tunic of the finest white linen. Even the simplest of my sandals were incised with gold designs on the leather insole, but at least these were hidden when I wore them.

Oil lamps cast a gentle wavering light as the stars looked down on my endeavours. The gods, I had begun to suspect, did not. In every temple I had visited I had prayed to its god for divine help. The gods had remained as silent as they had for my entreaties about the Nile. The harvest had been poor and the people had suffered. I had seen them lurking thin and wraith-like in the shadows, as I had ridden by in my sedan chair.

Something filled my chest, making it difficult to draw breath. My heart was fluttering like a trapped bird.

I had sent the servants away so when I heard the footsteps, I knew she was coming, led by Dedifer. I turned away as though entranced by the glittering constellations that hung in the sky to the east.

Dedifer cleared his throat and I turned. Though more than two hundred days had passed since her husband's death, Peseshet still wore mourning clothes. Her head was covered with a white cloth tied by a red band. A red dress hung by straps from her shoulders, its high waist coming to just under her bare breasts. The waistband was tight, allowing the dress to curve over the swell of her full hips.

I motioned with my finger and she came towards me, hands clasped over her stomach, her head down. I flicked my head at Dedifer and he disappeared silently.

"Thank you for coming, Peseshet," I said.

"I am at your command, my King." I recognised her perfume as Mendesian, with the sweet tones of myrrh and cassia. With her head bowed I could look frankly down at her, at the softness of her shoulders and the hints of the delicate bones beneath. Near the strap over her right shoulder a single small mole exquisitely undermined her smooth perfection and it was all I could do not to bend down and kiss it.

"I had hoped that you would have wanted to come even without my command."

She glanced up, confusion on her face. All her past assurance had fled, for now she was faced by a god.

In this whole damned country, only I knew I was no such thing.

"Come!" I said. "Sit and I will get you some wine."

Her fingers came to her throat and she looked aghast. "Please, my King, permit me!" and she made her way quickly to the table. Her hands were shaking as she poured a cup of wine that looked purple in the candlelight. She turned and offered it.

"Drink!" I commanded.

Startled, she took a gulp and when the cup came away it left a stain to one side of her lips. Without thinking I wiped it away with a thumb. Her eyes widened and she swallowed quickly. "My King..."

I had been spoiled with women. My wives and concubines, fractious, demanding, querulous though they all were, none dared resist my carnal wishes. Peseshet might intimidate me with her intellect and I certainly feared the power of the love I had finally realised she had ignited within me, but she was nevertheless simply a woman while I was a god, in name if nothing else. I stroked a finger across her cheek and the elegance of her cheekbone. Her eyes remained wide but whether with shock or the beginnings of desire I could not tell.

I held her chin between my thumb and forefinger and leaned in to kiss her. I tasted the sweetness of the wine as I pushed my tongue against her closed lips. My hand found her shoulders and the smoothness made me push harder until her lips parted reluctantly.

She raised an arm but seemed too afraid to touch me. Her other hand was still holding the wine so I took it from her and hurled it away. She gasped as it disappeared into the gloom, crashing down onto marble. "My King..."

"Egypt allows seventy-two days for mourning, Peseshet, my love, but I have waited nearly three times as long. I love you. Can I hope that you feel love for me? All those days we spent with the poor and the sick. Were you simply indulging my interest or did you take pleasure in my company?"

She hesitated and, for a second, I thought I saw the suggestion of a shy smile. Whether I did nor not, it was all the encouragement I needed. I drew her to me and kissed her again. Her lips, tremulous against mine, parted once more. The feel of the smooth skin of her back poured oil on the flames of my desire.

She did not resist (but then I was a god, so how could she?) as I pulled her down on the cushions.

Lying there afterwards, satisfied beyond imagining, I turned my head to find her looking at me, her eyes wide, the pupils enlarged. "I was afraid I might die," she whispered.

I turned fully towards her and put my hand on her shoulder. "Why, my love?"

She looked away, her cheek colouring. "A mortal woman being taken by a god."

For the first time, hearing the fear in the voice of this incredible, accomplished woman, I did feel like an all-powerful god. In my magnanimity, I laughed. "Come, Chief Physician, where is the seeker after truth I know so well? Djedefre's wives are all still alive. But for Meritities and my own mother, even all of Khufu's wives lived to grow old and fat."

At the mention of the dead queen a look of anguish passed over her face. I had not realised she had felt so close to the old woman. Perhaps Peseshet came to love all her patients.

"But the queens were married my lord, they had the protection of the gods. I had no such protection and was at the mercy of your desire."

I grasped her hand. "Then we must give you that protection."

Later, the wild dogs howling as they hunted amongst the crops across the river, she must have caught the smell from my anointment. "Acacia!" she said accusingly. "You meant all along to seduce me." Then she gave me a naughty smile that would have made even Khufu's cock, dead these many years, rise up and break through his wrappings.

Strangely, I have no dreams of the wedding, though I know I married her and it must have been the most joyous day of my life. I loved her more than life itself but, even to her, I could never admit that I was no more a god than she. Perhaps I feared that was the only reason she loved me.

And she continued to treat me like a god until the very day I had her killed.

Modern Day

I'd marvelled at how calm the Nile had been but Lake Nasser has a serenity that is almost uncanny. Somewhere far, far upriver the Nile is flowing in, but down here at the dam end the surface is like a mirror. As our little patrol boat cuts through the water, I watch as the arrowhead-shaped waves flow away, expanding forever. I'm thinking it's like the passage of a god-king through life, his bow wave flowing out for eons. After all, my pyramid is still filling people with awe four thousand years after my death and even the Sphinx is mystifying people to this day.

It's this metaphor of the bow wave that finally gets me out of my funk. My handlers aren't gods despite their dams and colossal man-made lakes, their trucks and gun-demons and metal birds. If Amr or the others died tomorrow their memories would fade faster than the ripples of a stone thrown into rapids.

The engine chugs away as we zig-zag across this vast expanse of held-back water. They're right in one thing: if the dam burst this would scour the twisty Nile valley all the way to the Great Green.

"This is boring," says Ragab. We're all sheltering under the gun platform that provides the only shade on the tiny deck. It's big enough to hold just us and the guy for the great big mounted gun who is also sheltering there.

"It's a waste, that's what it is," says Amr. "There are hardly any ships for us to check. That's the trouble with subsidising fuel."

"What do you mean?" Mazan must be bored because he hasn't left it alone even though he must realise Amr is teeing us up for a lecture.

Amr swings his arm out to encompass the lake. "Empty," he says, "Even worse than the Nile. Long stretches of navigable water but as a nation we don't use it. It's way cheaper to transport goods by water, but the country bankrupts itself providing a fuel subsidy that gives motor transport a competitive advantage. This is a crazy nation."

I guess he's right because in two weeks we've boarded only a handful of ships, most of which were like the Nile cruisers, full of pale-skinned old people crisping in the sun.

Along the Nile there is a solid strip of green either side, but this far upriver Lake Nasser has submerged even this and much of the surrounding desert as well. The lake hasn't been here long enough for vegetation to get a grip on the new shoreline. Here and there, however, are bursts of green where farming has begun. The monster that is the desert is slowly being driven back.

"Look at that!" Amr is pointing to an inlet whose sides are too straight to be natural. "They're driving a channel through the desert to make a second Nile. Farms and towns are already springing up around it."

A second Nile! Now that's what I call a breathtaking ambition. I feel intense, if unearned, pride.

The steersman sticks his head out of his cramped little wheelhouse. He has the darker, Nubian skin tones of people in the south. Though their skins are black, their spirits are lighter and their bearing more relaxed than their northern cousins. "There's something ahead."

The men get stiffly to their feet and peer over the wheelhouse. "It's a little freighter," the steersman says. The gunner, another Nubian, climbs up onto his gun platform, wincing in the midday sunlight.

The ship that swings into view is a mess. It lies low, a single deck barely an arm-length clear of the water. Large irregular bundles wrapped in white material are stacked precariously high on the deck. Drop a stone into the water and you suspect the ripples would overturn the whole damned thing. Three Nubians are watching our approach with sun-dulled curiosity.

Our helmsman sticks his arm out of the wheelhouse windows and raises and lowers it repeatedly. The chugging of the freighter's engine cuts out and it slows. The ship is about fifteen man-lengths long with a little wheelhouse right at the front. We come alongside amidships and our patrol boat noses gently in, the tyres that hang over our side squealing as we grind to a halt.

Amr leaps aboard first and nearly falls right back. The stack of parcels almost covers the whole width of the deck, leaving only a narrow track along each edge to move forwards and back. By holding onto the parcels Amr is able to edge along the deck towards the wheelhouse. Mazan follows, then Ragab who pulls me along behind him. Not having hands to grab at the parcels, I have to teeter along the edge as best I can.

My sense of smell goes into overdrive and it soon becomes apparent what's in the parcels: everything. I smell linen and linseed, meat and dried fish and fruit, motor oil, cooking oil and oils to soften a maiden's skin. I smell jasmine and pomegranate, old clothes and cushions sat on by a thousand backsides. I smell cloves and coriander, marjoram and mace, cumin and fenugreek, kief and opium as well as spices and herbs I cannot even begin to name.

Dizzy with this storm of fragrances, it's a miracle I manage to get to the bow without tipping into the lake. The three Nubians in gallabiyahs stand looking at my handlers. "What's this about?" asks the one in the least dirty of the tunics. The captain, I'm guessing.

"Routine search," says Amr.

The captain scratches his arse. "Routine? We've never been stopped and searched when we're underway before. We've been searched at the docks before by cops wanting..." and he rubs his thumb, fore and middle-fingers together. He raises his eyebrows.

My gift for reading changing micro-expressions unrolls Amr like a papyrus. There's a fleeting impression of greed before offence triumphs. He frowns. "This isn't a shakedown by your butt-fuck local cops. This is an anti-terrorist operation."

The captain blinks twice then waves an arm to take in the ramshackle boat and the teetering pile of poor peoples' crap. "Seriously?"

"What are you carrying and where are you taking it?"

The captain scratches his arse again and seems genuinely confused. "We carry everything, anywhere on the lake. From El Ramla to Tushka. Slow but cheap." He pauses as the penny drops. "You're not from around here, are you?"

Amr turns to Ragab. "Keep an eye on this lot while we search." Mazan takes my lead and shoves me towards the first line of parcels.

You'd think that against a backdrop of such a myriad of smells even my doggy nose would be useless, but that's not how it works. It's like looking at a crowd but suddenly, somehow, you recognise a familiar face. Amongst all the other hair and eyes and eyebrows and noses and mouths, one person suddenly stands out as though waving at you. In any case, natural and man-made smells are so far apart I can focus easily on the latter.

Nothing in the first row of parcels stands out. The ship is quite narrow but nevertheless most of the parcels are buried under and amongst others. I stick my nose between the parcels trying to huff up signals from deep inside the stack. "Good dog," says Mazan appreciatively and he starts to pull parcels aside so I can get my head in further.

With little room it's a difficult business and Mazan is soon sweating with the effort as we work our way down the port side. Amr follows behind, readjusting the disturbed parcels so they're more stable. It's amazing nothing falls into the lake. If it did, I don't see anyone on this boat jumping in to get it back.

I smell tea, then lemons. Mazan pulls aside another bag and now there's room for me to leap up onto the sacks and probe further in. There's something sugar-sweet and then the bitterness of tamarind. I smell paper, then perfume, then the musk of many women. Someone has filled a parcel with their used clothing. Enough of a disguise, a human might think, to turn a dog's mind to other things. But humans think wrong, for the smell of the gun-demons cuts through it like an arrow through air.

I give a low growl and bite at the plastic wrapping. Mazan raises a hand and whistles. At the bow I can imagine Ragab taking a firmer grip on his gun.

Amr squeezes past me and pulls out the package. Standing upright, he tosses it forward then edges along the side of the deck until he can grab it again and fling it even further forward. He repeats this until the package is lying at the feet of the crew by the wheelhouse.

Amr kneels and fingers a note taped to the side. "Name and delivery address. Take a note!" he says to Mazan who kneels down beside him and gets out a pen and his notebook.

Amr takes a knife from his pocket and starts to cut. The package has many layers and I suspect pilfering must be a big problem on a boat like this; it would be a hell of a job to repack it to make it look like it hadn't been opened.

The Nubians look more curious than tense, though already their interest is drifting. One goes to light a cigarette but Ragab holds out a hand, palm forward. "Confuses the dog," he says. It's not true but it helps him establish his authority.

Amr recoils a little when he realises he is handling unwashed women's underwear. He paws these delicately aside and finds some more substantial fabric and lifts it up. It's a light blue dress, delicate and off both shoulders to reveal the armpits and possibly even yielding a hint of the top of the breasts. Delicately embroidered flowers sweep down from the neck almost to the hem.

"Walidah would love that," muses Mazan thoughtfully, though nowhere near thoughtfully enough. The sun may be near its zenith but the temperature on the boat plummets. Ragab swings slowly to face Mazan. He's been cradling the gun in his arms and the muzzle swings with him. I back out of the line of fire.

Mazan has that did I really say that out loud look. I'm willing him to say something, anything that would defuse this situation. It's tough enough being a dog without your handlers going to war with each other.

However, words fail the dunce and he looks back down at the package, trying to pretend it's business as usual. The heel of Ragab's palm slams against his shoulder and spins him back round, but then Amr gets back up and pushes Ragab's gun muzzle aside so it's threatening only Lake Nasser. He cups Ragab's chin in the palm of his hand and squeezes so even Ragab's thin cheeks swell up around his fingers. "Later!" Amr hisses.

The Nubians don't know what the fuck is going on but they do know that three heavily armed and deeply upset men are on their boat. They shuffle back as far as the little foredeck will allow.

Amr is looking from Ragab to Mazan and back again. Mazan isn't looking at anyone so Amr snaps his fingers to get his attention. "Search!" he says.

Mazan stoops and fumbles around in the underwear. A look of nausea comes to Ragab's face. Amr, reaching back, puts a hand on Ragab's gun barrel.

Mazan, feeling away, hesitates then frowns. He digs more firmly and comes up with a pistol. It's black but the surface is scored and rusting metal shows through.

The three policemen turn their heads to look at the captain, whose day has taken a very sharp downturn. Lightning is sparking between my handlers and needs somewhere to strike.

"In the name of Allah, I didn't put that there." He points to the mound of packages swamping the deck. "I don't know what's in all those things. I just carry them from one place to another. Like the postal service except on water."

Amr nods his head, a font of understanding. "So, you're not a terrorist, you simply aid and abet them."

The look of woe on the captain's face is comical. In the old days the actors had to slather themselves in makeup to get that exaggerated effect.

"Turn around! Put your hands behind your back!"

Soon all three are immobilised with little plastic bands wrapped tightly round their wrists. There then follows an exchange between gritted teeth which reveals that none of my handlers are confident about steering this ship to the nearest port. They don't even know where that is anyway.

Annoyed, Amr cuts the captain's plastic band and gestures to the wheelhouse. "Keep an eye on him!" he tells Mazan. The glass in the wheelhouse is reflecting the sun so Mazan and the captain disappear from view. Ragab turns and steps to the edge, feet apart, gazing out over the lake. The engine starts and the boat turns in a long, slow arc.

Ancient Days 2554 BC

"*I love you so much*, my King!" I felt Peseshet's arm around my neck as I looked out over the Giza plateau in the early morning sun, my eyes drawn inevitably to Khufu's pyramid. Even I had to admit its gleaming limestone splendour was as close to the sublime as you can get in this life.

An unworthy thought crept like a thief into my mind. Perhaps I could burn Khufu's mummy as kindling and use the pyramid as my own tomb.

Tempting, but I had to cast that thought aside. The people of Egypt would never tolerate such an outrage. As time had passed the hard lines defining Khufu's life had softened in their memories.

"What are you thinking of, my love?" Peseshet, arm still on my neck, swung around until her eyes filled mine.

"Nothing, my dear," I said. I stroked her cheek and kissed her, the taste of her mouth so fresh and pure I felt ashamed for the troubling thoughts that tugged at the corners of my mind on sleepless nights.

I turned my gaze to the site of the new temple of healing I had ordered built as a gift for Peseshet. It was further down the incline leading away from the pyramid. Its stone was warm and brown and behind it rippled the blue waters of the Nile. Khufu had excavated a long canal so the boats could bring the stones for his pyramid from the river. Now that same canal would bring the sick to the Temple of Healing.

Peseshet turned to follow my gaze. "It looks so beautiful. Nobody has ever given a woman a greater gift."

"Or one so expensive," I said, unable to disguise my querulous tone. This was as rebellious as I got, for I found I was unable to resist her wishes since she had become my queen.

"We want it to last forever, Great Khafre. Like other temples but for once worthy of the effort and expense."

I raised my eyebrows in admonishment. We may have both felt this but it was rash to state it.

She smiled impishly, so confident now of her power over me.

Marble and sandstone are expensive and the population had started to grumble. They'd grumble even more when they found that Peseshet had plans for many more such buildings all along the Nile.

The physician priests had resisted her entreaties to help support this new enterprise. Many still regarded her new methods as heresy but took pains to keep this to themselves as Neferhotep and his web of spies now worked for me. They also did not like the precedent of spending so much money on places for the living, rather than on the gods or the dead. They feared the gods would be offended.

Peseshet had been forced to train others, unqualified in the ancient ways of medicine. When wine had loosened her tongue, she was wont to say the priests would have been useless anyway. She was discarding old ideas like a snake sheds its skin.

With priests and populace troubled by Peseshet's new ideas, she was not well liked and Neferhotep said his spies had heard the word 'witchcraft' on many lips. But for my protection and support she might have been stoned to death long since.

"Come, my love, our first patients await." She led me by the hand from our vantage point below the pyramid. I waved away the slaves who rushed to cover our heads with their parasols, Ra's light and heat still being benign so early in the morning. Below us was the muscled back of the Sphinx and resting on it was the gold and lapis blue of its headdress. As we walked down the side, the full lips and wide nostrils forming my brutal, rather bullish features came into view. The golden heads of eagle and serpent jutted out over my forehead while below my chin was a long blue beard and the crossed flail and crook. Once again, I found myself cursing the conceit that had led me to instruct the builders to faithfully reproduce my features. Too late I realised I should have looked prettier for the ages.

The Sphinx had been Peseshet's idea. She wanted it to represent me as a man-lion, the Father and Guardian of the new medicine. The new Temple of Healing nestled at its front paws.

"By Maat, I'm an ugly bastard," I said.

Peseshet smiled and her hand tightened on mine. "I could love you no more if you were the most handsome man in Egypt. Do you love me, my King?" She stopped suddenly to face me so I had to halt as well.

"Of course, how can you doubt it?"

"Because you still go with your other women."

I sighed. "You mean my other wives. I wish you would stop this, my love. We've been through this so often. I have… responsibilities. Diplomacy, alliances, succession, you know what I must do."

Her eyes were wide, almost frightened, for this was difficult ground but Peseshet was never one to falter when she wanted something. "You already have seventeen children, my King. You also have two brothers who you could marry to your wives and so perform your royal 'duties' in your stead. You do not need to consort with them at all."

"Peseshet, my dear, please be content. I have after all named you my First Wife, something unheard of in a woman who has not yet produced issue."

A tear fell from her eye and I felt my heart melt away like candle wax in an oven. "What is wrong?" I asked anxiously.

"I had meant to wait… it is still too early and much can go wrong, barely two full moons since my blood last came, but I have been yearning to tell you."

In that instant I felt many things. Fear for her was foremost. Childbirth was always difficult and she would not have the one person I would trust to attend her - Peseshet herself. I felt pride that this wonderful woman had consented to bear a child with me (Khufu must be turning in his grave as it was supposed to be the other way around). I also felt intense interest at what the child would be like and found myself hoping it would be like her and not like me.

So, I felt a wealth of emotion yet also a nagging sense of something else I did not expect and so could not at first identify. It was only later that I realised it had been a touch of fear.

I took her in my arms. "My prayers have been answered. But you must rest. I will take you back to the palace, keep you cool, feed you myself."

She laughed, as I had hoped. "I am not missing the opening day of my new temple. There is no need to treat me like a child to be protected, my King. If I have to lift anything, I'll get my helpers to do it.

As she pulled away and I followed her eager steps, I began to smell the Nile after the dustiness of the plateau.

Little boats bobbed on it gently, the first of the sick having arrived soon after first light.

I had missed my work with Peseshet. It had stopped once I became King. I could no longer leave the palace without an armed guard the size of a town.

However, this new Temple of Healing was well-guarded and the patients thoroughly searched for weapons. I could walk freely around it, albeit with five bodyguards staying closer than my shadow.

Many patients, no matter how sick, had been too frightened to come on this first day. It was known that I would be attending. The people believed I was a god and they feared me, feared me more than anything else except death itself. I saw it in their eyes sometimes when they gave me looks of both terror and adulation. I could understand how, over time, that could have turned my dear old father Khufu into the monster that he became.

Peseshet's helpers had winnowed out the patients even further by sending back all but the most seriously ill. On this first day there were but three patients. A child with a broken leg, a man with a grapefruit-sized abscess on one leg and a woman whose womb was protruding from her vagina. They looked at me with eyes so wide I could see the whites all around them.

Tadukhipa, her medicines now spread on gilt tables rather than on the reed mats of a tavern floor, awaited instructions. One of Peseshet's helpers was already setting the broken leg and binding it to bamboo splints. Draining the abscess would hardly tax my wife's skills so I was not surprised when she paid all her attention to the woman.

"Milk of the poppy, Tadukhipa!" she commanded. Then she turned to me. "If it pleases you, My Lord, you might administer the milk, but first I have a surprise for you. There is a new medicine I have found that I will use here for the first time. You could administer this with the Fang, if you so wished."

Peseshet was always working on something so I was not surprised but I was, as ever, intrigued. I led her away out of the patient's earshot and asked her to explain.

Yet again, the enthusiasm that was always so attractive burned fiercely in her eyes. "I must make stitches within the woman. Sending her to sleep is not enough, as you know, my Lord. Though the milk of the poppy brings sleep it does not still movement. I cannot have the patient move while I stitch deep inside her. We must relax her completely and also make the muscles of her abdomen and vagina loose, to allow me room to work."

I had seen many of her surgeries and could attest to the movements the unconscious could make, like dreamers walking in their sleep. "This new medicine of yours which does these things, where did you learn of it?"

She smiled. "I had heard tales of a tribe far south of the Great Cataract that used medicine from a local root as a final resort when a baby would not allow itself to leave the womb. It paralyses, for a while at least, but gives enough time for the midwife to reach in and pull the baby out. I must warn you, my Lord, that on administration the woman will void… well, everything."

Childbirth was never unsoiled and it no longer concerned me. "The root, how did you get it and where exactly did it come from?"

"From the foothills of Mountains of the Moon. Its name means loosening in the local dialect but I will not try to pronounce it. As to how I got it, I simply placed a reward on its supply, some good land in the Delta that belonged to…"

I held up a hand, not keen to hear Hapiwer's name.

"It was enough to send some of our more adventurous traders deep into Africa to find it. One returned with a sack of the dried root." She took my hand and led me over to Tadukhipa's table. Picking up a small pot, she said. "Crushing the root in water is all that is required. I have experimented on many dogs first, of course. It was just as well because, like the milk of the poppy, too high a dose can still the breath."

I looked into the pot and was surprised at how clear the fluid was and could easily make out some residue spread across the bottom. "Don't draw up the sediment!" she said. "Just the clear fluid above it."

"How much?" I asked.

We both walked across to another table on which the array of bladders rested. Up to now the Fang had been used only with the milk of the poppy and bladders ranged from a cat's for a child, to a small dog's for a full-grown man. The new, even smaller bladders already had their thorns attached, each sewn up carefully where the upper end of the thorn entered. She chose one and handed it to me. "Remember, my love…"

"Fill it fully, yes, yes, I know. Before or after the milk of the poppy?"

"After would be kinder to the patient. Being paralysed but fully conscious would be alarming."

Peseshet went away to the side room where the attendants had taken the man with the abscess. I squeezed out all air from a mid-sized bladder then filled it with poppy milk and took it over to the woman. She looked up at me, frozen with such fear that the root from the Mountains of the Moon seemed unnecessary. She opened her mouth to say something but then thought much better of it. She winced when I stuck the thorn into a vein in her upper arm but dared not make a sound. When I withdrew the thorn, the milk had mixed with the blood, and it appeared as the faintest of pink globules on the puncture site.

The milk worked quickly and her eyes had started to flutter even as I set the Fang aside. By the time I was back with the smaller bladder full of the crushed root, she was already unconscious and breathing heavily. I inserted the thorn further down the vein and carefully squeezed in the clear new fluid. Though already unconscious, I swear I could see her entire body slump as though the flesh had been made more liquid.

I was about to turn away when something caught my eye. On the puncture site, the colourless liquid had done little to diminish the colour of the bright globule of blood. It lay there like a little red pearl and, when I realised what this meant, it destroyed my happiness forever.

Modern Day

The trapped air, wet and fuggy with sweat and farts, presses in. Hemmed in by Nile brick, like countless generations before them, my handlers pass an uncomfortable night, as do I. The room is tiny and bare but for their thin bed-rolls and the dog blanket I'm lying on.

Too many police and soldiers are being moved to Aswan and there's nowhere for them all to stay and certainly nowhere with enough kennels for dogs like me. I'm guessing this used to be a storage hut just inside the wire of this big military base. My nose tells me it held bags of soil and fertiliser for the little green islands of vegetation that dot the base. I've seen older soldiers watering these and tending the flowers and shrubs that grow there. Perhaps these simple tended gardens are a reminder of what the desert troops are fighting for.

Now the little hut is full of three men and a dog who are all supposed to be asleep. I listen to their breathing, slow and regular, but they can't fool doggy ears. Now and again I catch Ragab's suppressed sniffles and flinch every time he stirs. Sometimes he just has to move, turning in his pretend sleep but with a violence that hastens my heartbeat.

Mazan and Amr too are wide awake. Mazan fearing for his life, Amr fearing for Mazan. 'Later' had not come, the confrontation delayed, hanging like a sword over Mazan's head.

I'd overheard Ragab's conversation with his wife on his votive device. I think these things scare me even more than the metal birds. Do they hold little demons skilled in mimicry? Demons that fly from one device to the other relaying messages?

Ragab had left me in the hut, too ashamed to have even a dog listen. Nevertheless, what he said was still within my sharpened hearing.

"... but how does he know what you like? You only met him once!"

He'd got the thing pressed too hard to his ear for enough sound to leak out. He didn't speak for a while and I guessed Walidah was not making it easy for him.

"How can you call me that?" His voice was high, peevish, wronged. "You are the one who is..."

Fuck me, I thought. Go out, steal a car, drive back to Cairo and slit her fucking throat, you wimp!

I couldn't hear what she was saying but I could hear her outraged whine like a fly caught under a cup. She definitely wasn't going down without a fight.

"No, no, it's not like that. I'm not being paranoid and suspicious. OK, maybe, just maybe, it's something anyone might have said but it's the way he said it. He..." But again she was off. Ragab was soft as clay and, as I listened, Walidah moulded him into a pot into which she could piss.

This devil-relayed conversation had kept up for a long time and perhaps had helped suppress his concerns in the light of day. Now, however, it was only a few hours past midnight and doubts and worries and fears have come crawling out of the shadows and are stirring Ragab's roiling pit of hate and shame.

Something is welling up from the depths of that pit because Ragab's control of his breathing falters. I hear the rustle of a hand over cotton and fingers fumbling at something. There's a very faint thud which I struggle to place, then more rustling.

Amr hasn't been dumb enough to leave either of them armed while they sleep. He's taken their pistols and assault rifles and is keeping them by his side, safely between him and the wall. So, it isn't a gun Ragab is...

His pen-knife! He keeps it in his breast pocket and the cushioned thud has been the button popping. I strain my ears and, sure enough, I hear metal slowly being pulled across metal. He's opening it!

Watching these clowns kill each other would be entertaining but what would happen to me then? My behaviour being so exemplary, these guys treat me better than any other dog could hope for. It has taken time but they appreciate that I don't bark my stupid head off and they appreciate that I'm better toilet-trained than they are themselves. I make their life easy and in return they make my life as easy as it can be.

If I have to begin again with other policemen it would be a different story. For a start, the arseholes would spend weeks kicking me around to establish they were the bosses. Like all men in power they'd take out their frustrations on the powerless like me. Their screeching wives, their ungrateful wailing children, their brutish superiors, all of them breaking their balls day after day. Dogs were made to absorb all that anger.

It had taken an eternity of making hopeless, innocent wide eyes at Amr, Mazan and Ragab to get them to stop doing that to me. I couldn't face breaking in another bunch.

Ragab is turning over on his mattress and I hear him begin to pull off the cover. Mazan's tender throat is no more than a metre away from the knife. Ragab is so wound up he forgets to breath.

I bark.

"What is it, boy?" asks Amr.

I hear Ragab pull the cover back over himself and gently slide the blade back into the handle of his knife.

We're not at our best when the morning comes. Amr has been making Ragab drive the truck everywhere so his hands are always occupied. Inevitably, of course, Ragab has lost the keys. The men hunt around for an eternity until they find them behind a coffee cup.

Ragab and Mazan are surrounded by invisible shields that prevent them getting too close.

Amr, a man of regular habits but now determinedly costive, gets Ragab in the driver's seat and Mazan in the back with me before risking going for his morning dump.

All this tension is getting to me and one part of me begins to wish these idiots would just get it over with, even if one winds up dead and the other in jail.

Amr comes back, his steps lighter, and gets in the front with Ragab. Dawn is painting the sky red (probably). The truck starts up and I'm alone with Mazan. He starts to talk to me, as my handlers invariably do once we're alone. It strikes me that they are all lonely men who have thoughts they are too scared to voice.

"I wonder what happened to those poor bastards we arrested yesterday on that boat. I feel sorry for them. They'll have a tough enough time with the local cops, but if those anti-terrorism boys really do take an interest…"

So far so boring, but then Mazan completely changes tack. "I don't even like her that much." He pats my head. "In fact, I don't like any woman that much in... in that way."

Up to now Mazan's relationship with me has been purely professional: him policeman, me dog. Now what am I? A priest?

For an army base, the road leading to it is pretty run down. We crunch over the potholes and ruts. He scratches me behind the ear, always a winner with me, though his heart clearly isn't in it.

"It's like... it's like I have something to prove. Other men's wives. This isn't the first time, may Allah forgive me."

He leans forward to whisper in my ear. The engine is loud, the vehicle is rattling with every bounce. Even if I, with my magic ears, had been in the front with the others I still wouldn't have been able to hear him no matter if he shouted. This must be bad.

"I even tried it on with Amr's wife. She didn't want to know and, Allah be praised, she never told him."

Yup, that's a bad one alright. Lovely woman though she is, Amr's wife is no catch and must be at least twenty years older than Mazan. Whatever's driving this idiot, it's got little or nothing to do with sex.

"And I hate myself for it. Ragab's a nice chap. Why am I doing this?"

There's a delightful silence as he shuts the fuck up for a while, but then, "I blame my father, Cheops, I blame him for everything." There is both so much wrong and so much right with that sentence that my mind reels. I wish I could tune out what the fool is saying but, with such fierce hearing, that's not something you can do as a dog when the guy is right next to you. I pretend to look at the desert, tongue out, wishing I were deaf.

"He left one day. Didn't say a word. Just walked out and never came back. My mother told me the secret police took him but that has to be bullshit. Guy never had a political thought in his life, probably didn't even know who Hosni Mubarak was. No, I reckon he just got fed up with us."

From what I've overheard in previous conversations I think that Mubarak was the pharaoh who came before Sisi, but I'm not totally sure. The only thing I'm totally sure of is that I don't care for all this mewling.

"So, I was brought up by only a woman and four sisters." His voice is rising. "So is it any wonder I turned out like this?"

His Kalashnikov is lying on the bed of the truck. I've been around these things long enough to have an idea how they work. Could I use my teeth to draw back the slide, aim the gun and hook a paw into the trigger? Unleash the demons and blow this idiot into a red mist?

No chance. A dog's forelegs just aren't designed for that level of coordination. I whimper in frustration.

"Thanks, Cheops. You're the only one I can speak to." Since when? I see a hint of moisture form in the corner of his eye and I turn away in disgust.

The smell of a lot of water is suddenly strong and I realise with surprise how far we must have travelled while Mazan was singing me his sad songs. Lake Nasser lies as calm and serene as my father used to be when he had the might of an army to back up his every decision. To the left I can see the dam and, further upriver, some docks we haven't been to before. On them are man-height mounds of carefully stacked white sacks. A little vehicle with long arms held down low drives into one of these mounds. Its arms lift and it pulls back, now cradling some sacks. It backs and turns until it is facing the water and the single boat pulled up at the dock. The boat is bigger and higher in the water than the little loose cargo vessel we stopped yesterday. A broad gangway has been laid down from the deck to the dock. The little vehicle charges up this and adds to the piles of sacks on the deck.

The road we're on now is much better and it takes a slow incline down to the dock. We're still a long way away but already I'm aware of the rising smell. It's not natural and is very bitter.

Further out into the desert, a chain-link fence surrounds the dock on three sides. We stop at the gate and two policemen with guns give us the once-over. Amr sticks his head out of the window. He takes out his wallet and displays his magic piece of paper. "Detection Dog Unit," he says.

One of the local policemen comes forward and takes the paper. He looks nonplussed but I'm guessing even a hangnail would be a challenge to comprehend. "Detection Dog Unit," he says with great perspicacity.

"Uh huh," says Amr. "One of our units will be on every boat that leaves here from now on, or for the foreseeable future anyway."

Both Mazan and the local man look equally puzzled. Perhaps annoyed by the behaviour of his men, Amr hasn't been forthcoming about our latest orders. "Is this news to you?" Amr asks the local cop.

"Wait a minute!" says the other policeman and retreats into a little hut by the gate, leaving his sidekick to stare at us dully.

After a minute or so the first one returns. "The Detection Dog Unit, from Cairo," he says, like he's on top of everything.

I'd thought my handlers were the lowest of the low, but a whole sub-stratum of incompetent police is now revealed.

"So, what are you looking for exactly?"

Amr sighs. "You see all this fertiliser. Ammonium nitrate. Mix it with fuel and it becomes a massive bomb."

The copper blinks. This is clearly a revelation, though he's been guarding this facility since God-knows-when. "Right..." he says in a rising inflection that is begging for more.

"The dam," says Amr a little irritably. "The ship becomes a floating bomb, it blows up and breaches the dam and everyone in Egypt gets their feet wet."

I've underestimated the local man because he shakes his head firmly. "Bullshit!" he says. "Have you any idea how thick that dam is? Take all your pyramids, Mr. Cairo, and multiply them by ten or more, and you still wouldn't be able to make a wall that thick."

Amr doesn't respond well to having his lectures returned to sender. "You need to get on the phone!" he says urgently. "Demand to speak to Hamid Abdallah. He's the Director of the National Security Agency, as I'm sure you know. Tell him that in your considered hydrological opinion that boats carrying fertiliser all over Lake Nasser constitute not the slightest threat to the Dam. Please!" He points at the hut. "We'll wait."

The copper bends down a little, puts his hands on the window sill of the car and leans in to take a closer look at Amr. "Tell me honestly, mate. Is everyone from Cairo such a cunt?"

It could go either way but Amr can't help but laugh. The copper grins and signals to his guy to open the gate. "Have a nice trip."

"Seriously?" says Amr. "You really didn't know about fertiliser bombs?"

"Fuck off," says the man as we ease forward through the gate.

Ragab parks next to a couple of beaten-up vehicles and we all disembark. The men collect their overnight bags. Amr between the other two, we all head along the dock. The smell of this fertiliser stuff they were talking about fills my nose like the sun fills your eyes if you stare at it. It's nearly as sore as well.

A tall man, not so dark as the Nubians, is standing beside the gangway directing the little truck back and forth. His white hair is cut to within a finger's width of the scalp. The hair is so thick it makes him look like he's wearing a helmet. As we approach, Amr pulls out his card again. "Detection Dog Unit."

The tall man gives a reluctant nod. "Yes, we were told."

"You don't seem pleased to see us."

"I'd be pleased if you could train your dogs to use the lake rather than shit all over the deck. I'd be pleased if you brought your own food rather than eating ours. This isn't a hotel."

Amr casts a weary eye over the rust and the peeling paint, the smears left by oily hands all over the superstructure, and nods wisely. "You may be right there."

The man picks a votive device out of his pocket. I notice two fingers on his left hand are missing and it makes him a little clumsy. "Let me get someone to show you to your room," he says icily, then starts talking into the thing.

"How long are we on this rust-bucket?" Ragab asks Amr.

"They don't exactly run to a timetable but it sails all the way down to Wadi Halfa which is about three hundred kilometres. We're doing two round trips so... oh, I don't fucking know." Amr has never been good at arithmetic.

"I look at this boat and the word speedy doesn't spring to mind," says Mazan.

Another man comes down the gangway. He's broad-shouldered but a little on the short side. He wears dingy oil-stained trousers and his filthy baseball cap has flames licking back from the brim. He has a beard but it's well-trimmed and it looks strange in someone so sloppily dressed. His eyes are so dark brown they are almost black.

The tall man indicates Amr. "Hamid, take them to the captain!" Then he goes back to supervising the little two-armed vehicle without a word. We are dismissed.

Without a word Hamid turns back up the gangway and makes a beckoning gesture over his shoulder.

The gangway is metal and has warmed in the sun; it burns my paws. We are led past the reeking bags of fertiliser to the blocky metal hut at the bow. We enter through the wheelhouse where a man in a dish-dash and keffiyeh is sitting smoking.

"This is Captain Al-Amin," says Hamid, though I imagine even Ragab has worked that out. Amr steps forward, hand outstretched. "Sorry to trouble you, Captain, but orders are orders."

The captain's head goes back a trifle in surprise, but Amr's unexpected display of charm seems to work. A grudging smile comes to his lips and he shakes the proffered hand. "We all have our orders," he admits. "I am afraid the accommodation I can offer you is..." He shrugs as his words tail off but we all know what he means. There will be no slave girls to smooth our pillows and help idle away our evenings.

"I am Corporal Amr Negem." They shake hands in their formal, grave, masculine way. Serious men doing serious business. As if!

Amr's tone is almost mild. "Your itinerary, Captain? Just to Wadi Halfa and back, is that correct?"

The captain takes a drag on his cigarette. With my nose, I cannot help but be a connoisseur of Egyptian cigarettes but I don't recognise this one. "No, I have just received new instructions from the owner." He points to a votive device resting precariously on the sloping panel from which the steering wheel protrudes. "We are stopping at the inlet that will one day lead to Toshka New City. There are many farms up there."

"Ah yes, where they are digging the second Nile. How's that going?"

The captain shrugs. "It is a city in the middle of the desert. Nobody wants to live there."

Amr is clearly disappointed. He's a big Sisi supporter and this second Nile is an idea that clearly ignites his imagination.

"Come!" says the captain, struggling off his high chair which squeaks as it pivots, "I will show you where you will sleep."

There is a curtain at the back of the wheelhouse which the captain pulls aside to reveal a rectangle of blackness exuding the smells of dirty clothes and rotting food. He fumbles for a switch and the interior is revealed as a single foetid room with a curtain that can be pulled to cut off one half from the other. On one side are three thin mattresses, on the other there is a single bed-roll, a stove and a big plastic drum which I'm guessing is where they keep their water.

"You can have my cabin," says the captain grandly, pointing to the half with the single bed-roll.

"Where will you sleep? We do not want to cause you too much inconvenience." This is something I've noticed before. Amr will say just about anything to his men and most everyone else, but if someone has even a hint of rank, even the captain on this rust-bucket, then suddenly he gets rather stately.

"Don't worry, Corporal. I will sleep in the engine room at the stern. It is something I have often considered doing anyway. My crew are not quiet sleepers. Did you bring bed-rolls?"

Amr nods. "Yes, back in the truck." I hadn't noticed any bed-rolls and I'm a little surprised at myself. The drama of last night and my lack of sleep must be making me less watchful.

The hell with this! I lie down and close my eyes. Dogs can do this and not be considered rude.

"He's settling in already," says the captain. "What's his name?"

"Cheops."

"Ah, the Great Pharaoh. Wait, isn't this the dog that..."

"Yes, this is the hero." I can hear the pride in Amr's voice and am surprised at the warm feeling bathing my heart.

"We are honoured. Fetch your stuff, leave Cheops here. I'll look after him."

I hear my handlers bumbling off the boat and crack open my eyes. Al-Amin is regarding me frankly but his face is immobile and I cannot tell what he is thinking. He sits back on his high chair and lights another cigarette.

Another man appears, wiping his hands on a rag. His brow is unusually narrow, making him appear ill-developed and stupid but there is the light of intelligence in his intense brown eyes.

"Well?" he asks in a deep, husky voice. He's a stocky man and his fingers are thick but he is wiping them delicately on the cloth.

Al-Amin shrugs. "We could have done without this. We'll just have to adapt. Is it sealed?"

"Welded tighter than a mosquito's arsehole."

There's silence for a while. "Unclean creature though it is, that's a good-looking dog," says the man.

"Better looking than you, certainly," says the captain, and they laugh.

Ancient Days 2554 BC

Like a patient thief who had waited for a moonless night, I made my way silently through the darkness of the garden. Sometimes, when the manicured trees hemmed me in and hid me from all light, I had to feel my way along the sides of the water fountains. Occasionally, from between the leaves of the trees, lights from the other royal palaces, like constellations in the night sky, gave me some vague sense of where I was. Slowly, falteringly, I made my way to the long marble balustrade which overlooked the Nile and the farmlands beyond.

An urgent whisper brought me to a halt. "You are making too much noise, my King." It was Dedifer, the only bodyguard I was reasonably sure I could trust. Dedifer's piety was sometimes unsettling, especially coming from such a bloodthirsty ex-soldier. The change had taken place overnight when I ascended to the throne and, sometimes, I would catch his looks of disapproval at something ungodlike I had done. I'd cemented his loyalty, such as it was, with gold enough to gild a pyramid.

I followed the direction of his voice and, sure enough, it brought me to a bower enclosed by palms and grapevines and supported by columns that were decorated with images of animals and poppies and roses. A bench strewn with comfortable cushions allowed one to sit here or make love in privacy.

A sigh escaped me, for this was a favourite spot of Peseshet and myself, a place where we had made love under the stars, the gods looking down in approval.

Or so I'd thought.

A figure rose from the bench and I reached out a hand to grasp Dedifer's sinewy forearm. Gently he led me to the bench and sat me down.

"All is ready, my King," he whispered urgently. "My brother has placed a ladder against the wall below. High Priest Shadra awaits."

"Bring him up!"

Dedifer slipped away and I heard a faint whistle then creaking and grunting. Though there were only one or two pinpricks of light from the many acres of farmland before me, it was enough to make out a darker patch of blackness rising from the wall.

"Good Selquet ease my way!" I heard the High Priest murmur as he struggled over the parapet with Dedifer's help. He was making enough noise to wake the dead, never mind my household. I heard Dedifer hushing him as respectfully as he could.

Their combined shapes staggered towards me like a monster, Shadra's deep breathing sounding like the work of the creature's mighty lungs.

"There is a guard beyond this grove who patrols along the wall," whispered Dedifer. "With your permission, my King, I will go and engage him in conversation. If I cannot prevent him making his rounds then I will cough loudly. You would see his torch approaching anyway. Take shelter under the bench. He will not see you."

"Go!"

The blackness that was Dedifer moved away. Shadra was still standing, no doubt perplexed and worried.

"My Lord..." he began.

"Sit down and be quiet, please."

He did as he was told. I could not make out his features in the darkness but we had met before. Several years ago, I had worshipped at his temple of Selquet, goddess of venomous bites and stings. He was a small man but running to fat, and the climb up the ladder would hardly have been something he was accustomed to. I imagined his soft brown eyes struggling to make me out in the gloom.

"The truth is I need your advice."

"Of course, my Lord, but why...?"

"The secrecy? Because I can't trust anybody. It is not a question of who is a spy in my palace but, rather, who isn't."

"Spies?" He sounded so genuinely surprised I could have kissed him on his naive old cheek.

"Don't trouble yourself about that, High Priest. I have summoned you here to ask you questions. You will answer, you will go, and then you will forget and never speak of this to anyone. Do you understand?"

"Are these questions of a religious or medical nature, my Lord?"

"Medical."

He hesitated. "But, my Lord, you are married to..."

"Yes, the greatest physician in the Kingdom. She must never know of this visit. That is on pain of your death, I'm afraid, High Priest."

I heard him swallow. "I will tell nobody, I swear on Selquet's honour." Selquet was traditionally shown wearing a deathstalker scorpion as a crown. She was the god who kept the snake-demon Apep in check. Taking her name, especially if you were her high priest, counted for something even in my cynical world.

My fears and suspicions had first appeared only obliquely in the shadow world of dreams. They came as undefined feelings of unease. As time passed this unease transferred to my waking moments, forcing me to seek their cause. I began to remember things I had carelessly cast aside. Then I had seen the blood pearl on the patient, so similar to the one I had seen on Djedefre's corpse. We had previously only used the Fang to administer opium, at least that's what I had thought, so the globule of blood that formed over the puncture site was milky. Now I realised that if the drug was colourless then that globule of leaking blood would look red.

Fears you have kept to yourself lest a careless comment seal your fate are not easy to reveal, however obliquely. Could I really trust Shadra? Neferhotep's tentacles were everywhere. How long would I last if he or Peseshet ever found out?

On the other hand, if I couldn't ascertain what was really going on, then how much longer would I survive? Peseshet was with child, its umbilicus a strangler's chord tightening around my neck.

The silence stretched but Shadra was either too respectful or too afraid to disturb it. In the cold of the night the stars were hard, remorseless points of light, the eyes of a million gods looking down. Either I was quite mad or my life was in grave danger. If the latter, I was sure the good physician beside me held the answer to a conundrum that had slowly but ineluctably clouded out the sunbeams of my loving thoughts.

"I want to talk to you about death."

"Osiris can guide you far more effectively than a humble priest such as myself, my Lord."

That Osiris, or indeed any god, would talk to me was as likely as me conversing with a mosquito but, of course, neither Shadra nor anyone else could be allowed to know that. Bad harvests and angry Egyptians were already a terrible combination and they would hardly react well to being ruled by a god who was a sham.

"Think of this as a test, High Priest."

Genius! I thought to myself. Tables suddenly turned, old Shadra would not want to be found wanting by a god.

"A man is healthy," I continued. "He's old but lean and fit. Vital, in fact. Highly sexually active, swives anything in sight."

I was aware that Shadra had stopped breathing heavily, his mind now occupied with wherever I was going with this. "But this man suddenly sickens and he becomes drowsy, his eyelids droop and he struggles for breath and dies within the hour. What has killed him?"

"Had he offended the gods?" asked Shadra tentatively, concerned that one wrong comment could bring about his own death.

"Let's assume for a minute that the gods are not involved."

"Had he been bitten by a snake or an insect?"

I sat back on the bench, holding my knee in cupped hands. "There were no obvious marks on his body, though there was something odd, whether significant or not. His stomach and intestine were black, as were their contents. This was revealed during mummification. You perform such preparations, don't you, High Priest?"

"Of course, my Lord. In truth that is how so many physicians make a living."

"So, you know what the undiseased stomach and intestine should look like."

He sighed. "Oh, indeed."

I waited, but my patience is short. "Well?"

He sighed again. "I assume you summoned me because of my expertise with the bites and stings of insects and snakes. Indeed, the deterioration you describe is reminiscent of the bite of a cobra but the lack of bite marks, the swelling and discolouration of which would have been evident, mandates against that. However..."

My patience had found its limit. "We don't have all night, Priest."

"Indeed, my apologies. What you describe of the stomach and its contents are indeed not normal. The stomach lining sounds as though it has been insulted. It has bled and the blood has coagulated after death. The blackness of the stomach and intestine indicate they had, in effect, died even before the patient. There is no single disease that can do all that. However, perhaps I can provide a theory but without close inspection of the stomach, a theory is all it can ever remain. I fear in some way I cannot anticipate that I may appear disrespectful."

"These are simply hypothetical questions. You may answer this and subsequent questions purely hypothetically without fear and with a clear conscience."

"Subsequent questions?" said Shadra faintly, perhaps realising he was sailing over the Great Cataract in a papyrus boat.

"You were saying about your best theory," I reminded him.

Another sigh. "Cobra venom makes the area round the bite go black but, of course, it could not bite inside the stomach unless the serpent was swallowed. However, the venom can be milked from the snake and smeared on sharp objects. If swallowed, these can lacerate the insides and..."

"The man who died would not have swallowed anything sharp. He was not stupid."

"The objects need be but tiny. If placed in food, they could be eaten unawares."

"What sort of objects?"

"Tiny fragments of bamboo, perhaps. In fact, in Djoser's time this was an entertaining means of execution. Starve a prisoner then give him a feast in which slivers of bamboo had been secreted. The prisoner wolfs it down, the bamboo lacerates his insides and he bleeds to death internally over the following days but yet not a scratch appears on his body. However, if the spines are dipped in poison that would kill, and much more quickly."

It was a neat explanation but it didn't account for why Khufu's food tasters had not suffered the same fate. They ate everything the King did, though four hours beforehand. Surely they too would have sickened and died by then?

"Another question. A woman, old but in good health, dies suddenly. There has been vomiting. Her legs are so contorted as though she died in pain. This spasm has happened at or just before death."

"Was there a bite mark, my King?"

"I don't know. I didn't… one was not searched for."

"These are conundrums Your Majesty is setting before me, though I am at a loss to understand why you are testing me in such a way. Perhaps you are trying to trick me. What you describe sounds like henbane poisoning. It is a popular drug that produces sensations of flight, amongst other things, but it strikes back in just the way you describe if abused."

I gave him a few seconds before continuing. "Another man dies. Like the woman his limbs are arranged as though in spasm, but unlike hers they cannot be unlocked. The joints have to be smashed so he can be laid out straight. His mouth is full of saliva. What was the cause of his death? This man had perhaps been bitten by something."

"It could be henbane poisoning again but such severe locking of the limbs... that is very reminiscent of the bites of certain snakes, of a water snake or of a black mamba."

Who knows how long I sat in silence, thinking. Eventually Shadra summoned up the nerve to clear his throat. We had been in the dark so long that I could almost make out his features, though I had to imagine the brow wrinkled with concern.

"You may leave me now," I said.

"May I ask... did I... were my answers correct?"

I shook my head, breathing out heavily. "Not entirely, but they were sufficient. Go!"

My thoughts, all-consuming as they were, were interrupted by Shadra's struggles down the ladder. He was an old man but, as it turned out, he would not get much older. Before the following evening he would be found in the cobra pit at his own temple, the snakes wrapped almost lovingly around his chilling body.

Maat looked down on me. Five times the height of a man, the goddess wore a red dress that left her small breasts bared. Two jade-coloured wings appeared from her back and swept round to be attached to her wrists with green bands. In one hand the ankh, in the other a long thin sceptre that denoted her power. Maat's temple was open-aired and the sun gleamed off the golden ostrich feather she wore in her luxuriant black hair.

High thick walls surrounded the temple and made the sounds of Memphis seem so far away it was as if they came from a different world.

More easily heard were Neferhotep's steps as he made his way towards me. He was in no hurry.

Mid-morning and the sun was not yet at its full height so the heat was bearable. I drank in the yellow light, wondering if this day would be my last.

I turned away from Maat and watched Neferhotep approach. Our bodyguards had been left at the main gate and I had instructed the priests to wait with them. The High Lord and I needed privacy and I had chosen this temple in the hope that the presence of the Goddess of Justice and Order would stir whatever vestigial conscience he might retain.

Perhaps it worked, for Neferhotep's hawk-like eyes went from me to the statue and back again. His tongue licked teeth worn to stumps over a long lifetime. He put his hands together and bowed his head almost penitently. "I have answered your summons, my King," he said.

I waited, letting his discomfort build, then opened my mouth to bring forth my words of full god-king majesty.

He quickly held up a finger before I could say anything. I blinked in surprise as he stepped up to the statue of Maat, lifted his tunic to reveal a penis rather less mighty than I would have expected, and pissed all over Maat's feet.

I stood astonished. The silence I had been exploiting now betrayed me for it brought to me every splash and tinkling drop of Neferhotep's water. I don't know what was worse, the shock of seeing the proud, dignified, lordly Neferhotep pissing so wantonly, or dismay at seeing the God of Justice desecrated in such an off-hand manner. It took an effort to close my mouth that had fallen fully open.

Still pissing, he turned to look at me. "Did you seriously think I would not hear of your meeting with Shadra? Sometimes, Khafre, you disappoint me."

So, I was no longer King or even Prince, Lordship or Highness. It seemed certain now that my life would go down with the setting sun.

"Address me as your King!" Even to my own ears this command was as substantial as gossamer.

He nodded his head. "I would gladly do that, Khafre, were you but to act like one."

He lowered his kilt and stepped back. I noticed that his impressively wide pool was already beginning to evaporate.

"I am your god!"

He shook his head. "My cock is mightier than your godhood and, I have to confess, it hasn't managed to stand erect in years."

This conversation was so at odds with what I'd expected, that I began to suspect I was dreaming. I actually pinched myself but it made no difference.

Keeping his sandals clear of the water, he leaned against Maat's statue. I could tell he was revelling in his blasphemy. "It's time to talk, Khafre. Properly for once."

"I don't understand."

"To begin with, you're not a god. You never were and you never will be. The thing I find so engaging about you is that you know this perfectly well yourself. Even your father Khufu knew he wasn't a god, the first time he beseeched Horus in his temple and the god gave fuck all by way of response. But, over the long years of being worshipped and pandered to, even Khufu was beguiled by the siren song of his godhood. Weak little Djedefre lasted barely two years before his empty head was turned."

He stopped, his eyebrows raised, as though politely waiting for me to interject, but I was too lost.

"So that's why I had Peseshet kill them," he intoned, like a teacher schooling a child by rote. Then, more gently, still like a teacher, but one now trying to tease a response out of a shy child, "That's why you summoned me here, is it not? To accuse me of these things."

Wrong-footed and comprehensively bettered, words were still not forthcoming and all I could manage was a few startled blinks.

Neferhotep nodded as though he had understood what I hadn't said. "Perhaps you want to know how I anticipated this. Well, between you and me, Shadra will be going into the Field of Reeds in a rather damaged condition. He was very forthcoming about your conversation."

My curiosity finally won the day and brought my tongue back to life. "Why would Peseshet murder my father?"

He shrugged. "Khufu started the war that killed most of her family. Simple revenge but from a very complex woman. You may have loved her, Khafre, but you had no notion of just how remarkable she was. Growing up as an orphan in the wine merchant's household she had been indiscreet about her feelings. Word got back to me and, though many years passed, I did not forget. When she became a priest, I had her arrested. She thought I would have her executed but I had other plans. Khufu was going slowly mad, spilling the blood of countless Egyptians in foreign wars and bankrupting the Kingdom with his endless temples and his absurd pyramid. It was a simple thing to bring her into the household as Royal Physician. When the time was right, she gave him the poison as medicine. That was the only thing that the royal poison tasters need not try first, Peseshet being so well trusted by then. She is a good physician, is she not?"

"But why poor Djedefre and his mother? They didn't start any wars."

Perhaps the movement of his lips was to show a smile but, if so, it was as dry as the desert. "Over the years Peseshet and I have come to an understanding for it turns out we both want the same things, more or less. We both want the people of Egypt to flourish. We don't want them to squander their resources building useless things to propitiate gods..." and he indicated Maat with a snap of his fingers, "... who exist only in their dreams."

I was finally getting angry. "What in Seth's name do you care about the people of Egypt? How many years has it been since you even talked to one?"

The Lord High Treasurer crossed his arms. "Being lectured to on consorting with the poor is priceless coming from a coddled princeling such as yourself. Have you ever talked to a pauper?"

"I'm not claiming to be their saviour."

"Neither am I but I do care about them. Khufu with his wars never did. He didn't care how many of our soldiers were killed, how many families were plunged into grief. Just as long as his foreign wars brought booty. The same with Djedefre, eventually. He had designs on the lands at the Eastern end of the Great Green, for he wanted a pyramid even grander than Khufu's. Silly little man. He was taking so much medicine for his many illnesses that it was easy for Peseshet to poison him. With the promise of a cure for his scrofula, he was more than ready to submit to that dreadful Fang device of hers and whatever exotic new poison she had discovered."

"Meritities wasn't silly. Why kill her?"

He gave a dry laugh. "Indeed, for unlike Khufu and Djedefre she thought she was a god from the beginning, or at least she acted like one. I couldn't have her as regent for she bent to nobody's will but her own. Her love of henbane made her unpredictable and completely ungovernable. She didn't even know the poor existed. All it required was a simple overdose which she took willingly."

This was getting painful in ways I had not anticipated. "So, after Djedefre, you needed someone whose will you could bend."

Neferhotep held both arms up towards me. "Your puppy-dog attachment to Peseshet, though you denied it to yourself, was a gift from the gods, were they to exist. Between Peseshet and myself we could get you to do whatever we wished. Hapiwer was an obstacle but easy to get rid of. Did you really not suspect he was innocent?"

I realised that over the years Peseshet and Neferhotep had slowly but inexorably wrapped me in their web. What could I do to escape? I could shout for the soldiers and bodyguards waiting at the entrance and demand that Neferhotep be executed on the spot. I was a god-king and I could do as I wanted. But, once the soldiers rushed in, who would they kill? Dedifer was the only one I thought I could trust but he would be outnumbered. Then again, how had Neferhotep got to hear of my meeting with Shadra? It could only have been from Dedifer or his brother.

I was, once again, a prisoner in a gilded cage. I couldn't keep the leaden dullness out of my voice. "Now what?"

Neferhotep shrugged. "Nothing. You know the truth but this changes nothing. However, there is one matter we both must deal with, for our lives depend on it."

Modern Day

*I doze fitfully for severa*l hours as men bumble in and out of the cabin. My handlers return and lay down their bed-rolls and the crew wander in for tea. Apart from the captain and Saffir, there are two others. Their names are Ghannan and Totah, who was the one on the gangway. All the men are watchful but then this is a culture, not unlike my own, where people are unafraid to stare frankly.

You'd think I had a second head by the way they look at me.

Ghannan is soft-spoken with fine regular features betrayed by a lag when the left side of his face moves. His left eye never seems to entirely close and the line of his mouth on that side only approximately reflects what the other half is doing. He seems too young to have had a stroke so perhaps he was born with this problem.

All the men have a lightness of skin that indicates they have little or no Nubian blood, yet the lake is within the old boundaries of Nubia. That they are smuggling something is beyond doubt. These southern regions are too hot and dry and I imagine growing kief must be almost impossible, so smuggling it will likely make up a lucrative part of their trade. For the inhabitants of the lifeless desert city they have been talking about, I imagine it must be a blessing.

The noxious fertiliser is still being loaded but at least my nose is becoming used to it so other smells are starting to come through. Ghannan smells of kief, Totah of unwashed clothes. I'm happy to leave the cabin as Ragab leads me on a tour of the ship, Saffir following behind.

The fertiliser sacks are stacked taller than a man and I can feel the boat tilt as the little two-armed vehicle continues with the loading. The lake has made the Nile balloon out to swallow the whole river valley but then has spread out to cover flat desert. The edges of this new inland sea must be as shallow as the Nile in summer and so the draught of this boat cannot be deep. With all the sacks stacked on the deck and forming a wall, I'm worried that even a gust of wind will overturn the boat.

We walk down the narrow space left all around the edge of the deck. We go down the side facing the lake so we don't get squished by the loading vehicle. A gentle and very welcome breeze is ruffling the water. Come the evening the breeze will reverse, bringing hot desert air and it will not be so pleasant.

The boat has two metal huts fore and aft and I've been on enough of these modern boats now to realise that the engine will be in the one at the back. The door to the engine room doesn't just have the handle that lets you into the wheelhouse, but also metal wheel that has to be rotated before the door can be opened.

Ragab looks surprised as Saffir swings the heavy door open. "That's pretty solid," he says.

Annoyance flickers across Saffir's face, probably too fast for Ragab to catch. "It's for fire. If the engine goes up, we can cut off the air, starve the flames."

We enter the blessed cool of the engine room, though when the engine is running, I know it won't be so pleasant.

The place stinks of oil and rust. Tools lie scattered everywhere. A small chugging motor is at the rear and to the left.

Ragab, too stupid to realise he's revealing his stupidity, says: "So that's the engine? It's a bit small."

Saffir frowns. "That's the bilge pump. The engine is below the waterline."

"Show me!"

"I was. Give me time!" Saffir bends and hauls back some metal deck plates and reveals the engine: a blackened bulky beast, a filth-caked hippo squatting in a metal hole. Pipes and cables lead from this, diving into bulkheads and back towards the bow.

"Even this seems very small for such a big boat," says Ragab.

Saffir frowns. "How fast do you think this thing travels? I hope you're not in a rush."

"And where's the fuel?"

Saffir leans into the well where the engine lurks and slaps his hand against the forward bulkhead. There's a *wwomm* sound and then a leaden echo. "It's full, as you can hear. We've just bunkered."

Ragab leans down, pushing aside the AK so it doesn't poke him in the ribs. He slaps the bulkhead to the right of the engine and the sound is louder, the echo sharper. "So, what's behind here?"

"Nothing. Nothing but air. Below decks is just air, apart from the engine and the fuel tank. It's what keeps us afloat." Saffir picks up a rag and starts to wipe his hands.

I can't believe a metal boat like this would float at all. I never paid much attention to what my boat builders said, though they built me several sublime wooden solar boats for my journeys with the sun. Bow-shaped in outline, they were beautiful, each with a smooth single thirty man-lengths of arc lifting the prow and stern out of the water. I doubt that any boat since has looked more elegant.

The trouble is I never believed that even they would actually float. The priests assured me that they would sail with the solar wind through azure heavens and maybe they were right, but try to sail them on the Nile and I'm guessing you'd get wet. Big-time as Ragab often says.

My handler's thought processes are slow but sometimes he gets there. "How do you get into the under-deck?"

"There are a couple of hatches in the deck but they get covered with cargo. There's no need to go down there anyway."

"Suppose there's a leak. Suppose you hit a rock or something." Ragab's brain is working overtime today. Lack of sleep and hatred of a colleague seems to have gingered him up.

"All boats leak, that's why we have bilge pumps. If it's too much for the pump to cope with then you steer to the side and run her aground. Then you fix the leak."

Sailor's bullshit or not, Ragab's mind has moved onto other things. "What time are we leaving?"

"Dawn tomorrow," says Saffir, bending to re-seat the engine plates.

"Tomorrow?"

Saffir looks up at him. "Is this your first time on a boat?"

Ragab stiffens a little. "Of course not. I have done countless trips on Nile cruisers."

"Even on the Nile nobody sails at night, though there are a few lights along the water's edge to give you some idea where the hell you are. On the lake all we are surrounded by is desert. No lights. We travel by day from one mooring spot to another. Sometimes there are little villages or, more usually, just a jetty. By the time we finish loading today it will be too late to reach the first one before dusk."

Ragab nods. He probably stopped paying attention after the first sentence. "Are you married?"

"Yes," says Saffir, but in a way which conveys a reluctance to pursue this further. Not that it matters for Ragab isn't listening.

"I too am married," he says. "She's beautiful. We love each other very much."

Saffir nods his head politely.

Ragab sighs. "But sometimes couples... it is not always easy."

From the look on his face, Saffir intuits that he has wandered into a world of pain and wants none of it. "Have you finished, can I shut this place up? I have to lock it down tight because those damned Nubians nick all our tools."

Ragab looks at me and I look at him. With all the fertiliser and oil, I doubt I could smell anything anyway. I don't give my signal bark.

"Yeah, let's go." He looks at me again. "May as well give you the run of the ship." He bends and unclips me. I follow him out of the engine hut and into the brutal sunlight.

The more I walk on the ship the more confident I get. The little clear space along the edges of the deck doesn't seem quite so precarious now. Even distracted by his own personal grief, Ragab strides along it easily.

We lift the curtain in the wheelhouse and, for a second, all inside freeze. Mazan is unrolling a third bedroll, an act of kindness which he finds suddenly embarrassing. He swiftly shuffles over until he's on his own thin mattress. Amr has been tinkering with the little stove and hands Ragab a coffee. Ghannan and Totah are lounging against the far wall, both reading books.

"Everything OK?" asks Amr.

Ragab nods. "Did you know we weren't leaving until tomorrow? We didn't have to come here today."

"Wrong! These boats are to be guarded all the time. In port, between ports. This boat has just been recommissioned. It's been out of action for repairs so it hasn't needed a guard until now."

"What repairs?" asks Mazan idly.

Four bulbs hang from cables taped around the room near the ceiling so the light is good and the changes to the crewmen's expressions are stark, to me anyway. Though they quickly hide it, neither of them is happy with this question.

Totah shrugs. "It's an old boat. Engine, steering linkages, you name it."

Amr sips at his coffee. "Three eight-hour shifts," he says. Mazan you first until eight. You, Ragab, eight 'til four tomorrow morning, then me."

"Cheops?" asks Ragab.

"If there was anything on here, he'd have told us by now. We only need to bring him into play when someone or something new comes on board. Where's the fuel stopcock?"

Ragab looks away quickly.

Ghannan sits forward in the uncomfortable silence. "Aft, port side, just forward of the engine room. There's a plate on the deck you can remove."

"Familiarise yourself with it! Keep an eye on it!" says Amr to his men then glances at Ghannan. "When do you next bunker?"

"Not for a week at least."

"OK, so nobody should be doing anything with it until then. Mazan, your watch starts now so off you go!"

Mazan puts on his blue policeman's baseball cap and heads out into the sun. I can hear him clomping down the deck to the stern.

Somehow, I doze off in the muggy little cabin and am only awakened when Mazan comes clomping back. He pulls back the curtain but, instead of letting in harsh sunlight, he is framed only by blackness. Ragab and Amr have also been asleep for they are sighing and massaging their brows.

Doggy intestinal tracts aren't the same as humans. This may be too much information, but the truth is that humans can get quite a bit of notice when they need attention, with dogs not so much. I give my little 'I really need a shit' whimper.

Mazan beckons me out of the cabin and grandly sweeps his arm around, offering all of Egypt for me to dump in except for the boat. Gratefully, I brush past his legs, lope back along the deck's edge then down the gangplank and ashore. The whole enclosure round the dock seems deserted, though there is some activity at the entrance. Two of the guards are talking to each other by the gates that are closed and barred.

On the opposite side of the enclosure to the gates, and almost backing onto the fence, I find a pile of ripped fertiliser sacks that have been rejected. They are spilling their bitter contents so the smell is very sharp and bring tears to my eyes, but at least behind them I have some privacy. I do my business. Again, doggy guts are different and I have to arch my back as though in agony to force out the ordure. Osiris knows I've crapped in front of servants often enough before but these wracking, grotesque contortions I have to go through now make me so much more self-conscious.

I lope back. Normally there'd be all sorts of smells I'd want to investigate but the eye-stinging whiff of the fertiliser has erased them.

The captain and Ghannan are standing ashore by the gangplank. They're looking towards the gate and haven't noticed me approach.

"Four against six," Ghannan is saying. "That's not good."

I slow down and stop, not wanting to alert them.

"It is all about timing," says the captain.

"So what..." Ghannan has turned to face the Captain and sees me. He points in my direction. "Seven," he says.

"Ah yes. Come here boy!" The captain bends down, rubbing his fingers together.

I know my part so I play along. I edge forward so he can stroke my head. Looking right into my eyes he says, "A man with a gun, or a dog with sharp teeth. Which do you take out first? That's tricky to prioritise."

Ghannan shakes his head. "Man with gun. Always."

"Maybe. The choice will be yours."

There are lights in the compound but because of the way the men are standing their faces are in shadow. There is something so serene about their voices it counteracts the menace and makes me wonder if I'm being paranoid. Could they be talking hypothetically to pass an idle hour?

"I will start, inshallah," says the captain, "and you will all follow." He shoos me back on board and, though I linger by the wheelhouse, they say nothing else and instead just stand there smoking.

Now would be a good time to be able to communicate my uncertainty to my handlers but that boat has long since sailed. Then again, if I'd ever tried to communicate in a way that spoke of real intelligence, I'd probably be pickled in a row of glass jars in some Cairo museum by now.

I hear Ragab's dry little cough from far aft which means they have changed shifts already. The desert air is blowing from land to sea now and I find myself panting hard.

I suppose I could bark my head off but what would that achieve? There'd be a shakedown sure enough- my handlers know I don't bark without a really good reason- but what would that achieve? Hurt aggrieved looks from the crew and embarrassment for my handlers at coming on so strong.

So, whatever the crew are up to they need to be caught in the act.

I lope back into the cabin, which is getting muggier and sweatier. I settle down to the right of the curtain which has been pulled back to let in some air. All I can do is wait.

Ancient Days 2554 BC

Peseshet lay beaten and helpless. Jailers were never gentle, especially to those who had fallen from grace, and Peseshet had fallen so very far. Her eyes, their makeup faded and smeared, looked up at me as she lay on the floor clutching her stomach.

I was staring down at her through the bars. Oil lamps on the wall behind me would be throwing me into shadow as far as she was concerned.

"This is your baby I am carrying, yet you let them beat me." She spoke with the same gentle tones whose magic, even now, tugged at my heart, but now they came freighted with disappointment and betrayal.

"Did you ever love me?" I found myself asking.

"I love you now!" She sounded so convincing but, then again, she always did.

It would have been easier never to have seen her again, to have allowed Neferhotep and his minions to finish her, but I was cursed with the need to understand.

"My father and my brother allowed you to administer your lethal 'medicines', while my step-mother allowed you to give her a surfeit of her precious henbane. In their different ways they trusted you enough to let you kill them. You would have killed me too and it would have been so easy for I too was so trusting. If you had offered me medicine, I would not have hesitated to take it. Killing Neferhotep would have been harder. He never trusted you."

She turned her head away. "Neferhotep is mad. A lifetime of palace intrigue has turned his mind. These are fantasies, my King. He has turned you against me for his own dark reasons."

"We gave you everything and you wanted for nothing. How could you turn on us?"

She got up painfully and came to place her hands on the cell bars so we were only a breath apart. "I did no such thing, my King."

I shook my head. "Tadukhipa and your servants lasted hardly at all under torture. They named the hunters who found you the snakes that furnished your poisons. When questioned, those gentlemen yielded the truth even without prompting for they had done nothing wrong. Neferhotep's men found the pits you kept the snakes in and the devices you used to restrain them as you extracted their venom. I went to see these with my own eyes. I saw the big fat viper you were no doubt going to use to dispatch me to the Field of Reeds."

As I spoke, I was conscious of the deadness of my own tone and the certainty it conveyed. There was other evidence, of payments to a slave in Neferhotep's kitchen in preparation for his poisoning. Either the heavy certainty in my voice or the beatings had their effect for she sat back down, cross-legged on the floor. For the first time ever, I saw her slump with weariness. "You are all monsters," she said.

"Khufu, Neferhotep and, yes, Meritities. But Djedefre? Me?"

Her eyes found mine and the look she gave was chilling. "You had my husband killed. So yes, you too are certainly a monster."

"He stole from a king's tomb. Justice had to be done."

"Hapiwer was no more a thief than you are a decent man."

I laughed at her effrontery. "And what of you? Dead or divorced, Hapiwer would have been discarded when he was of no further use. If I'm a monster then so are you."

"What is one man's life or happiness against fighting the evil that has poisoned Egypt for a thousand years and will, unless stopped, poison it for thousands more? A parasitic royal family bankrupting the country to indulge their every decadent whim. The nation always in debt so not enough grain can be put aside to see us through bad floods and to stop the children dying. The priesthood condemning any change, exiling any who bring forth new ideas. Treating the sick with nostrums which do not work, yet condemning treatments that do as blasphemy." She shook her head. "Beneath the grandeur of your dynasty there is nothing but rot."

"Egypt needs strong kings. Would you have been any better as a queen?"

"I would have surrendered my power to the people over time."

"The people? You're joking! What do they know about anything?"

"I would not have condemned them to a lifetime of ignorance as your family has. I would have set up schools, schools for learning, not for filling their heads with myths of non-existent gods."

Educating the common people! I had to laugh. I had not, up until that point, realised that Peseshet was mad. How had she kept this lunacy from me? I had loved talking to her, learning from her, yet all these crazy ideas had been carefully hidden. Every second of every day we had been together she had been deceiving me. That I had been so thoroughly taken in made my anger soar.

"I will see to it that your body is burned and cast to the winds. I swear by Osiris that you will never enter the Field of Reeds."

"There is no Field of Reeds, you royal fool."

I would have torn her limb from limb myself but found something worse to hurt her with. "Tadukhipa will be executed, all your servants and helpers will be executed, your writings will be burned. All records of your sacrilegious medical practices will be lost so your heresies will blow away with your ashes."

This brought her back to the bars. "If you do that then you will consign the world to the darkness of ignorance for thousands of years, perhaps forever if your cursed kind keep control. You will bring pain and suffering and unnecessary death to multitudes yet unborn. To destroy my work would be an act of unspeakable evil."

"Hah!" I snapped my fingers in her face. "I'm a monster, Peseshet. You said so yourself."

I had hurt and betrayed her as much as she had hurt and betrayed me. Laughing, I turned and left her to die.

My final dream is as indistinct as the memory of a long dead slave. Perhaps my mind was fading fast at that point or perhaps I just refused to remember.

I was on my deathbed. My aching, withered limbs were still, my breathing laboured. Every night as I slept, I felt a greater darkness falling upon me and I woke struggling to draw breath.

In my waking hours I found comfort in my old wives, especially Kham who had retained her sweet nature even with the heaviness of age and the cataracts that spread their milky poison over her eyes. Our son, Menkaure, was headstrong and sometimes, in my darker moments, he reminded me of Khufu and I felt the same coldness clutch my heart as when I had been a child. At other times the smile he gave me was all Kham's, revealing a kindness that neither Khufu nor I had ever possessed. I had named him as my successor.

In one way I relented about Peseshet. She was not dismembered and burned. Instead she lies in her own humble tomb amongst many others in a rock-strewn valley southeast of Minya, her unborn son extracted after her execution and laid by her side.

Neferhotep, aware of the fate she had planned for him, had been all too keen to have her killed. She had become too powerful, too quickly. She was my senior queen and all she was waiting for was to give birth. One nick of the clever little device she had used in her clinics to administer opium would have sent me to the Field of Reeds or, more likely, somewhere far less perfect.

Peseshet as Regent until our child came of age would not have maintained the stability that Neferhotep craved, quite the reverse. In any event, he had realised Peseshet was probably too clever for him. Once she became Regent, he knew he would not be able to control her. She had to die.

I razed her Temple of Healing and built a funerary temple for myself on its foundations. I had not executed the helpers she had trained but instead commanded their silence and solemn promises not to use her witchcraft on pain of death. After what I'd had done to Peseshet, they certainly paid attention.

It hardly mattered for I found out that Neferhotep had them executed anyway.

I had stayed my hand when it came to destroying the records of her work but one evening, after much drink and in a fit of spite, I made good my threat. I watched her work burn and laughed as I did so. I regretted this later but by then it was too late.

Afterward, I lapsed back into my old ways, drowning my sorrow in drink and the flesh of women. Meanwhile, Neferhotep ran the kingdom. Two bad years of harvests, perhaps the punishment of the gods for my actions, were followed by ten good years and the kingdom flourished. We started no wars, we made peace with the Nubians.

Though plunder no longer filled our coffers, sending half the army back to work in the fields produced its own wealth. Success brought its problems: demands for more public buildings, more temples, dredging of stretches of the Nile, expeditions against the bandits that preyed on the trade caravans from the south and east. Though Neferhotep and I had no hunger for building any more temples we could not refuse them all without angering a populace keen to influence fate by propitiating the gods.

All this took its toll on Neferhotep who was already in his fifties when I came to the throne. The work hollowed him out. One day, during a particularly fractious dispute among merchants, when the High Lord was giving his final tetchy judgement, he had suddenly clasped his upper left arm with his right hand, roared in agony, and had pitched forward dead on the marble floor.

Neferhotep had been the one solid presence there all my life yet it transpired that even he could die. For me there followed long nights of the soul. The deaths of Peseshet and my unborn son lay at my door. If the gods did exist then my sins were evident. I knew I would be found wanting in the Temple of Judgement when I faced the dying of the light.

And so, belatedly, over the coming years, I began to make amends.

I built funerary temples dedicated to my brother and mother and even to my father. I had Neferhotep's tomb desecrated and his mummy burned. I expunged all records of Neferhotep's rule as Lord High Treasurer, just as I had Peseshet's records as Queen. I named Nefermatt, a decent and kind man, to manage Egypt.

Where I had been thoughtless, now I was considerate. Would it be enough to save my soul?

Just in case, I began to build my pyramid and, to my credit, the people of Egypt seemed by and large to approve, though more because of the ten good harvests than from any affection for me. They wanted me in death to continue to intercede with the gods on their behalf, to keep the grain growing so the young could thrive.

Are you listening, Maat? Not everyone thought I was bad.

So, I built a pyramid at Giza. Weakness made me make it seem taller than my father's but my new-found piety insisted it be less than half the cost. Building on higher ground than Khufu's pyramid squared this circle and eased my heart about the expense.

My death when it came was unpleasant but commonplace. I can recall what happened next, some of it anyway. I had fallen asleep but never awoke. Instead I found myself in an underground hall that was somehow arched higher than all the stars. Before me lay the Scales of Justice. These were small enough to hold in the hand but big enough to balance worlds. The scales, in short, were everything, and in one of its pans lay my blackened heart. Even without holding it I could sense its terrible weight for it warped the light around it, pulling it down into its Stygian depths.

Maat, the Goddess of Truth and Justice, stood tall and proud. Carefully, raising one green-winged arm, she plucked the feather from her headdress and let it fall. With its unbearable lightness it took an eternity to settle in the empty pan. The scales moved not a jot.

My dismay turned to fear for I sensed something else with us, something slithering in and out of the shadows, a huge serpent whose jaw was open to reveal an inky-black mouth.

I hastily begin to intone:

I have done no falsehood
I have not robbed
I have not been rapacious
I have not stolen
I have not killed men
I have...

But the last words were lost as the mamba lanced from the shadows, thrusting its way into my mouth, blocking my throat and worming its way deep within me. The last thing I remember is the serpent curling up in the space left by my blackened heart.

Modern Day

Maat, I do understand now! Destroying Peseshet's work was a very bad thing. Even doggy medicine nowadays involves the use of something definitely reminiscent of her 'fang'. The vet has stuck me in the bottom with it often enough. Also, the stuff invariably makes me feel better even though I'm pretty sure no dung, from whatever animal, is involved.

The really surprising thing is that that's the quality of treatment I get and I'm just a mutt. Imagine the medicine they must use for people! That there are so many old people about shows just how incredibly effective it must be. By suppressing knowledge of Peseshet's first faltering steps towards this sort of medicine, how long did I delay its advance? I hope it was by only a few years before another Peseshet came along to show the way. I'd hate to think I delayed these developments by over four thousand years, because then countless lives would have been sorely affected.

If I really did delay it that long then my crime might be the worst ever. Easily bad enough to merit the punishment of being confined within a dog's body.

I contemplate my last dispiriting doggy dream of ancient days as the hours pass and the moon slides across the sky. I watch its progress through the wheelhouse window. From my place at the side of the doorway I am looking out onto the blackness of Lake Nasser and the desert beyond. I imagine the myriad stars shining down, as unconcerned for me now as they were forty-five centuries ago.

Ghannan comes in quietly and shakes the shoulders of Totah and Saffir. Both have been sleeping so soundly I have come to believe they can't have been plotting anything, that somehow, I have misunderstood.

Saffir and Ghannan slip out quietly, Totah lagging behind. His foot catches on the side of his bedroll and knocks over a cup.

"Mmph," says Amr and sits upright after a bit of a struggle against his paunch. "What's happening?"

"It has been a long night for poor Ragab. I will take him a coffee," Totah whispers. Mazan is still dead to the world.

"That's very kind of you," says Amr, as big a fool as ever. He settles back down.

A small torch clicks on in Totah's hand and he goes to the little table and turns on the kettle. As he finally stirs in the sugar, I can hear Amr's snores. Taking the coffee cup, Totah disappears quickly.

I crawl forward, out of the cabin, across the wheelhouse and look around the side and back down the length of the boat. The four crewmen are clustered by the gangplank, what looks like a couple of opened fertiliser sacks at their feet. Even as I catch sight of them, they split up. The captain and Ghannan walk towards the gates, Totah heads aft and Saffir turns and heads back to the wheelhouse.

I quickly crawl backwards and into the cabin and to the side of the doorway. Do I alert my handlers now or is it too early? In my weakness and hesitation, I give a low growl.

"What's up, boy?" I hear Amr say, his tongue heavy from sleep.

I growl again and I can just make out Amr shake his head and reach out to wake Mazan. With his other hand Amr is reaching for his AK.

A blast of light whites out my vision and I shrink back. The crash and hot gases of a gunshot smack me like a slap across the face. My vision clears enough so I can see a hand holding a pistol sticking through the doorway. It fires again and I hear the bullet slap into something soft.

The gun jerks to the left and fires just as Mazan rears up, AK in hand. The assault rifle roars, full auto, as Mazan falls back. His bullets shatter the wheelhouse windows, then the rising burst strikes the metal wall and ceiling of the cabin, filling it with sparks and whizzing bullets like angry bees.

Far away I can hear other guns firing: quick pistol shots, two bursts of automatic gunfire then many more pistol shots.

Meanwhile Saffir has staggered back, the pistol falling from his grasp. He starts fumbling in his pocket.

I've been frozen in fear, the sounds too loud and bowel-loosening. Even as I will myself to move, Saffir has found what he was looking for and has brought the grenade to his mouth. I launch myself forward but already Saffir is tossing the thing just as my teeth close over his thigh and I bite as hard as I have ever bitten.

Saffir, roaring in pain, crashes down on top of me then falls to the side. I scrabble upright and start running, all the way through the wheelhouse and onto the deck. I start to leap just as a deafening blast punches deep into my body, lifting me up and sending me tumbling over the water and down onto the hard concrete of the jetty.

Stunned, unable to breath, I barely manage to crawl away to the cover of the fertiliser sacks where I collapse, struggling for air.

"Saffir! Totah!" I hear the captain shouting. There are three more gunshots, widely spaced, achingly deliberate. I know then that the three guards at the gate are surely dead.

"Oh shit!" I hear Ghannan yell. "The boat's on fire!"

I have to shift my position so I can see. Sure enough, the grenade has started a fire and flames are licking out of the cabin. All the windows of the wheelhouse have been blown from their frames. I can make out Saffir lying, head back against the wheel cabinet. He's not moving even though the flames are biting at his ankles.

A tickling sensation makes me look down to my right. Either one of Mazan's angry ricocheting bees, or fragments from Saffir's grenade, has caught me in the side. It doesn't hurt, not yet anyway, but blood is trickling down into the dust.

I should wait here until the men and boat are gone. Wait for the port workers to come back tomorrow. The police will take care of me, life will go on.

Better still, I could creep along the fence to where it meets the lake, jump in, swim along until I can find somewhere to scramble out. Then I'd be free. I could make my way back to the Nile below the dam. Live off rats and cats and fruit. Be really free for the first time in both my lives.

Except there may be no rats or cats or fruit, or men or women or children. If the paranoid idea of breaching the dam isn't a fantasy, then everything will be washed away and all I'll have to eat are the rotting corpses of the dead.

In the end, neither option is attractive. The truth is, I'm sick of being a dog. Would oblivion be any worse?

I lope along the fence, following it round on all three of the desert sides. Sacks and vehicles and huts hide my progress from Ghannan and the captain who are in any case too busy fighting the fire. They've found buckets and are racing up and down the gangway, filling them from the lake.

I pass the gate. To my right a body lies sprawled in the dust. The door to the guard hut is open and light shines out but there are no sounds from within.

I get to the lake. I'm about twenty man-lengths from the stern of the boat. There's not much cover but the two men are too busy scurrying back and forth at the bow to spot me. Ghannan, younger, is faster than the captain at scooping up the water, running up the gangplank and into the wheelhouse. I wait until their cycles synchronise, and both are running back up the gangway at the same time, then I sprint along the dock. The stern is higher than the dock by about an arm's length but that's nothing for me now. I launch myself up and quickly get behind the engine house so they can't see me.

Two bodies lie at my feet. Ragab's eyes are wide open. His AK, its strap round his neck, lies across his body. He has been shot twice in the chest. There is little blood and I remember from my days with Peseshet that this shows he has died quickly.

Totah is lying back on the deck, his head hanging over the side of the boat. A burst from the AK has caved his chest in. Being a dog, and despite everything that has happened, I can't help sniffing at the corpses.

Something, perhaps a last belated flickering of intelligence, had warned Ragab that something was coming. The Gods sometimes helps even fools. They must have fired at the same time, killing each other almost instantly.

I hear grunting then a clang. I peer around the sacks on the jetty side and see that the two men have heaved the gangway back onto the dock. One moves forward while one comes back towards me. They're going for the mooring lines. These are quickly cast off and both men return to the wheelhouse. No flickering light from flames bathes them so they must have put the fire out.

We drift away from the dock. Straining my ears lest one of the men sneaks up on me from the other side of the boat, I almost jump out of my skin when they start the engine. There's a bang, then another, before it settles down into asthmatic chugging. The boat swings to the left and keeps on going until we're pointing downriver.

And that pretty much says it all. If this had been a smuggling operation we'd have been going upriver, smuggling guns or whatever into the heart of Africa. Instead we're heading towards the dam so Amr's tale is true. For whatever foul, convoluted reason, these people are intent on destroying my homeland.

That has to be why I'm here. All my suffering, all my humiliation, has been to bring me to this point. A single dog against two armed men with the fate of a nation hanging in the balance.

Why me? How many god-kings have there been? From some of Amr's lectures I know there have been at least twenty dynasties so there must have been hundreds of us.

Why should this fall on my shoulders?

Ghannan comes out of the wheelhouse and starts walking aft towards me. I'm about to retreat when he stops mid-way along and starts dragging the fertiliser sacks off the top of the pile and heaving them overboard. They make a big splash but have sunk even before the slow-moving boat has left them behind.

It's hard work and Ghannan has to stop every now and then to catch his breath. These intervals take longer and longer and soon he is bending down each time, holding his hands to his hips.

The lights of the jetty have disappeared far astern, but now the lights of the dam have appeared. We move out closer to mid-stream to avoid the looming mass of an island to port. It is peppered with lights.

Ghannan has halted for a rest but now, instead of pulling at more sacks, he starts walking down the deck towards me. I'm about to bolt to the other side of the boat but he stops again. He heaves more sacks overboard.

Ragab's conversation with Saffir comes back to me. Ghannan must be uncovering the hatches to the under-deck: one that holds the sea-cocks for scuttling the ship and the other for the part of the ship that was supposed to contain air.

The engine cuts out but we continue to drift forward on the still waters. The captain appears out of the wheelhouse and comes back to join Ghannan. The latter has his back to me and I can see a pistol tucked into his waistband. The captain must have a gun too. Both are wearing military style webbing around their waists and I can see at least two grenades dangling from the captain's.

"How's it going?"

Ghannan stops and wipes his brow with the back of his wrist. "The hatch to the sea-cocks is exposed. Nearly there for the other."

The captain starts to help him, each alternately reaching in to the little valley they have made in the stack.

It's already been a tough night for them and they have to stop to rest after moving only a few sacks. "Do you really think this will work?" asks Ghannan between gasps.

"We've been through this a thousand times," says the captain, though not unkindly. "Of course it will work but we've got to sink the boat first, otherwise the blast just goes straight up and the dam is hardly damaged. If the nuke explodes underwater, the huge blast of steam pushes out the dam like rodding out a drain. Even if it doesn't it'll poison the whole damned river."

Ghannan shakes his head. "That's not the problem. What I mean is that you've got to survive the sinking so you can activate the bomb. Is this little chamber we've rigged up really watertight?"

The captain puts his hand on Ghannan's shoulder. "It's barely a hundred metres to the bottom. It won't take long to get there so it doesn't have to be completely airtight. I might be wet by then but as soon as I feel the boat hit bottom, I start the activation sequence, inshallah."

Ghannan is still not placated. "The misdirection... I worry it will not hold up."

The captain smiles. "I have never seen you like this before. Please my friend, the trail of breadcrumbs has been carefully laid all the way back to the Israelis. They will get the blame. With Egypt gone and Israel a pariah there will be a new dawn. Iran will be unchallenged. Surely that is worth giving our lives for?"

Ghannan lowers his head against the captain's chest and what he says is so muffled even I cannot hear it.

The captain claps him on the shoulder and points into the stack. "I'll finish here. You go and open the other hatch, check the handles on the sea-cocks are still loose enough to turn easily, then come back and seal me in. Finally, all you have to do is open the sea-cocks and pray as the ship is scuttled."

They awkwardly shuffle by each other and Ghannan heads forward while the captain steps into the declivity they have made.

I guess this is where I come in. I turn and pad to the other side of the boat and move along it to the middle. The stack of bags is nearly two metres high but I'm trained for high jumps. It's tricky, though, because the ledge between bags and the edge of the deck is cramped so my take-off is restricted.

I leap, fuck up, and have to scrabble with my claws, sacks ripping and eye-watering clouds of white fertiliser puffing out. I still don't get enough traction and I fall back, landing on my back legs and tipping backwards. Somehow, I manage to twist and land on my side rather than splashing down into the lake.

I get to my feet and leap again, bearing down on the top of the sacks with all the power in my front legs. For an instant I'm launched into the air, my enhanced peripheral vision allowing me to take in the boat's whole length.

I land as gently as I can then pad across the top of the sacks to where I estimate Ghannan has entered. Sure enough, I can see the tight valley they've made just ahead. I nose over the top and see a square metal plate has been pulled aside to reveal a black hole with light from a torch flickering around inside.

I leap down onto the deck and, crouching, risk peering into the hole. There's less room than I expected and Ghannan is having to crawl. I can just make out his legs and, ahead of him, illuminated by the circle of light from his torch, I can see what looks like two large shiny taps on very thick pipes. I'm guessing these must be the sea-cocks that he'll use to scuttle the boat once he's sealed the captain in. That the captain can't seal himself in suggests to me there is some concern he might chicken out when the ship starts to sink. This way he has no choice; he's going to die anyway so why not do what he's supposed to?

I drop down into the underdeck and start crawling towards Ghannan. He's already turning one of the little wheels that opens the tap. A spurt of water spits out and splashes to the deck. He closes the tap then gently opens the other one. Again, there's a small spurt of water.

By now I'm only a couple of metres away but I haven't worked out exactly what I'm going to do. I can bite the hell out of his legs but he would just pull out his gun and shoot me before I could do any real damage.

My only hope is to slide over him from behind, grab the gun in his waistband with my teeth and pull it away. Once it's clear, he and I can go at it in earnest. In this confined space I don't fancy his chances.

Just as I'm about to surge forward, he turns, shuffling his body round, bringing his face within inches of mine.

What else can I do? Twisting my head to the side I close my jaws on either side of his head and bite down as hard as I can. Even as my teeth sink through soft flesh, he jerks his head back and away, but I've got a good hold. His face comes away in my jaws.

He's brought the torch round with him when he'd turned so I'm not spared the sight. The skin and fat have been torn from his cheeks and nose and eyes leaving only the red corded muscle behind. Now without benefit of eyelids, two huge white globes stare at what is left of his face hanging from my jaws. He's so shocked he makes no noise at all.

Even so, one hand is scrabbling at his waistband. I dart forward again, this time my lower fangs closing on his right eye, my upper ones between his left eye and his ear. He freezes, just for a second, but enough for me to make the bite of my life. I feel my own muscles tear with the strain. I taste fatty liquid washing over my tongue, while my upper fangs crunch through the thin bone of his eye socket.

Again, I pull back, bringing with me muscle and bone and sloppy lumps of eye.

Though he will never see again, his fingers have found his gun and it's swinging round in a horizontal arc. These pistols hold a lot of bullets and there isn't much space in here. If he starts pulling the trigger, he's bound to get me.

With my doggy reflexes it's as easy as catching a thrown ball. My jaws crunch down on his wrist and the gun falls from his nerveless fingers, clumping to the deck.

"Ghannan! What's going on?"

If the captain traps me in here, I've had it. I shuffle round and crawl back to the open hatch. Behind me Ghannan finally starts to scream.

It's awkward getting back out of the hatch and all the time I can hear the Captain's boots clumping down the deck towards me. He'll have his gun drawn by now and if I try to race away down the edge of the deck, he's sure to get me.

I'm in the narrow space they've made in the sacks and facing out to the lake. I turn around and launch myself upward. "What the..." I hear the captain say as my forelegs land on the sacks. I feel my claws punching through the fabric, giving me traction, and I start racing across the sacks as I hear him hauling himself up behind me. There's a flash of light and a gunshot and a bullet whizzes by my ear. I'm charging across the sacks to the other side of the boat, hoping to jump down and seek cover, when I realise my mistake. I'm travelling too quickly, the lip of the deck is too narrow. At this speed I would fly right over the side. Stopping, carefully positioning myself so I could drop down onto the narrow lip would give the captain all the time in the world to shoot me.

I swerve to the right just as another bullet zips by. I lengthen my stride, aiming for the wheelhouse and the bridge wings which are at least clear of sacks and have railings. I can leap down at speed and the railings will stop me flying overboard into Lake Nasser.

But he's anticipated that and the next bullet goes through my ear even as I leap. My momentum carries me forward and my head goes between railings but the lower one catches me across my chest and legs.

All the air flees my lungs and I stumble back and shuffle round. I find myself staring stupidly at the blackened doorway leading into the cabin, even though the last thing I want to see is the macabre scene within.

Far away I hear the crunching sound of boots stumping across the fertiliser sacks. Whatever way I go now he'll have a good shot from his vantage point. Running down either side of the boat constrained by the narrow ledge will make me a too predictable target.

I feel so weary, so out of my depth. Then I hear him almost above me and I panic and run. Perhaps I can destroy this nuke. Maybe it's some sort of Chaos-summoning amulet I can easily crush between my teeth. I race across the bridge and back down the other side.

"Where are you, boy?" I hear behind me, then the sound of him running over the sacks again.

I run as fast as I can, past the hatch and Ghannan's screams. Just as I come to the other hatch, the crinkling sounds of boots on paper stop and I know he's taking aim.

He's been too deliberate and I manage to turn into the defile just as another gunshot rings out. The hatch here is more substantial than the other. It's thicker, with a complex arrangement of metal levers, presumably for sealing it. I poke my head under the deck level. The captain has left a lamp but all it reveals is a narrow crawl space at the end of which lies a brooding mass. The light reflects off the metal of its body.

My teeth aren't going to be much use against that. Meanwhile, the crunching boots are coming nearer. I pull my head back out of the hatch, go back on my hind legs then launch myself upwards as hard as I can.

I see the captain's eyes widen with surprise as I come shooting up onto the top of the sacks. He's barely five metres away, his gun hand outstretched before him. I close the distance in two leaps, jaws open, ready for the bite. He twists aside as my jaws close, my teeth clashing just to the side of his waist. I scrape by him, running for my life.

"You missed, you stupid fucking dog," he roars and I hear the gunshots and feel the bullets. My back legs stop working and I tumble end over end. I come to a halt, looking back towards him. There's more than enough moonlight to make out his triumphant smile.

"Bad dog! Time to put you down." I find myself staring into the barrel of his gun and I see the muscles in his wrist tense.

The explosion cuts him clean in two, his torso cartwheeling one way, his legs the other. A mighty gust of wind kicks me hard and shrapnel strikes me all down my side.

As the echoes die away, I spit out the pin of the grenade plus bits of my teeth. I'd closed my jaws so hard that even though my fangs slipped through the little circle of metal, my upper and lower teeth had smashed together, shattering some of them.

But that's the least of my problems. I'm surrounded by blood and it's all mine. I can't seem to catch my breath.

I sense a darkness falling over me and it has nothing to do with the night. This darkness is horribly familiar, memories of it coming back to me like fading echoes, hinting at other times, other bodies, other deaths.

How often has this happened? It must stop!

Horus, Atum, Isis, Tefnut, any of you. Isn't this enough? You put me in the body of a dog. A dog! You humiliated me, cast me down further than any human being has ever fallen. And I swear to you that I can see why you are punishing me. This is about Peseshet and her medicine. By suppressing it I have wilfully deprived multitudes of medicines that would have saved their lives or at least eased their pains. How many hundreds or even thousands of years passed before people rediscovered her methods? Years of needless suffering and early death across the whole wide world. That's why I'm here. Perhaps I've always known. I'm not a god, I'm just a man with all a man's weaknesses. And now I've given my life to save this nation. A multitude of lives saved. Surely that is enough? Can't you forgive me? Can't you release me at last?

I can feel my blackened heart still lying in Maat's Scales of Justice. To my relief I feel it lighten. The mamba coiled in the space left by my heart stirs. I listen expectantly for the beating wings of death.

There are noises but they are coming from the dam. More lights are appearing and I can hear motors starting on trucks and boats. They've heard or seen the gunshots.

Yet no other sounds trouble Lake Nasser. Neither Horus nor any of the others deign to address me. Ra does not smile down on me. Hathor does not enclose me in her motherly arms. I am still to die a lonely dog's death, shunned by the gods, my fate to be reborn to endless suffering.

My heart in Maat's scales has not lowered her feather even by the breadth of a hair.

I have saved almost all the souls in Egypt yet it is not enough.

What else can I possibly do?

I have no choice but to examine my conscience yet further.

My breathing is deeply laboured now and my vision flickers like the shadows cast by the fronds of a wind-whipped palm. I don't have much longer. There is no time left to only flirt with the truth. I know exactly what I have to do but that means prizing open a box I have kept tightly shut for thousands of years. It means shedding my last illusion that somewhere within my cynical, jealous nature there yet beats the heart of an honourable man. A man more sinned against than sinning.

The pain in my spirit is as great as that in my body and I find I do not have the strength to open that final box. Perhaps, instead, if I can make another confession.

The innocent child, the baby in Peseshet's womb. I am responsible for its death. I may as well have been the executioner who used his strangler's cord on my queen and deprived them both of life.

I can almost hear the gods snort in derision. This isn't the issue at all. As soon as Peseshet's plot to kill the God-King had been revealed, her death and that of the unborn baby was inevitable. Egyptian justice routinely meted out punishment to whole generations if but one of their forebears had been guilty of a crime.

I might have used my power to stop this, but one way or another Neferhotep would have had Peseshet killed. She had threatened his life too.

Pleading forgiveness for that crime had been but a feint and the only person I managed to deceive was myself. It has lightened the weight of my heart not at all. The mamba has not moved.

The sealed box must be opened for it is the last thing I can seek forgiveness for, one last veil to strip aside. I have no human tongue yet I cry to the gods: Hapiwer was innocent. I knew that all along. Neferhotep did not have to convince me to put Peseshet's husband to death. He knew I was weak. He knew I loved Peseshet long before I was aware of it myself. He let me play my little self-deceiving game. I killed Hapiwer as though I had pierced him with that stake myself. I could have saved him yet I didn't, and all so I could possess his wife.

I feel my heart lighten and the mamba stirs again. To my surprise, complicity in the death of this unimportant man had made my heart almost as heavy as the spiteful eradication of Peseshet's medicine. I suppose the latter crime sprang more from ignorance and a want of imagination. There, quantity of those affected predominated, while with Hapiwer there was an altogether higher quality to the sin.

Despite this lightening, the Feather of Justice has still moved not one iota.

All that my confessions have achieved is soul-wrenching torment. I cannot bear to live with myself, now or in any future life. I want eternal oblivion as I have never wanted anything before.

I wait. Times passes, each moment another agony, but death will not come.

I have nothing left to confess but still I am found wanting. It is clear I am to remain tethered to this world, to live life after miserable life until Ra boils the oceans away. I cry out in frustration but all I hear is the barking of a dying dog.

Strangely, I find myself craving human company. Even the dead will do. I start crawling towards the stern, my back legs numb and useless. I'm so white with powder it's soaking up the blood. When I leapt up onto the sacks, to the captain I must have looked like a ghost dog emerging from the darkness.

After an eternity, I reach the engine house and haul myself over the side of the sacks, barely noticing the pain as I crash to the deck. I land beside Ragab who still stares into eternity.

Perhaps when the police find me, find my dead, broken body, they'll understand what I have done. Perhaps they'll venerate me, as we venerated our dead to keep their Ka alive. I don't want that any more. The truth is I have sinned and my Ka will never enter the Field of Reeds, if it even exists. Instead, the best I can hope for is that my Ka will dissipate and be lost forever over the still waters of this unnatural lake. Rather that than an endless stream of miserable lives.

I realise Ragab has something curled up in the palm of his hand. I fear my doggy eyes are at last failing but I know what it is anyway. It is the little bracelet Kiyo had given him. It looks so frail and delicate in Ragab's big hairy hand. Poor Kiyo, I think, poor Aleko and, most of all, poor Ragab. He tried to do the best he could but life was not kind.

My sight blurs as my eyes fill with water.

New pain roars to life like a monster. I thought I had known agony before but not like this. Agony for the suffering of Rajab. Agony for his family. Agony for people all over this unfair world. It pours into my heart until I think it must explode. Just for a second, I understand how Peseshet felt, why she cared so deeply for others, and why she despised me because I didn't.

To think that the gods had to bring me back as a dog to make me finally understand what it is to be fully human!

Something changes. Far away, in a vaulted room higher than the stars, Maat's Scales of Justice suddenly tilts under the weight of a single feather. The coiled mamba bursts into life, thrashing its way out of my body, taking with it my sin, and my final breath.

Then it is there, magnificent, glorious and terrible.

So pure it burns my eyes.

At last, I see the light of Ra.

finis

If you have enjoyed reading this book, please consider leaving a review. Some sites rate books by the number of reviews they get and, without your help, a really great book can be left to languish unseen.

Some notes on 4th Dynasty Egypt

Forty-five centuries have passed since those ancient days and so it is hardly surprising that we know so little about them.

One thing we do know is that there really was a Chief Physician called Peseshet (sometimes spelled as the less easy to pronounce Pesehet). She would have practised the ancient medicine described in this book. That she experimented with more modern medical approaches is, however, speculation. Nevertheless, she must have been a remarkable woman to become the leading physician in the most powerful civilisation of her day.

Khufu and Khafre (Khafra) were indeed God-Kings who built the two largest pyramids the world has ever seen. Before these pyramids were cannibalised to make other buildings, they were covered in smooth limestone cladding. Gleaming in the Egyptian sun, they must have been the most magnificent and sublime constructions man has ever made. Even though stripped back to their bare sandstone blocks nowadays, the pyramids are still breathtaking, as is so much of what remains of ancient Egypt.

There is much controversy about who actually built the Sphinx. Even so, the prevailing view is that it bears the face of Khafre.

We know little of Khufu but it is said that he sent his daughter to a brothel to pay for her own tomb. However, the source of this information seems to have been the Greek historian Herodotus who was writing two thousand years after the event and who may also have had his own agenda. It may well be that Khufu was not the monster alluded to in this novel. On the other hand, he did have the power and the will to drive the construction of the Great Pyramid. He was certainly no pussycat.

There really was a servant who had the title Keeper of the Royal Rectum.

Camels, horses, and fruit like bananas and mangos may be abundant in present day Egypt but were unknown in the 4th Dynasty. The word 'Pharaoh' was also unknown and would not be coined for at least another thousand years.

Acknowledgements

Many thanks to all the staff at Sparsile Books for their patience, help and encouragement, especially to my editors Jim Campbell and Alex Winpenny. I owe a debt of gratitude to Madeleine Jewett and Stephen Cashmore for their tireless work in proofing the final draft. And I would also like to gratefully acknowledge the support and literary criticism over many years from Gary Gibson, Don Ross and those scamps at the Glasgow Science Fiction Writers' Circle. Drinks are on me!

Further Reading

The Promise
When promises can cost lives

Simon's Wife
Time is running out, and history is being rewritten by a traitor's hand.

The Unforgiven King
A forgotten woman and the most vilified king in history

American Goddess
Ancient powers and new forces

L. M. Affrossman

Science for Heretics
Why so much of science is wrong

The Tethered God
Punished for a crime he can't remember

Barrie Condon

Pignut and Nuncle
When we are born, we cry that we have come to this stage of fools
King Lear

Des Dillon

Two Pups
What makes us different. What makes us the same.

Seona Calder

Comics and Columbine
An outcast look at comics, bigotry and school shootings

Tom Campbell

Drown for your Sins
DCI Grant McVicar: Book 1

Dress for Death
DCI Grant McVicar: Book 2

Diarmid MacArthur

www.sparsilebooks.com

Lightning Source UK Ltd.
Milton Keynes UK
UKHW010747060521
383241UK00003B/504